P9-DCC-892

Miss Westlake's Suitor

Chas cleared his throat and took a deep breath. "You do know that I love you, Ada, don't you?"

She laughed, relieved. "Is that all?"

All? It was all he had been thinking about since Leo had prodded at him. All that mattered, all that he had to pin his feeble hopes on. All of him. "Did you know?"

"Of course, you clunch. You love me better than your own sisters—haven't you always told me so?" She reached up to brush a lock of dark hair off his forehead. "And I'd know it anyway, by how you are always looking out for my interests, and how you worry when I do something foolish, like going to the Mermaid Tavern by myself." She stood on tiptoe to press a kiss to his uninjured cheek. "And I love you, even if you are like a mother hen with one chick."

A brother? A mother hen? She thought of him as a bloody relative! Leo was right, which made Chas all the angrier. His Ada did not even think of him as a man, as a mate. Damnation! Without a by-your-leave, Chas grabbed Ada in his good arm, tipped her toward the side, and kissed her firmly, fiercely, with fire and all the feeling he could fit in one—albeit lengthy—kiss. "Now," he said with a gasp as he left, "now tell me that I love you like a brother."

SIGNET

REGENCY ROMANCE

COMING IN MAY

The Blackmailed Bridegroom and The Luckless Elopement by Dorothy Mack

A REGENCY TWO-IN-ONE

"Ms. Mack has always shown a unique ability to make our hearts both ache and rejoice, while her sparkling wit and unerring romantic sensibility make each of her books a timeless treasure to be savored over and over again."

—*Romantic Times*

0-451-20357-7/$5.50

Broken Promises by Patricia Oliver

A widow returns to London and gets reacquainted with the man she left at the altar ten years earlier. Could this be a second chance for love—or a scheme for revenge?

0-451-20296-1/$4.99

The Unsuitable Miss Martingale by Barbara Hazard

Sent to London by her family in hopes she will marry respectably, Lili Martingale finds herself out of place in London high society. But she has a place in the heart of Viscount Halpern...

0-451-20265-1/$4.99

To order call: 1-800-788-6262

Miss Westlake's Windfall

Barbara Metzger

A SIGNET BOOK

SIGNET
Published by New American Library, a division of
Penguin Putnam Inc., 375 Hudson Street,
New York, New York 10014, U.S.A.
Penguin Books Ltd, 27 Wrights Lane,
London W8 5TZ, England
Penguin Books Australia Ltd,
Ringwood, Victoria, Australia
Penguin Books Canada Ltd, 10 Alcorn Avenue,
Toronto, Ontario, Canada M4V 3B2
Penguin Books (N.Z.) Ltd, 182–190 Wairau Road,
Auckland 10, New Zealand

Penguin Books Ltd, Registered Offices:
Harmondsworth, Middlesex, England

First published by Signet, an imprint of New American Library,
a division of Penguin Putnam Inc.

First Printing, April 2001
10 9 8 7 6 5 4 3 2 1

Copyright © Barbara Metzger, 2001

All rights reserved

REGISTERED TRADEMARK—MARCA REGISTRADA

Printed in the United States of America

Without limiting the rights under copyright reserved above, no part of this publication may be reproduced, stored in or introduced into a retrieval system, or transmitted, in any form, or by any means (electronic, mechanical, photocopying, recording, or otherwise), without the prior written permission of both the copyright owner and the above publisher of this book.

PUBLISHER'S NOTE
This is a work of fiction. Names, characters, places, and incidents either are the product of the author's imagination or are used fictitiously, and any resemblance to actual persons, living or dead, events, or locales is entirely coincidental.

BOOKS ARE AVAILABLE AT QUANTITY DISCOUNTS WHEN USED TO PROMOTE PRODUCTS OR SERVICES. FOR INFORMATION PLEASE WRITE TO PREMIUM MARKETING DIVISION, PENGUIN PUTNAM INC., 375 HUDSON STREET, NEW YORK, NEW YORK 10014.

If you purchased this book without a cover you should be aware that this book is stolen property. It was reported as "unsold and destroyed" to the publisher and neither the author nor the publisher has received any payment for this "stripped book."

To Volunteers

Chapter One

Money did not grow on trees. If sovereigns should, however, suddenly decide to sprout on shrubbery, they would not select Miss Ada Westlake's orchard. Apples barely grew on the stunted, runted, unpruned branches, much less money. In fact, Ada thought she'd be lucky to find enough fruit, after the bugs and the birds, the village brats and the various blights had wreaked their worst, to make preserves for the winter. She would have been content with enough apples for a pie or two, or even a tart.

Nevertheless, a coin had definitely struck Ada on the brow. She rubbed her forehead with one mittened hand and the silver coin with the other, looking up through the nearly bare branches. She spotted a shriveled apple or two, good enough to feed her pony or Uncle Filbert, but no orchard elf guarding a golden hoard. Ada had to smile at her own musings, that whereas she was not quite willing to barter her own unborn children for a sack of coins, she'd be perfectly willing to trade her sister-in-law Jane for a shilling. The fairies could have Jane's uncle Filbert for free. Ada shrugged and tucked the coin into her pocket.

Determined to retrieve the few salvageable apples on the upper branches, Ada pulled her pony around so the rickety wooden cart was directly beneath the tree, then she hiked up her skirts to clamber onto the back of the cart, without the least fear of being tumbled off. The old gray-muzzled mare had already gone back to mashing an apple between her nearly toothless jaws, her eyes closed. Lulu was not going anywhere until suppertime.

Hefting the long, forked stick she'd been using to rattle the gnarled trees into giving up their meager harvest, Ada batted at the highest branch she could reach. A handful of apples did tumble down, some even landing in the cart, one particularly wormy specimen managing to brush against Ada's cheek. She jumped back, scrubbing at her face with the now grimy mitten, then gave the branch another vigorous shake. This time the ancient apple tree showered her with leaves, twigs, a caterpillar—and a cascade of coins. A leather pouch fell at Ada's feet. The forked stick fell to the ground. Ada nearly fell off the back of the cart.

Sinking to her knees, she gathered the fallen treasure onto her faded skirts. Gold, silver, pounds, and pence—why, she calculated there must be a fortune here, and more in the still heavy, ripped leather sack. Ada leaned back against the wooden slats of the cart, careless of splinters in her heavy woolen shawl, careless of crushed apples under her half-boots. She did not even hear the squirrel scolding at her from the nearby branches.

A fortune, in her nearly barren orchard.

A fortune, in her nearly bankrupt fingers.

A fortune. But not her fortune, of course. There were, regrettably, no fairy godmothers, no pots at the ends of rainbows and, most definitely, no money trees. Ada tugged the scarf off her head, letting her light brown curls fall down around her shoulders as she began to transfer the coins from her skirt to the red silk square. What there were, she acknowledged, were smugglers. With Lillington so close to the Dover coast, and with times so hard, free trading was a common, accepted occupation for the local population. Westlake Hall's orchard must have served as a storeroom for barrels or as a shortcut for the packhorses. Either the landsmen had left the sack of money here as payment to the seafarers, or the gold was to recompense the Westlakes for the use of their land.

The problem was, Ada did not find smuggling an acceptable practice, not at all, not with her brother Emery serving on the Peninsula. Some of the so-called Gentlemen's profits undoubtedly found their way into needy local coffers, but the bulk of the blunt, Ada was certain, went to the French. The French were not buying bread and milk for their hungry children, which was the Lillington residents' rationale; they were buying guns, weapons to shoot at other Englishmen, at Emery. No, Ada could not accept trading with the enemy, and she would not permit her lands—Emery's lands—to be used for such a purpose, not even if the payment fell at her feet like manna from heaven.

She'd simply have to return the money. Ada did not even peek into the pouch to see how many coins were left inside. She just folded the small sack into her scarf with the rest of the money, lest she be tempted even more than she was, to keep some of it, any of it.

Ada was sorely tempted indeed. Lud knew she could use the funds as well as any freebooter could. With this much cash she could purchase new tools and breeding stock for the home farm, new roofs for the tenants' cottages. Goodness, if the farms saw an income, she could finally fix the roof at Westlake Hall itself, so they could use the upper floors again, before they fell in on them. She could finally pay off some of her profligate elder brother's debts, and see Rodney's expensive widow Jane installed at the dower house, along with Jane's freeloading uncle Filbert.

Ada raised her face to the weak autumn sun, enjoying the warmth on her skin and the air castles in her imagination. In her daydreams she saw her older sister Tess, dressed in pretty gowns and new bonnets, waltzing through a London Season, finding a gentleman worthy of her special nature. Tess's beau wouldn't mind that Ada's sister was somewhat . . . vague, to be polite. No, he would not even notice, Ada decided in her dreams. He'd simply cherish dear Tess and scoop her away to his magnificent castle, at the other side of England, with any luck.

As for herself—Ada came back to earth with the thud of another apple hitting the ground. No, she would not paint herself a rosy future, for there was no fortune, no repaying a wastrel's gaming debts, no refurbishing the manor or wardrobes. Perhaps when Emery came home he could take up the reins of the baronetcy, take care of Tess, take Jane to task for her extravagance. Then Ada could take up her own dreams again. Until that time, when Napoleon was finally defeated, she would simply muddle through.

Ada stowed the bundled scarf under the bench of the pony cart and encouraged Lulu to head for home. She was quite good at muddling, in fact. Didn't she have enough apples for both preserves and a pie?

While Lulu plodded along, still munching, Ada considered how she was to return the money to the smugglers. Well-bred, proper young ladies were frankly not on terms with men of that calling. The Westlakes might have fallen on hard times, but not hard enough to force Ada into the company of criminals and cutthroats. Still, she was determined to put the ill-gotten gilt back into the smugglers' hands—hands that were soiled with the blood of brave English soldiers—along with an admonition to keep off Westlake property, or else. Or else what? she wondered. Or else she would pelt them with rotten apples? Set her elderly servants after them, armed with pitchforks and brooms?

Botheration, Ada swore, wishing once more that her brother were here. Emery would know what to do. Even Rodney had been a dab hand with a pistol, when he wasn't too inebriated to aim straight. A young female without masculine protection was not likely to be an effective deterrent to anyone.

She could, of course, ask her neighbor for help. Charles Harrison Ashford, Viscount Ashmead, would come to Ada's aid at the drop of a feather, or an apple. At least he would have, before their argument yesterday. Chas was the kindest gentleman of Ada's acquaintance, her confidant, comforter, and estate-adviser since Rodney's demise. He was the best friend Ada had ever had, until yesterday. Now, just when she needed his support the most, Chas might never speak to her again, just because she'd turned down his latest offer of marriage.

Even Lulu was pulling in the direction of the Meadows, Chas's estate, where they so often stopped, and where the grooms lavished attention on the old mare.

"Not today, Lu," Ada told her, tugging the reins back toward the homeward path. "Maybe never."

She sniffled, from the chill in the air, Ada told herself, not because she felt bereft of her bosom bow. She'd begged him not to offer again, not to destroy their friendship with a proposal she could not accept, but he'd gone and done it anyway, the clunch. Chas had been so angry with Ada that he'd stormed out of Westlake Hall's shabby sitting room, shouting, "If you cannot see fit to entertain my honorable offer, dash it, perhaps you should not be forced to entertain me!"

Everyone had heard him, of course. Her old butler, Cobble, just shook his bald head, and Tess had patted Ada's hand, leaving plaster-dust fingerprints behind. Tess was sculpting yesterday.

Rodney's widow, Jane, however, was angrier even than Chas. "You'll never receive a better offer, you fool," she'd shrieked, "not stuck here in the back of beyond, and not with your managing ways. Why, even if you were not too clutch-fisted to pay for a London Season, you'd never catch the eye of a more eligible *parti.* Of *any* likely gentleman, by all that's holy, not even with my sponsorship and connections. For the life of me, I cannot understand why Ashmead even bothers with you. Your looks are barely passable. Your coloring is deplorable. Your shape is boyish, your manners are hoydenish, and your breeding is mediocre."

Jane was the granddaughter of a duke, which fact she never

let anyone forget, nor that she had married a mere baronet far beneath her. Jane would have demanded her sisters-in-law address her as Lady Westlake, if she thought for an instant they would obey anything she had to say. Tess and Ada were generally in the habit of ignoring Jane and her constant complaints, but Ada had been trapped in the drawing room, stunned by Chas's furious, noisy departure.

Jane, of course, was not finished. She'd curled her lip at Ada's plain muslin gown. "You have no taste, less style, and your dowry is nonexistent." She'd pointed one trembling—howbeit well-manicured—finger, at the door Lord Ashmead had so recently slammed. "Yet you turned down a well-funded, well-favored viscount!" Jane had ended her harangue with a sob, collapsing onto the sofa with her handkerchief clutched to her breast, her voluptuous, buxom breast. "You are a disgraceful, disloyal chit, not caring what's to become of the rest of us."

Her sister-in-law's uncle, Filbert Johnstone, had nodded sagely. Well, he'd nodded anyway, as much as he could with his shirt points up to his ears and his neckcloth tied higher than his three chins.

The worst of it was, they were right, Ada reflected on her slow, slogging way home. Chas was everything a maiden—or a matchmaking mama—could want in a suitor. He was handsome enough to make serving girls stare, with his fine chiseled features and dark waving hair. His broad shoulders and fine proportions were the envy of every gentleman in the neighborhood. His title was old, his fortune was deep, his acres were vast, and vastly profitable. Beyond those obvious attributes, Viscount Ashmead had impeccable manners—unless sorely provoked—a well-educated intelligence, and the devil's own smile, dimples and all.

Jane was correct, too, that Ada was entirely unworthy of such a paragon's notice. Ada did not have Jane's sumptuous endowments, nor Tess's tall, willowy grace. She was of medium height and medium build, and her hair was of medium light brown. Nondescript described her perfectly, Ada acknowledged. Not only did she not have Jane's golden blond ringlets or Tess's vibrant auburn, but she did not even possess the required porcelain complexion and rose-blushed cheeks, not when she had to help tend the kitchen garden. Chas always defended her to Jane, saying he found her freckles charming, but dear Chas would say that anyway, out of kindness, just as he lent her books to improve her scanty education.

Ada sighed and let Lulu crop at the hedges along the way, delaying her arrival home. No matter how long the journey took—and she could already see Westlake Hall's roof in the distance, missing slates and all—nothing would change. They were right, all of them, from her sister-in-law to the scullery maid: Ada's marriage to Lord Ashmead could have solved all of their difficulties.

Chas was wealthy enough to pay Rodney's debts as a bridal settlement, and oversee improvements to what was now Emery's impoverished estate, all without feeling the pinch of a single penny. He'd see to the tenants, the roof tiles, and Tess. No one at Westlake Hall would have to scrimp and save for the simple pleasures Jane demanded as Lady Westlake's due, such as year-round fires, ample wax candles, open accounts at the shops in Dover. As for Ada herself, she'd live at the Meadows in a style she'd never known, even in her parents' time, with servants tripping over each other to please her. If that grew tiresome, Chas also owned a London residence, a hunting box in Scotland, and a plantation in the Colonies. Travels, jewels, books, the *beau monde,* Ada could enjoy luxuries far beyond what the contents of her knotted scarf could purchase, beyond her imagination, in fact. What she'd enjoy most of all, Ada pondered, was never having to count coins again, never having to try to make her ledger books balance, never worrying over the future.

For all those reasons, because marriage to a man like Chas was every girl's dream, Ada could not accept his eminently honorable offer. Jane would never understand that Ada could not repay her friend's gallantry that way, for that's what his offer was: a noble rescue of a damsel in distress. His inherent chivalry, his goodness, his very strengths, made Chas want to extend his protection to those in need. His heart had nothing to do with the proposal.

Ada had to lock her own emotions away, her own dreams unexamined. She also had to bite her lip to keep from weeping. Charity, that's all his offer was, wrapped in the clean linen of friendship, with a scrap of ensuring his succession thrown in. Ada could not accept his largesse.

She liked Chas far too much to burden him with her problems, to tie him for life to a ramshackle family, to accept him for what he could do, not just for what he was. He deserved so much better, like a lady he could love. What if he found her someday, the woman of *his* dreams, but he was already wed to Ada, with her flighty—to be polite—sister, and grasping sister-in-law, her neglectful brother and rundown estate? Ada would never forgive herself for blighting her dear friend's chances for happiness, and so she would never marry him.

Perhaps when Chas did find his perfect bride, his soul mate, his heart's companion, perhaps then his pride could forgive Ada and they could be friends again.

And perhaps it was starting to drizzle, for Ada brushed away a drop of moisture from her cheek, leaving a trail of dirt through the freckles.

Chapter Two

The vultures were waiting.

"Did he accept your apology?" Jane pounced on Ada as soon as she walked through the drawing room door. "Is everything settled?"

Ada had put down her bundled scarf but hadn't yet handed her shawl to the butler, Cobble, who was waiting just as avidly for her answer. "Apology? Settled?"

"And not above time, my girl." Since there was no way on earth, by blood or by bond of matrimony, that Ada considered herself Filbert Johnstone's "girl," she ignored him as best she could, considering he was wearing a purple waistcoat with red cabbage roses embroidered on it. Mr. Johnstone was overfed, overdressed, and too frequently underfoot, when he ran out of his own funds, likely gambling winnings. He considered himself a man of the world, just as his son Algernon considered himself a sportsman when he blasted away at every bird, beast, and innocent passerby, and Jane put on the airs of a *grande dame.* Most days, Ada considered them all a flock of pesky pigeons, puffing themselves up, nattering on, roosting where they were least wanted. Today they were flesh-eating Harpies. At least Algernon was back at school. Heaven alone knew how Chas had managed to convince the university to rematriculate the moron.

Chas. Oh. "No, nothing is settled. That is, we settled everything yesterday. I have not seen Viscount Ashmead today."

Cobble turned and left the room, his shoulders stooped, his footsteps dragging, Ada's shawl forgotten.

Filbert went to pour himself another brandy, while Jane resettled her skirts on the striped sofa with a grumbled oath. "Dash it, I made sure you'd come to your senses at last. We supposed you'd gone to the Meadows to apologize."

"No, I was picking apples, as I told you all I was going to do last evening. Besides, I have done nothing for which I need apologize."

Mr. Johnstone had brightened momentarily at the thought of fresh apple turnovers, but Ada's fierce scowl sent him back for the bottle.

Jane inspected her fingernails. "Nothing to apologize for? I suppose calling a distinguished gentleman a jobbernowl, a jackanapes, and a jackass is a polite way of refusing his suit?"

Had she really used those words in the heat of their argument? She must have, or Cobble would not have repeated them to Jane from his position outside the drawing room, his ear pressed against the wood. Ada felt her cheeks flushing. "Yes, well, Chas knows I meant nothing by those terms. We've known each other much too long to be offended by a little friendly name-calling. Why, he always calls me Addled Ada, you know."

Uncle Filbert choked on a large swallow and muttered, "If he calls this one addled, I wonder what he calls t'other one?"

They could all hear Tess in the next door music room. The villagers in Lillington could likely hear Tess in the music room. They'd be complaining to Ada of soured milk again tomorrow, but she found Tess's latest composition . . . interesting. She raised her chin. "He calls her Miss Westlake, of course, since she is the elder daughter of the house."

Jane sipped at a cup of tea, without offering any to Ada. After three hours in the orchards, and three minutes in the drawing room, Ada needed refreshment. She briefly debated the merits of Mr. Johnstone's spirits before crossing to the tea cart and pouring out a cup of lukewarm, bitter tea, just the way Jane liked it. Ada added two lumps of sugar. Noting that nothing remained on the cake platter but one dry slice of toast, she added another lump before taking a seat. She did not bother ringing for a fresh pot or another plate of biscuits, not when she was in Cobble's black books.

Just when Ada was about to reach for the toast, Jane murmured, "I hear that Ashmead spent the night in an alehouse." Jane had an intricate network of informants, with her personal maid on intimate terms with every footman in the neighborhood, it seemed.

"I am sure it is no concern of ours where Lord Ashmead spends his nights, or days, for that matter. He is a grown man of seven and twenty. Surely he is entitled to his privacy."

Her repressive tones did not faze Jane one whit, who had seen her third birthday with a zero in it some few years ago. Lady Westlake did not intend to see her fourth decade celebrated in the country, in reduced circumstances, especially not when some stubborn, willful chit of one and twenty could rescue them all with two words. Since "I do" were the only words she wished to hear from Ada's lips, Jane continued as if her sister-in-law had not spoken at all. "An alehouse where he got as drunk as a, well, as a lord, in low company."

Ada's cup clattered on its saucer. She put the bread back, having lost her appetite. "Chas is not a drunkard."

"He never used to be, before you drove the poor man to drink."

"I say, Ashmead's a rich man, what? That's the whole point, ain't it?"

Jane ignored her uncle, too. "In fact, you ought to be sorely ashamed, Miss Too-Good-for-a-Viscount, breaking the poor man's heart that way."

"Oh, pooh. Chas's heart is as hard as his head. It was only his pride that was injured."

"Oh, and I suppose you didn't toss his heirloom engagement ring at his head?" It had been a huge ruby, surrounded by diamonds. Jane could have lived in London for a year on its worth. She pursed her lips.

"I might have, but it only left a tiny scratch."

Jane dabbed at her mouth with her napkin. "Besides, a gentleman's pride is no small thing. Why, having his suit rejected so adamantly might lead a man to any number of indiscretions, such as a barroom brawl."

Uncle Filbert nodded his agreement. "Steals his manhood, by George. Makes a chap want to prove himself. Young bucks butting heads, don't you know."

"Chas was in a fight? Is he . . . ? That is, was anyone injured?"

"I'd say your concern for Ashmead comes a little late, wouldn't you, Miss Holding-Out-for-a-Hero?"

"Was he hurt, by Heaven?"

Jane raised her perfect nose in the air. "How should I know? I do not gossip with servants."

At Ada's "Hah!" Jane did admit to making sure that his lordship was well enough for visitors. "Which is why we assumed you'd gone to call this afternoon, to see for yourself, to bring a restorative or some such."

What they'd wished was that Ada's senses were restored. Her hopes dashed once more, Jane asked her uncle to pour her a wee sip of his own brew, for her nerves.

Ada was certain she was the last person Chas would wish to see today, especially if he was feeling below par. Of course servants' gossip always made mountains out of molehills, especially when it concerned the gentry acting beneath their dignity. Likely Chas had shared a drink or two with some of his tenants, then took part in a friendly bout of arm-wrestling or some such physical proof of prowess men were so prone toward. Charles Harrison Ashford, Viscount Ashmead, was not a sot, nor did he need to prove his worth to anyone. For certain, his heart was not broken. Ada doubted if that organ was even slightly bruised.

The sight of the bottle in Mr. Johnstone's hands, however,

a bottle that held no excise label, reminded Ada of her own news. "Although I did not have converse with Viscount Ashmead this afternoon," she began, "I did accomplish something better. I gathered a decent quantity of apples. Mrs. Cobble is paring some now, so we should have a lovely pie for dinner."

"An apple pie is better than a *parti*?" Jane snapped. "Better than a peer with deep pockets? Is this whole family dicked in the nob?" She took a swallow of brandy. Perhaps it was not her first of the afternoon after all, for she went on: "One brother thought he could ride a wild horse, while the other one believes his presence on the Peninsula is the only thing keeping the Corsican from overrunning the Empire. This chit turns her back on the best offer she is ever likely to have, and the other . . . ? It's a madhouse, that's what this is. Bedlam at Westlake."

Now Ada might silently agree that her elder brother Rodney had been cork-brained, getting on an unbroken stallion and wagering the already mortgaged town house on his ability to stay aboard, besides. She would never have spoken such sentiments aloud, though, since Rodney had paid the ultimate price for his folly, but if his own widow wished to label him lunatic, Ada could not argue the point. She would not even debate the wisdom of Emery's insistence that his duty lay with the Army, when his inheritance was going to hell in a handcart. For herself, she'd been teased with Addled Ada so many times she took it as a pet name, a sign of affection for her independent ways. No one, however, no one at all, was permitted to question Tess's sanity, not while Ada had breath in her body.

"This is my family's home," she said, "Tess's home, and she will not be insulted here, *sister*. If you are so disappointed in your relatives by marriage, I am sure we will be pleased to help you pack."

"You forget yourself, miss. I am Lady Westlake, and until your rattle-pate of a brother returns from playing soldier, I am mistress of this establishment. I have let you deal with the servants and the estate, since dear Rodney seemed to think you could manage, but I shall not be pushed aside, not without my annuity, I won't."

"Rodney used the marriage settlements to buy you furs and gems. You know there is no money in the account or, by heaven, I would have given it to you long ago."

"Hmph. Well, I would have remained in the London house if you had not sold it from under my feet."

"I didn't sell it, Lady Westlake. May I remind you that the bank reclaimed it to pay the mortgage. Everything else, including the blasted unbroken stallion, went to pay gambling debts. If you and Rodney had managed to live within your means, we would not be in this fix now, and no one would care if I married the linen-draper, much less Lord Ashmead."

"Now, now, girls, no need to be pulling caps. We'll come about, see if we don't." Uncle Filbert brought the bottle, to tip some brandy into Ada's cold tea. She put her hand over the cup with a gruff "No, thank you." He shrugged and poured it into his own glass instead. "Aye, we'll manage. We're not doing so badly, what with an apple pie, a fine bottle of brandy—"

"That never saw the customs collector." Ada got up and retrieved her red scarf from the corner table. She untied the knot and dumped the contents onto a hard-backed chair no one ever sat in. "I found this in the orchard, too."

Jane moved faster than the time Tess brought her herpetology collection to the breakfast room. "Oh, my!" She started counting: "One new fan, two bonnets, three pairs of gloves . . ."

"No, Jane. We will not be spending the money."

"What, not spend all of this lovely brass? You mean to pay off more of those tiresome debts with this windfall? I won't have it, I tell you, Ada. I'll go speak to the trustees myself. I'll—"

"No, I mean the money is not ours to keep. I will be returning it to its rightful owners as soon as possible."

Uncle Filbert was leaning over Jane's shoulder, nearly licking his lips. "I say, finders keepers and all that, what?"

"No, I do not believe the money was accidentally misplaced. I believe it was left there in our orchard as payment for the use of our land by smugglers." She pointed at the bottle in Filbert Johnstone's hand. "And I believe I know who made the arrangement."

"Nonsense. You cannot think that we would traffic with such ruffians." Jane grew indignant, but her uncle was sputtering, dribbling brandy down his floral waistcoat. Now he looked more than ever like a bed throw in a bordello.

"How could you, sirrah?"

Filbert was trying to find a place out of Ada's sight to hide the telltale bottle. "It's just the one bottle, I swear. I don't know a thing about the brass."

"You don't know about sympathizing with the French? About aiding and abetting the enemy?"

Now he went pale. "I didn't . . . You can't . . ."

"Oh la, Ada, you are making too big a thing out of this. What's it to you if someone crosses our boundaries, when they pay so handsomely?"

"Rather ask my brother Emery what it is to him when the French have more cannons and more ammunition, warmer uniforms and better rations." She started to gather the coins into the kerchief again, prying Jane's fingers away from the ripped leather pouch. "The money goes back, and that is final."

Jane managed a smile without taking her eyes off the disappearing coins. "Well, I am sure you may try, Ada, but it is not as if smugglers place signs over their doorways like bootmakers or booksellers, advertising their trades. Nor will they step forward if you place a notice in the daily *Journal*. So do try to return the purse, if that's what it takes to satisfy your so-sincere scruples. Then we can spend the money."

Ada snatched the scarf away. "We will never spend it. It is soiled money; don't you see? Besides, everyone knows smugglers kill people who interfere with their business. Do you want us all to be murdered in our beds? I will donate it to charity before spending one shilling."

Jane moaned and fumbled in her pocket for her vinaigrette. She gave up looking and grabbed the bottle of brandy out of her uncle's nerveless fingers.

Ada glared at him. "I know better than to ask for the names of your confederates, but you can pass on my warning: if Westlake land is ever used for such a purpose again, I will go straight to the magistrate's office, then the excisemen and the sheriff." She took the bottle from Jane, opened the nearest window, and poured what little remained out onto the lawn. "And yours will be the first names I give them for questioning."

Chapter Three

Charles, Viscount Ashmead, swore that he would never touch another drop of Blue Ruin as long as he lived—if he lived through the day. The way he felt at this moment, such an outcome was neither likely nor necessarily desirable. Moaning took too much effort. Breathing took too much effort. That was the ticket, Chas told himself, he could stop breathing and put himself out of his misery. No, dying took too much effort.

He whimpered. Either that or his damned dog was mourning him already. The sound kept pounding at his head, as if some barbaric blacksmith was shoeing every blessed horse that ever ran at Epsom Downs. "Blast you, Tally, shut up before I shut you up."

Since his lordship could not possibly *get* up, his threat was an empty one. Since he hadn't actually opened his mouth, his threat came out more like a gurgle. It was enough for whomever was on the other side of the viscount's door, for the door creaked open—or was that the inside of his skull?—and a voice shouted, "Here you go, milord. Drink this and you'll feel right as a trivet in no time."

If feeling like a stiff, lifeless trivet was the best he could do, Chas would decline. When he opened his mouth to do so, however, that same fiendish torturer poured down his throat a noxious brew that promptly returned. The fortunate placement of a basin reminded Chas as to why he usually avoided overindulgence, as if he needed such enlightenment while in his extremities.

"Begone, you ghoul," the viscount groaned. "Let me die in peace."

"Tsk, tsk, milord. We are in a sorry state, aren't we?"

We? Chas hadn't noticed Purvis casting up his accounts. In fact the deuced valet looked fresh as a damned daisy, from what Chas could see through bleary, bloodshot eyes. "You're fired. Now get out."

"Very well, milord. I'll come back in an hour or so when you feel more the thing, shall I?"

"If you come back before dinnertime I'll have your guts for garters, I swear."

The valet wrinkled his long nose. "Dinner is in an hour, milord."

"Dinner tomorrow. Go."

Purvis bowed, unseen by Lord Ashmead, who had collapsed back onto his bed. "Very good, milord. But before I leave may I add my sympathies to those of the rest of the staff. We all regret that Miss Westlake has turned down your latest offer."

Chas pulled a pillow over his head and groaned. Oh, Lord, he swore as his memory reluctantly returned, he would have been better off dead after all. At least his vow never to overindulge would be easy to keep, because he was never going to offer for Ada Westlake again. Once a month, for as long as he could recall, he'd made her a proposal in form. Once a month, she'd turned him down, for some fardling reason or other, and every month he'd had a few glasses to ease the disappointment. He must have had a few bottles this time instead, but damned if he could remember anything between slamming out of Ada's house and waking up in his.

Never again, the viscount promised himself before he fell back asleep. Never again. No woman was worth this agony, not even Ada.

* * *

When the viscount next awoke—in itself a miracle of the body's will to survive—his memory was stronger, but so was his agony. Lud, no amount of drink could have made him this wretched. He ached not only with the hurt of Ada's rejection, and the entire shire's knowing of it, but also with more physical injuries. Chas tried to take stock by the faint glow of the fireplace embers, which meant he must have slept an entire day away, then. It wasn't enough.

He had the devil's own headache, for one, not surprising considering the quantities of cheap spirits he'd imbibed at Jake's Mermaid Tavern. His right eye felt swollen and sore, likely from the brief melee at the same venue. One of the dive's denizens had accused another of cheating at cards, at which fists and furniture had gone flying. Chas had ducked, but obviously not fast enough.

His left cheek burned as though he'd been shaved with a butcher's knife—by a blind barber. He tried to feel under the bandage there, but his left hand would not move, strapped as it was between two boards. Zeus, was his wrist broken, then? Perhaps he'd been concussed by the airborne bar stool after all, before Jake settled the argument with a belaying pin, and that was why Chas could not recall being knocked out, half scalped, and trampled. For sure at least one of his ribs must be broken, his lordship reasoned, since he was having so much trouble breathing.

No, that was Tally. The blasted bitch was lying smack on top of the viscount's chest. At least one female held him in affection. Nevertheless, Chas shoved the mixed-breed hound off the bed with his good hand, complaining, "Lud, you stink."

No, that was him. He recognized the odor from the last time his groom had doctored a bruised pastern—on a horse. What the deuce had happened to him?

He started to review the previous evening in his mind, skipping the argument at Westlake Hall, which was far more painful than the other aches and far more lasting, Chas feared. He began instead with his arrival at Jake's Mermaid Tavern, on the seaward outskirts of Lillington village.

Chas had gone to meet an old friend and sometime business partner, Leo Tobin. Both natives of Lillington, they'd been acquainted since boyhood, although they were from far different class and circumstances. Chas had been born to wealth and privilege, while Leo had been raised by hardworking fishing folk. The heir to the viscountcy was educated at the finest institutions; the heir to his father's ketch was taught by the local vicar and schooled by experience. Still, they dealt well together, from days of cricket on the village green, and rowing races near the shore. They even resembled each other in looks, each being tall and dark and broad-shouldered, although Leo had a swarthier complexion from his days sailing, and a few more years in his dish. Now that his new shipping business was so successful, it was Leo who dressed in the first stare, a diamond winking from his cravat, while Chas had donned his oldest riding coat and a spotted cloth tied loosely at his neck. In the murky light of the Mermaid Tavern, a stranger would be hard-pressed to name which was the aristocrat, which the smuggler.

Sitting quietly in a secluded corner, they'd been awaiting the arrival of a third man, but Prelieu had never arrived. According to Tobin, the rest of the expected shipment of goods had been delivered ashore earlier that evening, but not the Frenchman. Disturbed by the hitch in his plans, to say nothing of the wound to his heart, Chas had stayed on at the tavern, drinking the swill that passed for ale, then switching to the stomach-corroding Blue Ruin.

"Said no again, did she?" Leo had taunted with the unmerciful callousness of an old boyhood chum. With his sources, Leo likely knew of Ada's answer before Chas did. Then again, Chas and Ada had been yelling like fishwives, so it was no wonder the turning down of his tenderly tendered troth was so quickly common knowledge. But the viscount wasn't going to think about that now.

Leo had gone on to tease about monthly curses, and how Ashmead had found the only female in the kingdom who was not fickle. "Damned if your Miss Westlake isn't the steadfast sort."

He'd ignored the viscount's muttered, "She's not my anything."

Leo'd grinned. "Didn't want you last month. Doesn't want you this month. Won't want you next month. I admire a woman who knows her own opinion and sticks to it, don't you?"

Chas hadn't bothered mentioning that there would be no next month, that addlepated Ada had made him swear not to ask again. He'd just gritted his teeth and called for another bottle, trying to distract his now-former friend with speculation as to the Frenchman's whereabouts. Had he missed the boat? Found another way across the Channel? Changed his mind about selling his information to the Crown?

Trying to find a more comfortable spot against his pillows, Chas tried to make a mental note to ask his valet about the sack of coins that was to be Prelieu's payment. He knew he'd had it at the alehouse, because he'd made sure the purse was tucked away when the fight had broken out.

Nursing what he was sure would become a lurid black eye, Viscount Ashmead had started riding for home on his young chestnut gelding, Thunderbolt. Try as he might, his lordship could not recall meeting up with the Frenchman or being set upon by thieves. If Purvis hadn't taken the pouch of coins from Chas's pocket, then the small fortune must still be in his saddlebag. Leo was the only one who'd known of the planned payment, besides Prelieu, of course, and Chas trusted the smuggler with his life, if not with his pride.

On his way home, Ashmead's whiskey-riddled mind had chosen to trot through the orchard that separated Westlake Hall from the Meadows, where he knew Ada would be picking apples the next day. She'd told him so before the argument, promising to save one of Cook's apple tarts for him if she found enough fruit. Before she'd sent him to the rightabout,

Chas had thought of surprising Ada there, perhaps stealing a kiss or two in the privacy of the empty orchard.

Chas remembered Thunderbolt being spooked by an owl, but he hadn't fallen, not then. He'd played the mooncalf instead, mourning those lost kisses, regretting that he would not get to admire the sun on Ada's face, her gown stretched taut as she reached for a branch, her skirts showing a hint of ankle—No, he would not think about the heartless jade. Or her orchard. Or standing up on the back of a nervous, highstrung horse. Oh, God.

No, his lordship assured himself, he would never try such a totty-headed stunt, not even in his cups.

He next remembered arriving at his stables, where his head man, Coggs, was waiting up to put Thunderbolt to bed, no matter how many times the viscount had told the old man he was perfectly competent to rub down his own mount.

"Aye, I can see how competent you are tonight, lad." Coggs took the chestnut's reins, muttering, "The fumes on your breath be enough to set the stables on fire. Turned you down again, did she?"

Then Coggs had noticed how awkwardly the viscount dismounted, and how he had his left arm tucked between the buttons of his coat.

"What's this, then, lad? Here, let's take a look." Coggs had let the tired horse stand while he led the viscount toward the hanging lantern and an upended barrel. He whistled through his teeth when he saw the raw scrape on the viscount's cheek. "B'gad, looks like a peeled tomato." He gently reached for Ashmead's arm, starting to feel for swelling. When the viscount winced, the old man made clucking sounds, as he would to soothe a restless horse. "There now, lad, what the devil happened to you?"

Chas had shrugged, a painful mistake. On an indrawn breath, he gasped, "Must have been a rabbit hole."

"A rabbit hole, you say?" Old Coggs, who had put Chas on his first pony, dropped the viscount's aching arm like a hot iron to rush to the horse's side, checking for injuries. Lord Ashmead's injured wrist bounced against the barrel.

Somehow he'd reached the kitchens, where his valet and his butler, Epps, another old family retainer, had clucked their tongues. "Don't say it," Chas had ground out while they searched the housekeeper's stores for salve to spread on his cheek and the cook's pantry for a beefsteak to lay on his discolored eye. The dog was pressing herself close to his side for comfort, or for the beefsteak.

When Coggs came in from the stables, he pronounced the viscount's wrist badly sprained but not broken, as far as he could tell. He decided they'd ought to put it in a splint anyway, to keep the arm from being jostled. "Else the gudgeon's liable to damage it worse, don't you know." Since the old horseman had done more doctoring of man and beast than any sawbones, the others nodded in agreement. By now half the staff was in the kitchen, watching their jug-bitten master being trussed up like a plucked goose, but Lord Ashmead was beyond caring.

"Odd kind of rabbit hole it must of been," Coggs noted as he spread some foul-smelling substance on the viscount's fingers to take down the swelling. "Didn't leave a mark on a single one of the gelding's legs, not even a smidgen of dirt."

Lord Ashmead hadn't commented. He'd passed out ten minutes earlier when Purvis started pulling tree bark splinters out of his cheek.

Where was that blessed oblivion when he needed it? Chas wondered, there in the dark. In his houseful of servants, he was alone and aching. His cheek was burning, his wrist was throbbing, and his blasted dog was back on the bed, snoring. The fire was nearly out, and the bellpull might have been on the moon for all the good it was doing him across the room. His throat was too parched to call for help, not that any of his lordship's loyal retainers would bring him a cup of hemlock. And he stank.

Besides, Viscount Ashmead's pride was battered worse than his body. His mission for the War Office was a failure, to say nothing of his intended engagement. He'd lost Prelieu's reward, the respect of his associates, and Ada's friendship. No one loved him except his dog . . . and his mother.

Bloody hell.

Chapter Four

"Turned you down again, did she?"

Chas winced, and not just from the bright light in the morning room. His darling mother's voice grated on his raw nerves like an unoiled wheel. He felt like stable sweepings, and knew he looked worse, there being only so much damage even Purvis's hare's foot could cover. He also knew he had to attend the viscountess this morning or she'd be rapping on his bedroom door. Purvis did not have the spine to deny her. Lud knew, the scarecrow in Cook's kitchen garden, with a broom for a backbone, couldn't have stopped Lady Ashmead on a mission. Chas's diminutive, elegant, well-dressed mother was like a force of nature, going where she wished, shoving aside everything in her way, meanwhile looking like the sweetest, most genteel of ladies, busy about her embroidery.

Lady Ashmead had returned to the Meadows for a visit two years ago, to take her wayward son in hand, she'd declared. She had not left yet, despite frequent lamentations on the gay life she was missing at her home at the Royal Crescent in Bath. Chas lamented louder, but in private, being a dutiful son. Previously, the viscountess had divided her months-long visits between her two daughters. Chas could swear his sister Emily and her family had moved to Boston just to avoid the next maternal stay. His other sister Beth had convinced her diplomat husband to take a posting in India. Chas considered them both traitors, deserters, and lucky.

Chas preferred to meet his mother's attacks from a position of advantage, by mail being his first choice, but at least standing up, barring that. Hence his appearance in the morning room, where the smell of bacon was roiling his stomach, and the sight of kippers was enough to make both eyes shut, not just the empurpled one.

Having broken her own fast some hours ago, of which fact she reminded Chas by pointedly consulting the watch pinned to her lavender gown, Lady Ashmead was seated on a chintz-covered chair next to the window, her ever-present needlework in hand.

Pouring out a cup of coffee, Chas carried the steaming brew over to the seat beside his mother's, instead of sitting at the breakfast table, where he would have to view the piles of muffins and eggs.

"Is that all you are having?" Lady Ashmead demanded.

It was all he could carry, with his other arm in a sling, and Chas preferred not having servants about to hear his mother's diatribe, which was not long in coming.

"When are you going to come to your senses, you muttonhead?" his loving mother snapped. "When are you going to give up this caper-witted nonsense?"

"Good morning to you, too, Mother. Which nonsense might that be? Coffee for breakfast? I know you prefer chocolate, but I cannot think—"

"Obviously," she said with an inelegant snort. "I meant, as you very well know, when are you going to stop making a cake of yourself over that bacon-brained chit?"

The viscount's stomach really wished his mother would not keep mentioning food. "Oh, that nonsense. You will undoubtedly be pleased to note, ma'am, that henceforth I shall no longer be courting Miss Ada Westlake." There, he'd said it without the words trying to strangle him in sorrow. He might even chance a sip of coffee, past the lump in his throat, once the steam dissipated.

"Courtship?" She snorted again, jabbing her needle into the

fabric on her lap. "Is that what you call slamming doors and throwing jewelry at each other's heads?"

Chas had almost forgotten the tiny cut near his eye, a drop in the ocean of agony. His mother had immediately noticed it, of course.

"I never thought a child of mine could be so cow-handed."

Since that comment seemed to require no reply, Chas took another small sip of the hot liquid, praying the coffee would stay where it belonged. Disgracing himself on her favorite Aubusson carpet would find Chas in even less favor with his formidable mother, if such were possible.

"Why, we are the laughingstock of the neighborhood. I cannot hold my head up at the Ladies' Guild meetings."

Chas rested his own aching head on the back of his chair, hoping she'd run out of complaints before he ran out of patience. No such luck. When she got down to the vicar's wife's sister's mother-in-law's opinions of young people's morals, marriages, and manners, he gave up the effort. "Mother, do you know how old I am, that you address me as you would a child?"

Lady Ashmead put down her sewing and bestowed one comprehensive, entirely unsympathetic, glance upon her son's sorry state. "Perhaps when you act your age and your station, you will be afforded the dignity they deserve. Tavern brawls, indeed."

Leaving his midnight mishaps misunderstood seemed a wiser course than trying to explain. He tried wiggling the swollen fingers of his left hand.

"And of course I know how old you are, Charles, to the minute. But do you know how many hours I labored to bring you into this world? Days, I swear, days of agony your piddling injuries cannot come close to duplicating. Your sisters at least recognize the cost, having gone through childbirth themselves. But a son? A son feels he owes his mother no respect, no recompense for the sacrifices she makes."

He should have had the tea that Purvis recommended.

"If you were a daughter, Charles, you would not be this constant disappointment to me. Your sisters married well and have already provided their husbands heirs. Granted the children are being raised like savages, but—No, do not distract me with your drivel. The least you can do is listen when your own mother speaks."

Chas had groaned. He apologized, thinking that perhaps he was the one who should have gone into the diplomatic corps.

Lady Ashmead nodded her exquisitely coiffed head. "Where was I? Oh, yes, daughters. Well, if you had been another daughter, then I'd have had to do the whole thing over again, wouldn't I, to ensure your father's succession? I knew my duty to the family. Unlike some others I could name."

Chas wished he'd thought to check the time, to see how long it had taken his mother to get to her inevitable point. Then again, he wished he had a cool cloth to put on his forehead. He grunted in pain, which she took as participation in the conversation, and continued.

"As did your father, of course. Ashmead knew his duty, and did not shirk his responsibilities. Why, if he were alive, and the old baronet, you'd be hitched to that bran-faced female before the cat could lick its ear. If that nodcock Sir Rodney had lived long enough, you could have arranged with him to wed the chit. The wastrel would have been willing enough to hand her over, if you settled a few of his debts in exchange."

"What, you think I should have forced Ada into marriage?"

"Why not? Gal doesn't seem to have the sense of a slug, living hand-to-mouth while moneybags wait down the street. Nothing wrong with an arranged marriage anyway. That's how it was done in our day, and good enough for your father and me. Good enough to see you brought into the world."

Good enough, when Lady Ashmead lived in Bath, her husband lived in London, and the children were left in Lillington to be reared by servants and schoolmasters? That was not what Chas wanted for his offspring, not by half. Besides, the thought of marrying Ada Westlake against her will was even more nauseating than the coffee.

"Marriages of convenience might have been the norm in your day, ma'am, but I would find such an arrangement dashed inconvenient. I would never consider marrying a woman who did not lo—like me enough to marry me of her own free will."

"Love? What's that got to do with anything? Niminy-piminy emotion's got no place with carrying on the family line. Your father and I managed well enough without that romantical claptrap."

Of course the previous Lord Ashmead had died in the arms of his mistress, while the viscountess filled her own empty arms with endless embroidery. In an effort to change the subject, Chas asked, "What is that you are working on now, Mother?" The house was already filled with wall-hangings, fire screens, and decorative pillows. Chas had a new pair of slippers every year for his birthday, all embellished with the family's coat of arms of red and white roses, separated by a winged lion. His closets were filled with them, for how many slippers could a fellow wear out in a year? Chas had a lifetime supply. Handkerchiefs with his monogram, too. The church got a new altar cloth every year, and the dining room chairs had been recovered twice in the last three years. A hoop or a frame or a work basket was never far from the viscountess's side. The only thing she directed more energy toward, in fact, was her son's future.

Lady Ashmead held up a small scrap of fine white cloth to which she was adding delicate flower blossoms in tiny stitches.

"Lovely," Chas said, attempting another swallow of the still too hot coffee. "But what the deuce—That is, what exactly is it, Mother?"

"It's a baby bonnet, of course, you clunch."

"Ah, one of the cousins having another child? Be sure to

let me know, so we can send a bank draft along with the bonnet."

The viscountess scowled. "This one is for closer to home."

"The church bazaar? I thought that was just past. Of course, no reason you cannot work ahead."

"It's for *your* infant, you gossoon! At the rate you are going, my fingers will be too stiff with the arthritics to see the boy dressed according to his station."

"With flowers?"

She held the fabric out to him and, unthinking, Chas reached out with his splinted arm. The other, after all, held his coffee. It did, at any rate. No matter that his biscuit pantaloons were ruined, or that his privates were so scalded he might never be able to father a child at all, or that his injured wrist was flinging fireballs of hurt through his lordship's eyeballs, a drop of coffee had landed on the baby bonnet.

Lady Ashmead screamed as if she'd been the one boiled alive. She kept screaming while footmen rushed into the room. "So that's what you think of me and all my efforts on your behalf. Nothing I do is good enough for you, and you never listen to my advice. All I have ever wanted is my children's happiness, and this is the thanks I get!" She stalked out in a cloud of spilled threads, scattered needles, and scowling servants, knowing they'd be the one to suffer now that her nibs was in a snit.

While the footmen worked around him, Chas contemplated the tiny garment he still held. Could an infant truly be so small that its head fit in this scrap of cloth that was almost lost in his hand? He turned it so he could see the intricate needlework on the bonnet's brim. Those flowers were the roses of the family crest, by Jupiter. What a heavy weight for such a poor little mite to be born carrying . . . if he was ever born at all.

It took the staff a few anxious hours to restore the viscount and baby bonnet. The little cap was soaked, soaped, sponged, and pressed, and looked as good as new. The viscount looked only slightly worse than he had before. By lunchtime, however, he was actually hungry, and able to present the pristine bonnet to his mother.

At least the viscount's knees were not injured; he could still grovel for the sake of domestic harmony. "I do appreciate your efforts, Mother, and I swear to try to be a more dutiful son."

Lady Ashmead tossed the cap aside in her eagerness. "Then you'll let me speak to the Westlake chit about a betrothal?"

"Zeus, no." Chas wasn't *that* repentant. "Ada and I have agreed to remain friends, nothing more."

The viscountess bit into her veal pie with gusto. "Good."

Chas was being more cautious about his meal. He put down the buttered roll and repeated, "Good? I thought your life's mission was to see me in parson's mousetrap."

"Do not be vulgar, Charles. I wish to see you wed, naturally. What mother wouldn't, especially when there is the question of a succession? But I am quite pleased you have decided not to pursue that particular connection."

Chas lost his appetite again. "Oh?"

"Yes, I cannot like the blood in that family, you know. The gamester baronet, now that hey-go-mad youngster with no sense of responsibility to his family name. That impossible Lady Westlake who is forever acting above herself."

"I don't think you can blame Jane Johnstone on the Westlake blood, Mother."

"Sir Rodney married her, didn't he? Bad taste, bad blood, it's all the same. You wouldn't want that greedy female hanging on your sleeve, anyway, and you can rest assured she would be if you wed the sister-in-law. Then there is Tess, of course."

"I am quite fond of Tess, ma'am," Chas said in a tone of voice seldom heard by his mother.

"As I am fond of organ-grinders' monkeys. That does not mean I would enjoy having one in the family. I should not like having a grandson who believes he is the reincarnation of some dead Austrian composer."

"I believe it is a dead Italian sculptor this week, but I could be mistaken."

Lady Ashmead nodded her regal head. "I know you and Ada insist on seeing no ill in Tess, but not even you can gainsay the gal has a deucedly odd kick to her gallop."

"We prefer to view Tess's quirks as the eccentricities of a creative genius."

"Nuttier than last month's fruit cake, is what I call it, but that's irrelevant now, thank my stars and salvation." She took another bite, then put down her fork. "So, Charles, if you aren't going to wed the Westlake chit, whom are you going to marry?"

Chapter Five

So who *was* he going to marry? Chas knew he'd have to wed in the near future, to provide heirs to the Ashmead estate and titles. That and nurturing his properties and dependents were his *raisons d'être,* according to his mother, drummed into him since birth. Begetting more little blue bloods was one of the prime obligations that the country demanded of its nobles.

The viscount wouldn't even mind having children, little lace-capped infants, sturdy sons to trail after him about the estate, dainty moppets who would look just like their mother. The problem was, he could put no face to this future bearer of his heirs.

Chas had spent most of his life—since thinking he would become a pirate—thinking that he would marry Ada Westlake, when the time was right. He'd believed she was his, his friend and companion, his laughing bride, the loving mother to his children, when the time was right.

He'd thought wrong. That time was never going to come.

Still, he could not retire from the world, nursing his broken dreams along with his perhaps broken wrist. His mother would nag him to death, for one thing, and his father's memory would haunt him. Uncertain of their futures, his many dependents would feel betrayed. And his house would grow quieter and emptier, like a museum or a mausoleum. No, he would have to marry.

Chas could not, however, think of a single woman he wished to spend the evening with, much less eternity.

So what was he going to do? For one thing, he was going to retrieve Monsieur Prelieu's parcel, in case that well-placed and thus highly valuable gentleman ever managed to get himself and his information out of France. The leather pouch was not on Lord Ashmead's dresser, nor in the stables, confound it, which meant that Chas's inebriated imaginings were less fanciful and more likely fact. He cursed all castaway clunches and pot-valiant visionaries. At least the money was his own and not the Crown's, the government having other odd notions as to the obligations of its more wealthy citizens. They were delighted to have him oversee the small espionage trade from Lillington, at their request but at his own expense. Now he would only have to explain the loss of a Frenchman to the Foreign office, not a fortune.

Telling his concerned valet that he needed to clear his still muddled mind, Chas donned his most comfortable boots and tossed a cloak over his shoulders, so he would not have to disturb his injured arm, now in a sling. He also accepted from his anxious butler a packet of bread and cheese to sustain him.

Chas thought he might be able to manage a horse with one hand, if Coggs was willing to saddle one for him, which he doubted. He believed he could handle the curricle, if the bays were not eager to run, which he also doubted. He refused to be driven in one of his mother's carriages, or trundled around the estate like a sack of grain in one of the carts. Besides, he had no intention of letting anyone know exactly how big a fool he'd been. So, whistling jauntily, Viscount Ashmead strode smartly down the ash tree–lined carriage path, his dog for company. Tally, whose actual name was Tally-ho, since she was always so keen to be running, as usual refused to be left behind.

As soon as he was out of sight of the windows and outbuildings where Chas knew his devoted retainers kept watch, his step faltered and the whistle turned to ragged breathing, as every muscle in his body protested this new jarring. The blasted dog kept circling back to him, looking up accusingly with those big, brown hound eyes, wondering why he wasn't keeping up. Chas fed her the bread and cheese.

When he hobbled off the carriage drive and onto the lane that led to Westlake Hall, the Viscount couldn't help thinking of all the times he had walked or ridden this way, to Ada. He sighed loudly enough that Tally came back from whatever scent she was investigating to rub against his leg. Or to look for more bread and cheese. Chas sighed again. Those times were past.

Perhaps he should let his mother fill the house with her friends, as she'd been threatening, complaining of loneliness for female companionship. It went without saying that all those friends would have marriageable daughters in tow. The chits would all be pretty, and presentable to polite company. Knowing his mother, they'd all come from exalted families and have extensive dowries. Any one of them would satisfy his mother.

None of them would satisfy Lord Ashmead. He didn't want any well-bred London miss, a pattern card of demure behavior. He couldn't bear a blushing bud, with neither confidence nor conversation, nor a dasher like Sir Rodney's widow, more interested in fashion and flirting than family. Charles Harrison Ashmead was not about to worry over cuckoo birds landing in his nest. He did not want an acknowledged belle, either, a woman who'd demand attention and adoration, and would never be content in the country.

No, what Chas wanted in a bride was a woman who was intelligent and loyal, who could share the simple country pursuits he enjoyed, who accepted him for what he was. When he tallied those qualities, he realized he'd just described . . . Tally.

If his mother was lonely—a loneliness he was certain could only be assuaged by a daughter-in-law—he would encourage her intentions to hire a companion instead of turning the Meadows into a Marriage Market. He could also try once more to convince his single-minded mother to return to her cronies in Bath, although Lady Ashmead had insisted that she would not leave the Meadows until Chas was wed, which made taking a stranger to wife a tad more appealing.

If his mother managed to keep a companion longer than the first quarter day, unlike the previous poor relations or unfortunates in her employ, she'd have someone else to commiserate with over a son's failures. A gentlewoman could also take on chatelaine duties her ladyship found onerous, although to Chas's certain knowledge, the only bits of household chores his mother managed were seat cushions and menus, both of which she changed constantly, to the staff's distress.

Having another gently born female in the house was not without complications of its own, since the poor lady was always about, not quite family, never a servant. Still, Chas had offered to pay the woman's wages, as the cost of the coffee stain on the infant cap, a stain, incidentally, which only Lady Ashmead could see. He'd vowed to be polite to the companion and do the pretty, and not even complain when his mother held a few small entertainments for the female, dinners and such, to introduce her to the neighborhood. For what that stain was going to cost Chas, he could have bought a coffee plantation.

By now he had reached the abandoned Westlake orchards, where withered apple trees loomed ahead of him, row upon row of identical, indistinguishable trees. "Come on, Tally," he called to the dog, "there are only a hundred or so." There were only a thousand or so niches where a pouch could be stashed by a drunken dunderhead who could barely recall the orchard, much less the chosen branch.

He held a duplicate leather purse out to the hound for sniffing, then had to hide the thing back in his pocket before the delighted dog ate it or buried it. "It's not a present, dash it, you useless mutt, it's something to go find."

Without high expectations, the viscount was not too disappointed when Tally located a half-rotted glove, a stick suitable for tossing, a surfeit of spoiled apples, and an angry squirrel. Always trying to please him, she'd laid them all at her master's feet, except, of course, the squirrel, but not for lack of trying.

Chas had been searching too, looking beneath the trees for any sign of disturbance where something—or someone—might have fallen from one of the cursed trees. The stiff autumn breeze had ruffled the fallen leaves, though, and the excited dog's tearing around had disturbed any other possible evidence.

Close to dusk, Viscount Ashmead had to concede defeat. As far as he was concerned, the orchard was as empty as his own future.

Ada was on a search that afternoon, too: she was looking for a smuggler. The farms and villages around Lillington were rife with them, according to rumor. The apothecary's assistant might be in the gang, or the blacksmith's son. No matter. They wouldn't talk to Miss Ada Westlake about the illegal trade, and she was not interested in any of the henchmen anyway. She wanted the head of the operation, the ringleader, the dastardly Leo Tobin.

How did she know the mastermind behind the local free traders was Leo Tobin? Because everyone said so. Because he could not have gotten rich with his father's fishing boat. Because he dressed like a gentleman. That's what everyone said, at any rate.

Ada was not, naturally, acquainted with Mr. Tobin. He might be wealthy, but he was not accepted in the polite circles of Lillington society. If the heathen even bothered to attend church, it was not Ada's own St. Jerome's where he put his ill-gotten gains into the poor box. He did not subscribe to the local assemblies, and he did not frequent the Misses Hanneford's lending library. He neither strolled the village streets, nor patronized the shops. Still, Ada knew where to find her quarry. The so-called Gentlemen gathered at a low tavern on the edge of town. Everyone said so.

Never one to shirk her duty, Ada hitched old Lulu to the pony cart and pointed the old mare in the right direction, alone with her thoughts since Westlake Hall could afford neither groom nor maid to accompany her. Since she was already breaking every tenet of proper decorum for an unwed miss by entering a thieves' den, Ada could not worry about being unchaperoned on the journey. Her sister-in-law refused to travel in the pony cart, but would have lain down in front of it before she let Ada return the sack of coins. As for Tess, Ada's sister was inspired today to study the worms in the apples.

Ada might be alone, but she did have her brother Rodney's old dueling pistol for protection. The thing was empty, but would look impressive to the raff and scaff she expected to encounter at Jake's Mermaid Tavern. At least Ada hoped it would.

She herself was not impressed with the dilapidated building. The roof sagged, the single window was grimed with smoke, and the mermaid painted on the unevenly hung sign outside was naked! Ada supposed mermaids usually were, but, goodness, they could have added a bit of seaweed for modesty's sake. This woman made Jane look like an undeveloped schoolgirl.

Eyes lowered, Ada tied Lulu to the post, adjusted her shawl, marched into the building, and announced to the barkeep that she had come to see Mr. Leo Tobin, and she was not leaving until she had done so.

"Bless you, ma'am, but Leo ain't here."

Ada crossed her arms over her chest. "Then find him." She peered around the murky, low-ceilinged room. "You there, Fred. What are you doing here in the daytime when you should be out fishing?"

Fred nervously shuffled his feet. "Tide bein't right, Miss Ada. But you hadn't oughtta—"

"Then you should be home with your wife, helping with the babies. And you, Sam Findley, didn't you promise to build a new pen for your mother's pigs? I nearly ran one over on my way here."

In no time at all, Jake's clientele had dwindled to one old salt asleep in the corner. Ada tapped her foot. Jake spit on the floor, but he sent a boy with a message.

No one had said how handsome Leo Tobin was. His dark hair and eyes reminded her somewhat of Chas, but the smuggler had a rakish, dangerous, devil-may-care quality about him that some women—not Ada, certainly—would find attractive. Ada preferred Viscount Ashmead's open, good-humored countenance. Chas never wore such form-fitting coats, though, nor such clinging pantaloons. The gossips never mentioned that, either.

The smuggler cleared his throat. "You wished to see me, Miss . . . ?"

Ada could have kicked herself for blushing, for looking, for seeing far more than was proper. "No. That is, yes, I did wish to see you."

"I am honored, to be sure, Miss . . . ?" he prompted once more.

Ada blushed again at her lack of manners. The man might be the devil's own disciple, but she was a lady. "Miss Westlake. Miss Ada Westlake," she added, not to be confused with Tess, although in this instance even Ada was worried as to which sister had her wits about her.

"Aha," was all he said, unhelpfully. He did smile, which did not settle her suddenly racing pulse at all.

"Yes, and I have come to give you this." She reached into her pocket and pulled out the pistol.

His eyes widened.

"I beg your pardon. I meant this." Ada gave him the gun to hold while she reached into her other pocket. Missing

Tobin's grin, she held out the sack of coins, repaired with her neat stitches. "From my apple tree."

"Oh?"

"You may as well take it, Mr. Tobin, for I will not accept it, nor your nefarious trespassing.

"No?"

"A thousand times no. I will not permit my land to be used to support the French cause. You may not be aware, sir, but my brother is a soldier, fighting to defend our shores while scum like you profit by undermining his efforts." She noticed his raised eyebrow, the same affectation Chas employed just before he called her Addled Ada. Perhaps she had been a shade overzealous, considering she was practically alone in an alehouse with a known criminal, and he still held her pistol. At least it was unloaded; she wasn't that much of a peagoose. "That is, I am sure you are a fine man. Everyone says so. You must simply find another route to ply your trade than through my apple orchard."

"Or?"

"Or I shall be forced to . . . to report you to the magistrate." Who must be hand in glove with the handsome villain, she realized, that he'd gone so long unapprehended. "Or else I shall have my good friend Viscount Ashmead make sure you do not use Westlake property again."

"How good?"

"How good?" At least no one ever said he had a silver tongue. "Oh. Very good." If Chas's name and title had the fellow quaking in his boots, then she'd use them for all they were worth. Silently apologizing to Chas and wishing more than ever that her words were true, she added, "Viscount Ashmead and I are very, very good friends."

"Very good." Leo handed her the pistol and took the pouch, listening for the satisfactory clink of coins.

"Yes, that's what I said. Lord Ashmead is a close friend."

"No, miss, I meant very good, Westlake Hall is out of bounds to the Gentlemen."

Ada was so relieved she held her hand out to shake the smuggler's, but he raised hers to his lips, the scoundrel. Blushing again, or still, Ada recaptured her hand and fled through the door to Lulu and the waiting cart.

Leo tossed the pouch, the familiar pouch—for hadn't he seen it just recently?—in the air, whistling. "Ah, Charlie, my boy, I can see why you're so smitten. It's a merry dance that little minx will lead you."

Chapter Six

When Chas returned to the Meadows, a red phaeton with gold wheels was drawn up by the stables, where the grooms were rubbing down a pair of showy but narrow-chested grays. The flashy cattle looked fine as fivepence, but Chas's expert eye told him they'd be winded before they reached Lillington. At least Leo had had the sense to park them out of sight of the house. Chas could not imagine what his mother would think about the gaudy equipage, but he well knew what she'd say about the ill effects of associating with the lower classes. In her estimation, none came lower than Leo Tobin.

The viscount hurried into the stables, where Leo was throwing dice with the head groom, Coggs, by the day's last light. Chas looked around, knowing only something of import would have led Leo to visit where he'd never been invited, and never would be invited in this Lady Ashmead's lifetime. "Did our friend arrive then?" he asked, peering into the shadows but spotting nothing except immaculate stalls and his own high-bred horses.

"No such luck." Leo put the dice back in his pocket and came closer to the entry while Coggs went off to the tack room, giving the two men privacy. Leo's brows raised when he caught sight of the viscount's battered visage, that had been barely nicked just two nights ago. "Good grief, man, what the devil happened to you?"

"Fell off my horse." No one believed him about the rabbit hole, so why bother? Leo would not swallow the bar-fight fustian, not when he'd been in the same brawl.

"You? The best rider in the county? With the best trained nags?"

Chas shrugged. "Yes, well, mishaps happen. I suppose that's why they call them accidents."

Leo shook his head, but took the money pouch out of his coat. "I suppose this must have fallen out of your pocket when you parted company with your horse, then."

"By Jove, I am happy to see the deuced thing! I've been searching half the afternoon, dash it. And, yes, I'd wager that was precisely what happened. I lost the purse when I fell. Too dark to see it at the time, of course."

"It would be dark as Hades, I'd guess, in Miss Westlake's orchard. That's where the brass was found."

"What were you doing—? That is, yes, it was quite dark. Foolish of me to take the shortcut through the orchard, I know. But as long as the blunt's recovered, no harm done." Chas motioned toward his injured wrist. "Well, no permanent harm, at any rate."

"In an apple tree."

Chas didn't know whether to pray for quick death, or for strength enough to wipe that knowing grin off Leo's face. He went on the offensive. "What the deuce were you doing in Ada's orchard?"

"I? Whoever said I was ambling about the apples? No, your little lady found it."

"She's not my anything."

"And brought it to me. At Jake's."

Now Chas knew what to pray for this Sunday, at any rate: patience not to murder the both of them, the smirking smuggler and his once would-have-been wife. If he ground his teeth any harder, they'd be down to nubs. "No lady goes into Jake's."

"This one did." Leo tossed the purse from hand to hand. "She seemed to think the brass belonged to me, ill-gotten gain from the French trade."

The viscount snatched for the pouch with his one good hand, and missed. "Well, it doesn't and it isn't."

"Aye, but who does it belong to, then? You? The little angel?"

"To Prelieu, if he gets here. The man will need it to make a new life for himself. And don't call Ada an angel."

"Why not? You did it t'other night while in your cups."

"Dash it, can't you forget that night? I said and did a great many remarkably idiotic things I do not wish to discuss, Miss Westlake being the foremost topic I do not wish to address."

"I might be convinced to lose the evening from my memory, my friend, if you'd explain how you came to lose both a fortune and a bout of fisticuffs to an apple tree, on the same day you lost your bid for the angel—for Miss Ada's hand."

Chas knew there was no putting his friend off, not when such a tasty morsel was so tantalizingly near. Leo was worse than Tally on a good scent. He was equally as trustworthy, too, though. Just as Chas would never need to count the money in the purse, he would never worry about Leo Tobin spreading the tale of his ignominy.

"Very well, I was not thinking clearly, thanks to you and your Blue Ruin, and there was Prelieu's purse, going begging. I got the knacky idea that if Ada had money of her own, she would not feel I was offering her charity by offering her marriage. She'd be able to relieve some of the worse burdens on her shoulders, and perhaps start thinking of her own future instead of her family and her brother's inheritance."

"Yes, I heard all about the noble Sir Emery."

"Noble, hell. If the cawker had any honor he'd sell out and come take care of his own dependents, not leave it for a barely grown sister. The dead brother wasted everything on cards and lavish living; now this living one thinks it's more honorable to die in Portugal than manage his estates. Steps can be taken to restore the properties and the income, but only Emery can make the decisions. If I could do it, I'd go shoot the nodcock myself—not fatally, of course—so he'd be sent home."

"I could . . ."

"No. Anyway, Ada would never accept the money from my hand—might as well marry me, otherwise—so I decided to leave it where I knew she'd be."

"In a tree?"

"That part of the plan was not my best, I admit. Nor standing up in the saddle to put it there."

"So what are you going to do about it now?" Leo had stopped tossing the pouch and was rubbing Tally's silky ears while the dog leaned against his booted legs.

"I am not going to do anything. You are going to restore the pouch to Ada."

"Like hell I am."

"Well, I cannot very well do it, can I? How would I explain having come by the blasted thing? Besides, the sight of my phiz is bound to frighten her half to death."

"Seems to me that any miss with backbone enough to walk into Jake's with an unloaded pistol ain't about to swoon at the sight of a few minor cuts and scrapes."

Minor? Chas felt as ugly as an ape, especially next to Leo's handsome face. "No, you send it with a message that she is free to keep the blunt. Tell her you made inquiries, and the money has nothing to do with you or your operations."

Leo stopped petting the dog to brush a piece of straw off his superfine-clad sleeve. "So I send the money back. How is that going to solve your problem?"

Like finding a woman to marry? Hah. Chas bent to pat Tally's head, so Leo could not see his despair. "My problems don't matter. The cash might buy Ada some time with the banks, or some new breeding stock. She might even buy herself a new bonnet or something."

"What about Prelieu?" Leo asked, lighting a cigarillo. He offered one to Chas, who refused. "I am not encouraged that we've had no word, but if another band had set him ashore, we'll hear soon."

"He knew the dangers, so he must have changed his mind. Or else the French changed it for him, deeming even an under-exchequer of the army too valuable to lose sight of. Hell, the man knew how many guns Napoleon was ordering and where they were being sent, how many officers were on the payroll, and which Englishmen were being paid for information." The viscount shrugged. "He would have been valuable, but we'll find the names we need some other way. I can easily get more cash if he does make an eventual appearance."

"That's it? You are just going to give up on Prelieu and Miss Ada?"

"I am not giving up, dash it, I am giving her back the money. Or you are."

"You are giving up your suit of her, though, aren't you? If she married you, she wouldn't need this piddling purse."

Chas kicked at a pebble on the well-swept floor. "She made me swear not to ask her again."

"Bah. You must have made a rare mull of your courting, Charlie. Why, if I had your title and fortune—and my face—I could have any woman I wanted."

"Not Ada. She isn't mercenary."

Leo ground his cigarillo out under his boot heel. He'd never met a woman whose favors could not be bought but he did not travel in the same circles as Viscount Ashmead. "Why doesn't the lady like you, then?"

"She likes me fine, as a friend. She doesn't love me."

"Gammon. Your kind is forever marrying for other considerations. You must have done something to give her a disgust of you. I thought you had better address than that, my friend."

"Oh, and I suppose you could do much better? I've seen you with Molly and her ilk on your lap. That's not courting, that's rutting. Any other female comes into the room, and you go mumchance. Fine address you have." He gestured to where

Tally was once more shedding dog hairs on Leo's fawn trousers. "I don't see you with a wife at your side and a passel of children at your knee, now that you can provide for them, only a mongrel hound."

"Well, you've been to London, you must know the proper way to court a lady."

"Faugh, it's all flowers and verse and morning calls. Ada wouldn't give a hang for any of that tomfoolery."

"You must have learned something about women at least, from your years on the Town, something to keep you from making micefeet of Miss Ada's affections."

"All I learned from the London Marriage Market was that I didn't like it. I didn't like the scrutiny of a man's background and bankbook. As for the frantic bustle to be entertained, the artificial laughter, the closed spaces, you can have them. And the women . . . Most of them are like trained parrots, repeating whatever a man says, while others are like crows, picking over bones of gossips. Then there are the jackdaws, collecting anything that sparkles. All of their feelings are false, fake, feigned. A man could not trust a one of them."

"Nothing fake about Miss Ada."

"No, Ada always says what she means." He sighed, remembering their last argument. "One is never in doubt as to her feelings."

"Unless the lady doesn't know her own emotions, of course. Why don't you just carry her off and have done with it? She'd ought to love you well enough by the time you reached Gretna."

"What, kidnap Ada? You might think such a thing is romantic, but I consider it an insult to any lady."

"How is a lady supposed to know if she can share passion with a bloke if they don't even share kisses? I suppose such fine gentlefolks as you don't . . . ?"

"Of course not. Ada's a lady, by George. Naturally there was last Christmas, under the mistletoe, and her birthday. And that bonfire at All Hallow's."

"Deuce take it, no wonder there are so few of you nobs. If you never kiss the gal, how is she supposed to know you love her?"

"I asked her to marry me, damn it. That ought to be enough."

Leo was musing, leaning carefully against an upright beam. "Or maybe you don't love her enough to try to convince her."

Not love her enough? He'd stood on a blasted saddle, hadn't he? "She doesn't love me, and that's the point."

"No, you said she had too many other concerns. That's why you thought the money might make her reconsider."

She was never going to reconsider, was she? Chas did not want to hope. "That's not what I meant at all. I just wanted to take care of her, if she won't let me do it the right and proper way."

Leo shook his head. "You've got the moon-sickness, Charlie. Even I can see you've got it bad." He pressed the pouch on the viscount. "Give it to her, tell the girl what you did for her. Tell her you love her."

Chas handed the sack of coins back. "No, it would never work. Ada's got too many scruples. Besides, she hates my dog."

Chapter Seven

Leo Tobin might not betray a comrade's confidence, but he was not above meddling in a friend's failed romance. Viscount Ashmead was almost as close as a brother to Leo, despite their different circumstances, and Leo felt duty-bound to help. Hadn't his lordship given him the funds to buy a bigger ship, to carry enough merchandise to make longer voyages profitable, to hire experienced seamen? No bank would have done that, not with a leaky old boat as collateral. Then Charlie had thrown Leo this plum, working for the government on the sly, ferrying information and turncoat Frogs back and forth, letting slip what information the toffs in London wanted fed to the French. In return the government turned a blind eye to the rest of Tobin's activities.

Leo was growing rich as a result, and he owed it all to his boyhood chum. He hated seeing Charlie so blue-deviled, besides black-and-blue. The least Leo could do was help get the viscount's ducks in a row, if those ducks were at all willing to be herded by a wealthy, well-meaning wharf rat who knew nothing about dainty women. The little Westlake chit seemed perfect for the lad, a true lady who'd walk through hell for one she loved. Leo admired how she stood up for that soldier brother, and held the rest of her family together in his absence. Charlie deserved a woman like that, by Jupiter, and Leo aimed to see he got her.

Leo thought about locking Charlie and Miss Ada in the captain's cabin of his ship, let them settle their differences like two strange cats, and not open the door till they had. Then he thought of having one of his contacts bring Lieutenant Sir Emery Westlake home, willy-nilly. Both plans were about as cork-brained as jumping out of apple trees though, if the chit loved someone else. That was the only reason Leo could see for any female in her right mind turning down his friend, no matter what excuse she gave.

There was nothing for it but for Leo to go in person to see which way the wind of Charlie's destiny blew: a soft breeze to rock his ship, a sprightly gust to fill his sails, a hurricane to see him dashed on the rocks, or no wind at all, leaving poor Charlie with no hope whatsoever.

Now Leo Tobin was a brave man. One had to be, in his profession. He'd rather run a loaded sloop between the French garrisons and the British blockade, though, than face a house full of highborn gentlewomen. His trepidation might have come from all the times he'd been given the cut direct by Lady Ashmead when she visited the village to drag Charlie away from Leo's befouling friendship. He might also be sweating because, while he could dress like a gentleman and speak for the most part like a gentleman, he was nothing but the bastard son of a gentleman.

Still, Viscount Ashmead needed him, and Leo had never let a friend down yet. He rapped on the door of Westlake Hall, looking back to make sure his grays were safe in the hands of the oldest pair of grooms he'd ever seen. He'd swear one of the servants couldn't see the horses, and the other one hadn't heard his command to walk them.

After an uncomfortable interval, a bald old man in house slippers opened the door. "The ladies ain't receiving," the butler mumbled, shutting the door. "It's past time for morning calls."

Leo had commanded a crew of cutthroats and churls; he was not going to be denied by one relic of a retainer with bad feet and a bad attitude toward possible bill collectors. Tobin might look like one of the deceased Sir Rodney's gamng partners, come to make good on the wastrel's vowels, but he was not going to be left on the doorstep. He pushed the door—and the butler—aside. "I have come to see Miss Ada Westlake on a matter of business, to return something of value to her, and I am going to do so. Now. Understood?"

Leo followed the old man's hobbling path down a dark hall to a closed door, which the butler opened without waiting to be given entry. "Some flash cove insists on seeing you, Miss Ada. Should I fetch the musket?"

Ada looked up from the novel she was reading. "Oh. Oh, no, that won't be necessary."

Relieved at the interruption, for in Jane's mind any company was better than her sisters-in-law's, Lady Westlake tossed aside the fringe she was trying to knot. The thing looked more like a cat toy than a lady's reticule anyway. The gentleman whose broad shoulders nearly filled the doorway was infinitely more appealing. "I should say not."

Seated at the pianoforte, Tess did not stop her playing. She'd hit one key, then write on the scored page in her lap. Plunk, pencil scratch. Plunk, pencil.

Leo swallowed, which left his mouth too dry for his tongue to move in it. Lud, there were three ladies. He stood in the doorway, silent as a statue.

"Invite him in quickly, Ada," Jane whispered in an aside. "He has the look of a determined suitor about him."

"He is no suitor," Ada hissed back, as she moved past Jane's chair. "He is a smuggler." Still, she took Leo's hat and gloves, which the butler had forgotten, and drew Tobin into the room, to make introductions.

"Why, Captain Tobin," Jane burbled, after Leo had made a proper bow. "I am delighted to make your acquaintance, having heard so much about you. And to think you have met dear Ada unbeknownst to me. Sly boots, our Ada." Jane didn't care if the man were a Captain Sharp. He looked prosperous and he was calling on cabbage-headed Ada. That was enough for Jane. Of course, if he was a real gentleman, with a title instead of a trade, Jane would have made a push to fix his interest for herself, he was that attractive, in a darkly sensuous, silently brooding way. "You must stay for tea, Captain. I'll just go tell Cook, shall I?" She waggled her finger in his face. "Nothing improper about leaving you two alone, of course, not with our Tess in the room. And you seem a fine, trustworthy gentleman, to be sure."

Aghast at Jane's blatant matchmaking, Ada followed her to the door. "He's not trustworthy! The man is a smuggler, I told you!"

"A prosperous one, by all reports, and certainly handsome enough, and the first caller you've had since turning down Lord Ashmead. He's the only one you're likely to have, too, with a reputation for being so hard to please." She gave Ada a shove. "Now get back in there and try to be pleasant to the man. Think of your poor family for a change."

Ada returned to the drawing room to find that Captain Tobin had not moved. He was staring at Tess, who was entirely oblivious to his presence. Frowning, Ada said, "You'll have to forgive my sister. Tess forgets her manners when in the throes of creativity." When he still remained quiet, she raised her chin, as if in defense of his silent criticism of her beloved sister. "Tess is a creative genius. She, ah, has not quite decided upon which Muse to follow. Today she is composing."

Plunk, pencil scratch. Plunk.

"Will you please take a seat?" Ada offered, trying to distract Tobin from her admittedly odd sister. The impossible man had still not offered a word, and what did he mean by calling on Ada in the first place? She'd made it as plain as the straight, slightly aquiline nose on the dastard's handsome face that she had no wish to have anything to do with him or his ilk. Well, she could be as rude as he. "Cobble said you insisted on seeing me?"

Brought to his senses, and the realization that for the moment he only had to face one female, Charlie's sweetheart and the least intimidating of the trio, Leo sat. He reached into his pocket for the money pouch. "Returning this, ma'am. Not mine, nor my men's."

An honest smuggler? She'd never be the wiser if he'd kept the coins. Ada was touched, almost glad now that Jane had thought to offer him tea. "Then whose could it be?" she wondered.

And wondered again at the blush that suffused the dark complexion.

"Yours now, finders keepers."

"Oh, no, I could never keep such a sum. Someone must be missing it. I'll have to ask around."

"Ashmead."

"Ashmead?"

"Said he was your friend. Ask him what to do."

Ada'd used the viscount's name to threaten a smuggler. She had no intention of asking Chas anything, not after the way they'd parted, but she was curious. "Do *you* know Lord Ashmead?"

Leo liked the way her eyes lit up when she said Charlie's name, and how she was as full of principles as freckles. Miss Ada was a trim handful besides, he could see now that she wasn't wearing that old shawl. Despite a faded dress that even Leo could tell was out of fashion, she had a shape just made for cuddling. The lady was too short for him, of course, but just right for Charlie. Leo nodded and relaxed a bit. "Like a brother. No finer man alive, I swear."

She smiled at the idea of a recalcitrant ruffian recommending the viscount. "I think so too."

"You do? Capital. That is, a'course you do. Everyone loves our Charlie, don't they?" He leaned forward, eager for her answer, but Jane returned then, followed by Cobble with a tea tray.

"How lovely that you are becoming better acquainted. Here, Captain, you must try one of Cook's apple tarts. Ada picked the apples herself, you know. Quite the industrious little bee, our Ada."

She went on, pressing tea and tarts and Ada on the man. Luckily, Leo had only to answer "Please" and "Thank you," then "Um," while his mouth was full to keep her conversation flowing. Jane found him quite delightful, since any gentleman who let her speak without telling her to stubble it was quite a novelty. "How many ships did you say you owned?"

Having saved the purse from Jane's clutches by stuffing it between two sofa cushions, Ada now tried to rescue Mr. Tobin. If he was a friend of Chas's, he could not be all bad. "Is Mr. Johnstone not joining us for tea, Jane?"

"Unfortunately not, for I am certain Uncle Filbert would enjoy meeting our new acquaintance. We see so few new faces, don't you know, Captain Tobin, compared to what we were used to in London. Alas, Uncle has gone out shooting. He fancied venison, I believe."

Ada hoped Uncle Filbert was a better shot than Cousin Algernon. She fancied her flock of sheep. Then again, if Mr. Johnstone managed to put food on the table, it would be a welcome contribution to the household, his first contribution, in fact. "Do you hunt, Mr. Tobin?"

Leo had been known to hunt deserters, informers, and the occasional French spy. "Aye."

So much for that topic of conversation. Ada was about to start discussing the weather—surely a seafarer would be knowledgeable about that—or horses, Chas's favorite topic, about which Mr. Tobin was surely unknowledgeable, judging from the narrow-chested pair she could see through the window. She was spared the necessity by her sister.

Drawn from her creative trance by the smells of tea and pastries, Tess drifted toward the tea cart, the thick sheaf of note-filled pages in her hand. Leo carefully set his cup and plate and napkin aside, to rise and bow. "Ch—ch—Charmed," was all he had to say at Ada's introduction, but he really was, charmed, that is: charmed, ensorcelled, his mouth magicked shut by a divine vision, or a witch, all in flowing, fluttering layers of multicolored fabric. With green eyes.

As for Tess, she took one look at the tall, dark, and wickedly handsome stranger, and tossed her papers aside. "Sebastian!" she exclaimed, rushing to throw her arms around him. "My pirate!"

"My gawd," Leo managed to utter from a flurry of cloth and paper and soft, sweet-smelling woman.

"My salts," Jane cried.

"He's a smuggler, not a pirate," Ada whispered as, mortified, she pried her sister away from the red-faced gentleman.

"Smuggler, pirate, pish-tush." Tess had her hands pressed to her chest—her own chest, Ada was relieved to see—as she watched Mr. Tobin bend down to gather up the scattered pages. "You don't understand. He is my hero, my Tristan, my Lancelot, my Lochinvar."

"My stars," Jane moaned.

"The hero of my opera, you ninny," Tess said, grabbing up one of the papers and making rapid, undecipherable notes on the back.

"You must forgive my sister-in-law, Captain." Jane tapped her forehead. "We humor her odd turns, don't you know."

"We admire her creative talents," Ada corrected. "Don't we, dearest?"

Tess shrugged, still making notes. "Genius is seldom recognized in the artist's lifetime. But you wait, I'll be the salvation of this family yet when I make a fortune for us with my masterpiece."

Jane whimpered into her handkerchief.

"What do you think, Mr. . . . ah?"

"Mr. Tobin, Tess, Mr. Leo Tobin."

Leo stood up, most of the pages firmly in hand, and bowed again.

Tess made a perfect curtsy. "Thank you. But did you think, Jane, that Mr. Tobin would not notice that the tea service is earthenware, not porcelain?" He hadn't. "Or that you moved those cushions to cover the stain on the sofa or that the draperies are faded and threadbare?" He hadn't, being too concerned with not spilling his tea. "Of course he noticed. Further, everyone knows your husband left us without a feather to fly with." She aligned the pages in her hand. "But that will change. You see, Mr. Tobin, I first set out to write heroic poetry, like that Byron fellow, until I realized how little money versifiers earn from their works. So I am setting *Sebastian and the Sea Goddess* to music. Now I can design the handbill for my opera! What woman would not spend her last shilling to see a hero with those shoulders, those legs, that—"

"Tess!"

"Do say you will pose for me, Mr. Tobin. You can keep your jacket on, for the preliminary sketches, anyway."

"Tess!" Ada was wringing her hands by now. Jane had started mewling like a lost kitten, but Leo finally got "Charmed" out.

"Good." Tess pulled a charcoal stick out of her pocket and turned over another page. "Stand there. No, there. Cross your arms and spread your legs as if you were on a sailing ship. La, I can see you are a natural at this. No, don't keep looking at me."

Ada poured herself a fresh cup of tea, and one for Jane, who had her hands over her eyes.

"You are still looking at me, Mr. Tobin. This is not working. I know, we must have you with the sea goddess in your arms, in the ravishment scene. That's sure to sell more copies. Jane, would you—Of course not. Ada, be a dear and let Mr. Tobin embrace you."

Jane's cup hit the floor.

"I can always put in Jane's face and figure on the final painting."

Jane's head hit the floor.

"She'll be fine, Mr. Tobin. She does that all the time. Go

on, Ada. Step closer so Sebastian can put his arms around you."

"Please, Tess, I am sure this is not necessary. Surely an artist of your caliber can imagine—"

"Bosh. Do you want to be scrimping and saving the rest of your life, Ada? This will make our fortunes, I know. Now go on, I just need a rough sketch."

Scarlet-faced, Ada took a step nearer to the smuggler. "Do you mind? Tess will be unconsolable if we don't model for her. And she is a quick sketch-artist, I promise."

Leo had wanted to take a hand in his friend's love affair, not take his friend's love interest in his own calloused hands. He could no more have refused Tess Westlake's pleas, however, than he could have stopped breathing. Now that he thought of it, Leo wondered if he had taken a single breath since she'd dropped her papers and landed in his arms. For sure he was dizzy enough to have gone without air. He took a deep breath and nodded his acceptance of the inevitable.

"Excellent. Over there, please. That's right, both arms. Now bend sideways, balancing her back over your right arm. Ada, you are a graceful sea goddess, not a fireplace poker. No, Mr. Tobin, you are supposed to be looking at your lover, not at me. Ada, gaze up at Sebastian adoringly. No, do not giggle, worship. That's it, perfect. Hold that pose."

And that, of course, was when Viscount Ashmead entered the room.

Chapter Eight

"Bloody hell!"

Chas had spent all morning debating whether he should visit Westlake Hall, whether his face was healed enough, whether enough time had gone by that Ada would have forgiven his harsh words, whether Leo was correct and he was giving up too easily. Whether, he'd told himself, the orchard money had arrived safely or not.

It had arrived safely, all right, in the hands of a despicable, double-dealing dastard. This was betrayal of the worst sort. Chas felt as if his heart was being torn out of his chest, with his mother's tiny embroidery scissors. Losing Ada was one thing, but losing her to Leo, who hadn't wanted to return the money, who didn't like talking to ladies, who claimed to be Chas's friend, was outside of enough. That Leo was handling Ada as if she were one of his barmaids, after a visit to one of the upstairs rooms, was far beyond the powers of any mortal man's restraint.

"Get your filthy hands off my woman, you bastard!" Chas shouted, his good hand clenched in a fist.

Ada shouted back, "I am not your woman."

Tess shouted back, "He is not a bastard."

Leo just grinned. Oh, he was enjoying himself now. He did set Miss Ada back on her feet, though, and took a step away from the little lady, tugging down his waistcoat and smoothing back the dark lock of hair that had fallen across his forehead. Then, because he really was a smuggler and a bastard, by George—or by Geoffrey—he helped tuck a soft brown curl back into Miss Ada's topknot.

The growl that came from Chas's throat would have made a wolf take notice.

"Oh, Charlie, get off your high horse," Tess chided him, patting his arm and leaving a streak of charcoal down his sleeve. "It's not what it looks like. Mr. Tobin—or is it Captain?—has agreed to pose for the advertisement for my opera. You refused to portray Sebastian, if you'll recall."

"You wanted me to pose half naked, if you will recall." He ignored Leo's sudden cough. "And I should have known you would defend such havey-cavey goings on as poetic license or some such."

Having put herself to rights, Ada beckoned him over to the sofa. "Give over, Chas. There was no impropriety intended, not with Jane in the room."

Chas was already lifting that lady back onto the sofa. She opened her eyes, took one look at his scraped and scabbed face, and swooned again. This time she fell back onto the cushions.

"Yes, I can see what a proper chaperone Lady Westlake was," Chas grumbled, going to pour Jane a glass of wine to restore her nerves, and one for his own, with the familiarity of an old family friend.

By now Ada had a chance to get a better look at the viscount's appearance, and she winced. "Oh, dear."

Tess, predictably, wanted to paint him. "For when Sebastian vanquishes the evil kraken to rescue his princess. Where are my pastel crayons? Or should I use watercolors? Don't move, Charlie, and don't fade."

Chas fixed his eye, the one that was not swollen and lurid enough to send Tess into transports, on Leo, who decided that perhaps he had overstayed his welcome.

"Oh, no, Mr.—Captain—Botheration, Leo. I am not done with the sketch." Tess saw that he already had his hat and gloves. "Or you'll simply have to come back."

Ada and Chas chorused "No," with Jane rousing herself enough to add an echoing denial. The last thing Jane needed was for some adventurer to encourage Tess in her artistry. The captain would already be sure to tell the world what an odd household they had at Westlake Hall. Then too, if Viscount Ashmead was back to calling, they did not need any jumped-up fisherman on their doorstep, much less a smuggler.

Ignoring all the others, Leo looked toward Tess. "Ma'am?"

"I need you for the painting. You will return, won't you, sir?"

"Aye," Leo said with a smile, a bow to the ladies, and a wink toward his lordship.

Ada walked him out while Tess hunted for her drawing pad and Chas assured Jane that he looked worse than he felt.

"You know, Mr. Tobin," Ada began softly as they reached the door, where Cobble waited to see the caller on his way, "my sister is not like other women."

"Aye, she's an artist. Never known a real painter before, nor a poet."

"And I daresay she has never known a smuggler before. Still, her emotions and enthusiasms . . ."

"Be you warning me off, ma'am?"

Ada blushed. "I am not my sister's keeper, Mr. Tobin. It's just that her reputation is already so . . . so . . ."

"Squirrelly?"

She nodded. "Nuttier than a whole forest full of squirrels. I should not want to see her laughed at or belittled."

"I wouldn't do that, Miss Ada, though your protectiveness does you credit. I'd never hurt the lady."

Ada looked into his eyes and saw honesty there. The smuggler had brought back the money, too, so perhaps he could be trusted with her sensitive sister. She was almost confident of his motives, morals, and mental state, until he added, "Besides, no one will laugh at Miss Westlake when our opera is a success."

* * *

"Leo Tobin is not a proper person for you to be entertaining, dash it."

"How dare you act rudely to a guest in my house, sirrah. You have absolutely no right to be telling me who or who not to see. Besides, who are you to be criticizing me for the company I keep, Lord Lowlife? I'm not the one who was mauled about in an alehouse brawl with a bunch of foxed sailors and out-of-work fishermen."

Jane fled the room. Tess was already gone, mixing colors in her attic studio. Ada and Chas were alone in the parlor, squared off like prizefighters at opposite corners. She had her hands on her hips, he had a glass in his good hand.

"I was not in any tavern fight. I fell off my horse, confound it."

"Hah, a likely tale. You'd have to have been tossed off down the side of a mountain, then been rolled on by the horse, to look the way you do. Besides, you have not fallen off a horse since you were twelve and took out your father's stallion without permission. Even then you were hurt worse by the beating you got than by the fall. Moreover, the egg man's sister's husband was there that night and he saw you in the rowdy melee. At least you don't have a missing tooth, like he does." Ada took a step or two closer to look at his poor face. "Does it hurt?"

"Not at all," Chas lied.

She came closer still. "And your arm?"

Chas had done without the sling today so he could drive his curricle, but he was holding the tightly wrapped wrist stiffly. Now he wriggled his still swollen fingers. "Not broken."

"Well, if you expect me to feel guilty about your injuries," Ada said with a sniff, "you can just think again."

Chas took a sip of his wine. "Why the deuce should you feel guilty when I was the gudgeon?"

"Jane says that I drove you to drink, and her uncle says that you started the fight to restore your manly pride."

"Since when do you hold credit with anything Jane and her uncle say? They utter a great many remarkably foolish things, as you well know. Where is the pride in getting beaten bloody? Furthermore, I did not start any fight. I fell off my horse, which was no more your fault than the man in the moon's. In fact, had the moon been brighter, I might not have lost my footing, er, seat."

"You are just saying that to make me feel better."

"What, first I am trying to make you feel guilty and now I am trying to make you feel better? I take it all back, Ada; trying to follow your reasoning is enough to make any man take up the bottle."

"Then you *are* blaming me!" Her eyes were suspiciously damp.

Chas almost poured himself another glass of wine, but thought better of it. "No, I am my own man. No one drives me to do anything I don't want," he lied again. This woman drove him to distraction, constantly. Like now, when she flashed him a sudden smile, going from storm clouds to sunny day in an instant.

"Then you aren't angry at me anymore, either?"

He had to smile back. "Not if you aren't still mad at me."

"I am too glad you came to remember why I was so furious. I was going to write you a note if you hadn't called soon, apologizing for calling you a jackass."

"I came to apologize for calling you a turnip-head."

"I like donkeys."

"I like turnips."

"Friends?" Ada held her hand out.

Chas sighed inside, but he took her hand and squeezed it gently. "Friends." It was something, anyway. "I missed you." More than he missed using his left hand, or his right eye.

Comfortable with each other once more, they sat down to share the last apple tarts. Between bites, Chas said, "I do have to warn you, Ada, just as a friend, mind, that Leo Tobin really is not the kind of person you should encourage. I realize some women might be attracted by his reputation, excited by the threat of danger, and they might even find him good-looking, in a rugged, weathered kind of way. I suppose he dresses well, and his manners are passable, but, dash it, he is a smuggler!"

"But a very pleasant smuggler."

"There is no such thing as a pleasant smuggler, by Jupiter, for he would not last long at the trade. I saw the liberties Tobin was taking. No honorable man would have behaved in so . . . so warm a manner."

"Mr. Tobin was only trying to humor Tess. You know how intractable she can be when an inspiration strikes her."

"Petting the calf," he muttered.

"Excuse me?"

"He was playacting for Tess so he could impress you. Everyone knows how you dote on your sister."

"Why, Charles Harrison Ashford, I do believe you are jealous!"

"Of an outlaw? Do not be absurd." If he were any more jealous, Chas feared, his already discolored skin would turn green, so green that he felt no qualms whatsoever in blackening Leo's already shady reputation. "You and I are supposed to be friends, are we not? Well, friends look out for each other. I simply do not want to see you taken in by such a scurvy knave."

"Mr. Tobin seemed everything decent to me, and I did not feel that his kindness to Tess was a sham at all. He seemed quite gentle, almost shy, in fact."

Chas set his earthenware plate down with a force that would have shattered the fragile porcelain tea set, if it hadn't been sold months ago. "The man is a blasted free trader! Think of your brother, for heaven's sake."

"I am thinking of my sister, for her own sake. You know, it is odd how you have taken Mr. Tobin in such dislike. He speaks quite fondly of you, as if you were as close as brothers."

"We are brothers, dash it! Unacknowledged, of course, as

Leo was born on the wrong side of the blanket. I thought everyone knew."

"My parents might have known, but no one tells young girls things like that." Ada paused to take in this new revelation. The idea of the starched-up Viscountess Ashmead having an illicit relationship was too farfetched to consider, so Leo must be a product of the notoriously profligate Geoffrey Ashford, Chas's father. Now that she thought about it, the similarities in appearance of the two men to each other and to the late viscount's portrait were even more striking. She should have seen the relation for herself. Anyone could. If anyone could, then Lady Ashmead must. "Good heavens, does your mother know Leo is your father's . . . child?" Ada could not bring herself to call Tess's new friend a bastard, or even a by-blow.

"Of course, Mother knows. She has always known. That's why she won't let Leo in the house, and won't visit any home he's welcomed at. She shut every door she could to him, and I've had the devil's own time opening them since I came into the title, I can tell you that."

"Which must be why your brother thinks so highly of you. Otherwise one might have supposed he'd hate you."

"Why should he hate me? I wasn't the one who fathered a child by a woman not my wife. And no, he does not resent me for being the heir, despite the fact that he was born first. Leo was the son who got to be raised by a loving family, not left for servants to rear. He was the one who got to follow his dream and go to sea." Chas pulled the cuff over his bandaged wrist. It would well nigh kill him if his illegitimate brother got Ada, too. "I am the one who always envied Leo, you see." He took a swallow of wine. "By the way, what was the scapegrace doing here in the first place?"

Chapter Nine

Ada pushed some cushions aside to retrieve the leather sack. "It's the strangest thing. Your brother—No, I must not call him that, I suppose—was returning this pouch. It's full of money, astonishingly enough, that I found in the old apple orchard."

Chas was looking at the purse as if it contained a coiled cobra. If he never saw the thing again, that was too soon. Ada took his expression for suitable amazement, and continued.

"I thought such a sum of money could only belong to the local free traders, you see, for no one rightfully connected to Westlake Hall would possess such a fortune, nor so little sense as to leave it in a tree."

Chas was doubtful anyone anywhere had so little sense. Except him, and his Ada, of course. He tried very hard not to raise his voice when he asked, "So you . . . gave a large sum of money to a known smuggler?"

Ada was twisting the leather drawstrings that tied the pouch. "Well, I did not precisely know it myself, although I strongly suspected, from all the talk, you know."

"But you knew Leo, Mr. Tobin, that is? Not even you could be so totty-headed as to approach a possibly murderous, malfeasant, misogynistic makebait?" He tilted her chin up so he could look into her soft brown eyes. "Could you?"

Pretending interest in the last apple tart, Ada looked down, always a bad sign, in Chas's book. "I hadn't before, actually, but I do now and he is none of those things, I am certain."

"No, he isn't, but you are still a thick-headed turnip, my girl. He might have been all those and more."

"He couldn't have been, not if he is your brother."

"What has that to do with anything? I never trusted your brother Rodney with one of my sisters. Besides, you didn't know Leo was related to me at the time, Ada, so stop trying to wriggle your way out of a well-deserved scold. Wherever Leo was, was no place for a lady."

"Ah, but I knew some of the gentlemen there. I was never in any danger, I swear, so you can stop acting like an old windbags. I even had my brother's dueling pistol, just in case."

"Good grief, you weren't toting around a loaded Manton, were you? Those things have hair triggers, Ada. You could have blown your own fool head off."

"I am not entirely dim-witted, you know, despite your odious estimation of my intelligence. The pistol was not loaded, of course."

Chas groaned. "An unloaded weapon makes everything one hundred percent better. What are you using for brains, these days, breadcrumbs?"

Ada brushed the crumbs of apple tart to the side of her plate. "I do not wish to speak more of this." Not if it would lead to another argument. Now that Chas was here, she remembered what a warm comfort he was to her—not that she had exactly forgotten in the few days he was gone—and she did not want to jeopardize this restored closeness. "Anyway, Leo returned the purse today, which speaks to his credit, I believe."

It spoke more of the viscount's threats, but Chas did not say so. He took a deep breath. "Ada, what would you say if I told you that the money pouch was mine, that I put it in the orchard?"

She placed her hand over his. "I'd say that you were trying to protect me from doing anything as foolish as going into the Mermaid Tavern again. You cannot always be watching over me, you know, my friend."

Closing his eyes, Chas tried again. "But what if I swore I left the blunt there?"

Ada laughed. "Why, I'd believe that faradiddle as soon as I believed you fell off your horse. You know I would never take money from you. Heaven knows how many times you've offered to lend me what I need, with no hopes of getting it back. Besides, you would never be so foolish as to leave a fortune in a tree. You might be as stubborn as a mule, but I would never believe you could be that stupid."

Chas couldn't believe it, either.

She went on: "Why, anyone might have stumbled upon the sack, or no one, for years on end."

"I, um . . ."

"I won't ask you how much money is in the purse because your brother might have told you, but I'd wager a shilling you cannot tell me in which tree the pouch was hidden, nor even which part of the orchard."

That shilling was as safe as a stone house. Chas shook his head.

"There, now stop being so sweet and solicitous and help me decide what to do with the treasure now."

Sweet and solicitous? She'd just described a favorite uncle. Chas felt anything but paternal, fraternal, or friendly, sitting beside Ada. He could smell the lavender on her clothes, and some light floral scent that was all Ada's, along with baked apples. He could almost touch one of her soft curls, trailing out of the ribbons again, as it laid alongside her neck. He could nearly count the freckles on her cheeks, they were that close. He could take Leo's advice and kiss her—if he wanted his other eye blackened.

"So what do you think?" Ada jiggled the coins in the bag.

Chas thought she was the most maddening female of his acquaintance, and he was a hopeless mooncalf. "Think?"

"About the money, silly. What should I do with it?"

"I think you should keep it, of course. Use it to pay off some of those debts so you are not paying interest on top of interest. Use it to pay Kit Highsmith for the use of his stud ram. We've talked about a hundred things you could do to make this place pay for itself. Use the brass for any one of them."

"But it's not my money."

"It may as well be, if no one else claims it. You must have been correct, that it was left by some passing contrabanders. They would have used your orchard once, perhaps, in an emergency. They won't be back, I am sure, not with this area controlled by Leo Tobin and his men." Which was another reason Chas financed his half-brother's business, to keep actual criminals, ruthless and greedy cutthroats, from moving into the neighborhood. "The money was meant for you, I am certain."

"I cannot feel right about keeping it."

"Then give it to Tess, to stage her opera."

"What, and make us the laughingstocks of the county? You've heard her music. Besides, she'd most likely expect us to perform in the thing. I, of course, am not tall or voluptuous enough to play the sea goddess, she has already informed me."

"I think you'd make an excellent mermaid," he said out of loyalty but without much conviction, not liking the image of her in Leo's arms.

"You'd make a dashing Sebastian." Ada thought Chas would make a dashing anything.

"Not nearly as good as Leo."

"Can he sing?"

"Like a hungry hog."

"Poor Tess, she will be so disappointed. Or else she will have to rewrite her opera, making it *Sylvia and the Swine Prince*."

"Seriously, Ada, if you are uncomfortable about keeping the cash for yourself, why don't you give the money to Jane as her missing widow's benefits? That way you might at least get the leeches off your back and out of your house."

"No, she'd spend it in one month, but keep charging the

Westlake accounts for another three. Then she'd be back here, making more demands for funds I do not have."

"Then send some of it to Emery, dash it, to pay his ship fare home."

Ada shook her head. "He wouldn't leave his men. You know that. I daresay he'd think I ought to give the money to the War Office, to purchase ammunition for the troops. After all, the smuggling does finance the French, so it would only be fair that this bribe money benefits our own efforts."

"No!" Chas's protest came out a bit more vehemently than he'd intended. Give his blunt to those dodderers at Whitehall? They hadn't managed yet to get the men paid on time, much less equipped and fed. "The politicians would likely use it to line their own pockets." He maligned another group of friends, men he was working with to change those very conditions. "The soldiers would never see a shilling of it."

"I suppose you are right. I'll have to do some more thinking on the matter. Perhaps I will discuss the ethics of the thing with the vicar tomorrow."

Chas wondered what time he would have to get up to call on Reverend Mr. Tothy before Ada did. Ethics be damned, that money was Ada's, no one else's.

"You do that. I'm sure he'll tell you to keep it. By the way, you might ask him if he knows any gentlewomen in need of a position. My mother is considering hiring another companion."

"Really? Miss Ellen Hanneford at the lending library said she heard this morning that Lady Ashmead was planning a house party, with a formal dinner and ball."

"Confound it, and I swore to do the pretty by whomever Mother had stay, thinking she intended an elderly lady. A small entertainment, she said. Hah!"

Ada smiled in sympathy, knowing how Chas hated entertaining the type of guest his mother would be sure to invite. Ada could not feel comfortable with the viscountess's usual visitors from London and Bath, either, feeling dowdy and unsophisticated next to them, unable to converse about the latest plays, parties, and romantic pairings. "Well, Jane is in alt even if you are not, declaring herself out of mourning a month early. Considering the dire straits Rodney left his widow in, I cannot fault her."

"No, neither can I. Wouldn't it be a blessing for everyone if Lady Westlake lands herself a second husband while she still has a face and figure to attract one, since she has no fortune? 'Twould be a boon to everyone except the second husband, of course."

"That's mean," Ada said, but with a smile that meant she agreed with him.

"That's honest. Anyway, there are sure to be a few eligible gentlemen; not even my mother would fill the house with nothing but marriageable chits."

"Oh, it's to be that kind of party. I hadn't thought."

"Yes, well, now that you and I aren't . . . That is, Mother feels I should . . ."

"I see." Ada did understand, knowing that Chas had to marry to produce an heir, eventually. She just hadn't thought that eventually could come so soon.

"I had better be off, then, before she invites half the *beau monde*." Chas stood to go, consulting his pocket watch, straightening his waistcoat, making sure his neckcloth was secure. "Before I leave, though, I, ah, need to ask you a question."

Ada was on her feet, too. "No, Chas, please don't—"

"Don't worry, I am not going to ask you to marry me again. I swore I would never do so again, remember? The engagement ring is safely back in the vault and will remain there"—he almost said till Hell froze over, or until she asked him, which were likely one and the same—"until I find a suitable bride. But I just have to be sure of something that has been nibbling away at me. Something important."

A V formed between Ada's eyebrows. "I cannot imagine

what you are talking about, Chas. You know you can ask me anything. Except that other, of course."

He cleared his throat and took a deep breath. "You do know that I love you, Ada, don't you?"

She laughed, relieved. "Is that all?"

All? It was all he had been thinking about since Leo had prodded at him. All that mattered, all that he had to pin his feeble hopes on. All of him. "Do you?"

"Of course, you clunch. You love me better than your own sisters, haven't you always told me so?" She reached up to brush a lock of dark hair off his forehead. "And I'd know it anyway, by how you are always looking out for my interests, and how you worry when I do something foolish, like going to the Mermaid Tavern by myself." She stood on tiptoe to press a kiss to his uninjured cheek. "And I love you, even if you are like a mother hen with one chick."

A brother? A mother hen? She thought of him as a bloody relative! Leo was right, which made Chas all the angrier. His Ada did not even think of him as a man, as a mate. Damnation! "Do you know," he said now, before he had a chance to think about not saying it, "I have a mind to try that pose Tess had you and Leo in, just in case I am needed when mighty Sebastian is off killing dragons, or running from the excise men." With that, without a by-your-leave, Chas grabbed Ada in his good arm, tipped her toward the side, and kissed her firmly, fiercely, with fire and fervor and all the feeling he could fit in one—albeit lengthy—kiss. "Now," he said with a gasp as he left, "now tell me that I love you like a brother."

Somehow Ada's legs managed to support her back to the sofa. She couldn't imagine how, for her bones felt like blancmange. Her toes tingled and her lips burned and her mind—Oh, mercy, her mind had turned to mud. No, to mashed turnips.

That was certainly not a brotherly peck, nor even an affectionate buss under the mistletoe. Gracious, what did Chas mean by such a gesture, and had he been as shaken, as turned inside out, as befogged as she? Ada always thought of Chas as giving, always there with support and comfort and confidence, advice when she needed it, and even when she did not. He would have given her his wealth, his very name, to keep her safe. But this, this was a hungry kiss, as if Chas wanted so much more from her, as if he wanted a part of her soul.

Could it be that Chas had needs too, not just a man's lustful needs, or a viscount's need for an heir? Could he really be looking for his heart's completion, not just a convenient helpmeet? Could she be it? Ada'd never dared hope, and now it was too late. He said he'd never ask her again, and Chas never went back on his word.

He must have kissed her like that to show her what she'd be missing, Ada decided, to prove what could have been. Now he'd find a bride among those beautiful London belles, accomplished flirts every one of them, eager for Viscount Ashmead's title and wealth. They'd be eager for his kisses, too, if they knew Chas could make their blood flow backward. Unless it did not work for every woman, or with every woman. What was it he'd asked? "You do know that I love you, don't you?"

Ada didn't know anything anymore.

Chapter Ten

"Miss Ada Westlake is, possibly, going to make the church a sizeable donation, and if she does, I am going to refuse to accept it?" Vicar Tothy looked longingly toward his untouched breakfast. Even his sermon notes appeared more appetizing than this early morning interview with Lord Ashmead.

"That is correct." Chas tapped his riding crop against his high-topped boots, not that a whip would have done him much good on the horse Coggs deemed him capable of riding one-handed.

"May I ask why I am to turn away this potential bounty?"

"No."

The Reverend Mr. George Tothy was a third cousin to the viscount through the matriarchal branch. He was not in line to inherit any title, fortune, or property, only a great deal of instruction, interference, and embroidered items from his benefactress, Lady Ashmead. The viscount himself, who in fact held the living and who had appointed Tothy, had used to be a decent sort, the vicar always thought. The younger man had gained George Tothy's respect for his generosity, his sense of duty, for not putting on the airs of the lord of the manor, although he was, and for putting up with her ladyship.

Now Mr. Tothy eyed the whip and his lordship's impatience. He wiped a bead of sweat off his forehead, and said, "I am sorry to disoblige, my lord but, as a minion of the Church, I am afraid I cannot refuse any largesse, large or small. Bigger donations, with their concomitant broader opportunity to benefit the congregation, are, regrettably, more difficult to decline."

"Deuce take it, the church won't be out a farthing. I will match Miss Ada's gift, if you give it back to her. Or convince her to keep the blasted money in the first place."

"That is generous indeed, and yet the bishop would—"

"Hell—your pardon, sir—I will double the donation."

". . . Without a plausible excuse." Mr. Tothy did not understand, he did not suppose it was necessary that he understand, but if his lordship's dealings with Miss Ada were not aboveboard, the vicar knew his duty: he was to go directly to Lady Ashmead.

"Dash it, I merely wish her to have a proper dowry."

Tothy understood even less. "Not that I listen to rumor, of course, my lord, but Lady Ashmead herself informed me that there was to be no match between your houses. Therefore you would not be the recipient of said bridal portion?"

Chas thought he might have an apoplexy before he saw his blunt—and his bride—go to another man, but he nodded. "That is correct. Miss Ada is to have the money for her own, for whatever purpose she chooses, except giving it away."

"And you have no further involvement in the matter, my lord, except as a generous friend?"

"That, too, is true, Tothy." Temporarily, at least.

The vicar was, as a result of his lordship's visit, not at all surprised to receive a morning call from Miss Ada Westlake. He was astonished, however, to see her accompanied by old Lord Ashmead's brigand by-blow, and the baronetcy's batty sister, who barely took their eyes off each other. The good Lord certainly did work in mysterious ways, Reverend Tothy reflected.

Tess and Leo Tobin did not stay past politeness, preferring to view the ships in the harbor for their new project. Mr. Tothy preferred not to know the nature of that project. Over tea, he heard Ada's tale of finding the money in her orchard, and agreed that the origins of the purse were likely unsavory, and undiscoverable. That being the case, the vicar dutifully labeled Ada's windfall a godsend, a stroke of good fortune, a blessing. He abjured her not to look a gift horse in the mouth, which was, of course, precisely what the Trojans should have done, and trotted out any other platitudes he could think of. Then he asked her to marry him.

Why not? With Viscount Ashmead out of the picture, the Westlake girl was dwindling into an old maid. Who would take her with that skipwit sister? Miss Ada was a good manager, though, with a kind heart, just what the parish needed in a vicar's spouse. His own wife having gone on to her reward these five years ago, Tothy would not mind a reward for his own virtuous abstinence. A soft young body warming his bed at nights would be just the ticket, especially if it came with such a handsome dowry.

"It was the strangest thing," Ada told Chas later, when he came for tea. After the initial awkwardness that naturally followed yesterday's sudden soul-searing kiss, each had privately decided to pretend that such an emotion-fraught event had never taken place. A certain heightened awareness, however, did sit between them on the sofa, and Ada was quick to fill any silences. "Reverend Tothy would not take the money. He said I should keep it as my dowry, since I had given up mine to pay Rodney's gaming debts." She would have, had Sir Rodney not gambled her portion away long before his fatal wager.

"And so you should," Chas said while spreading slices of toast with apple jelly. "Wise man, our vicar."

"Then he said that the church was so well endowed, it had everything it needed. Whoever heard of such a thing?"

Chas scraped some of the jelly off. Laying it on too thick, Tothy, he said to himself. "Must be my mother's munificence."

"Hah! I'll believe that as easily as I'll believe you fell off your horse. I am certain it was your own generosity."

Chas shrugged and offered her a slice of toast. "You seem determined to believe what you will, no matter what anyone says."

Ada ignored that, as well as the tremor that fluttered up her arm when their hands touched. "Anyway, then Mr. Tothy proposed to me. Can you fathom that?"

Chas could not even swallow the bite of bread in his mouth.

"I know it is not polite to speak of a gentleman's proposal, but—"

"Why not? The world and its uncle seems to know you rejected my suit. What did you tell the villain—ah, the vicar?"

"I told him I was honored, of course, and that I would think about his offer."

Chas wondered if a man could hang twice for shooting a cleric.

The viscount's day went downhill from there.

"I thought you said you were going to hire a companion, Mother."

"No, dear, you said you thought I should do so. I merely said I would think about it. Then I got this letter from my cousin Margaret's sister-in-law, Harriet."

Lady Ashmead was related to half the families in England, it seemed to her son, who was trying to place Cousin Margaret, much less her sister-in-law.

"You remember Margaret. She sent you the lovely silver porringer for your christening."

"Ah, how could I have forgotten?"

"Harriet leased a house on Laura Place five years ago, or was it six? No matter. Her neighbors are the Wrenthams, Lord Ravenshaw and his family."

Chas brightened, recalling the earl's reputation as a well-schooled fencer. "Is that whom you have invited to come visit?"

"Unfortunately the earl had to travel to some foreign properties he owns, and the countess passed on some three years ago, I believe. Their daughter, who is Harriet's godchild, has been staying with her in Laura Place, but now Harriet's own daughter, Elizabeth, is increasing, in York, and you must see how such a long journey would be tedious, not to say unsuitable, for a young miss."

Chas began to see the end of rope, and it was looking a great deal like a noose. "Exactly how old is the daughter?"

Lady Ashmead stopped plying her needle long enough to wave her hand in the air. "Oh, I suppose she has seventeen or eighteen summers in her dish. She is to make her curtsy to the Queen in the spring."

"That is the companion you chose? A young chit barely out of the schoolroom?"

Lady Ashmead straightened her already rigid spine. "Harriet says that Lady Esther is a fine needlewoman. We shall have a great deal in common. Furthermore, this will be an excellent opportunity for the child to learn about managing a grand household, don't you see?"

What Chas saw was a clutch of old crones managing his life. "I don't suppose Lady Esther's family has fallen on hard times, has it?"

"Of course not. She is one of the premier heiresses in the land. That's why her father does not want her in London until he can be there to guard the girl from fortune hunters. Do not raise your eyebrows at me, Charles. You have nothing to complain of, since you shall not have to be paying any salary to some gray cipher of a hired attendant to keep me company. If you had been obliging enough to be married, I could return to Bath and take Lady Esther in hand there. This seems the perfect solution for everyone."

For everyone but Chas. "Do you know how particular this will look to the gossipmongers, an unfledged heiress visiting an unmarried man? Do you know how many opportunities there will be for the chit to be unavoidably compromised? Do you know how good a swordsman the Earl of Ravenshaw is?"

"Do not be more of a fool than you have to, Charles. Lord

Ravenshaw is an old friend of mine. Of course I know that having Lady Esther here on her own would appear as if you were singling her out for your attentions. That is why I have invited the other young ladies and their families."

"Others? You are filling my house with a gaggle of schoolgirls? I refuse. I will leave, go up to London."

"I never thought I would live to see the day that any son of mine turned craven. Besides, the party will not be all that large, not with the autumn Season in swing. And you can invite whatever gentlemen you like."

"Leo Tobin."

"Excuse me, I do not know any—"

"Of course you do, Mother. That's my price. I will stay and play host to your children's party, and you will invite Leo to the occasional dinner, to any dancing parties, to tea."

"When I am dead and buried."

"Which will be about when I return from London. I'd better go tell Purvis to start packing for an extended stay."

"The ball only. I can make it a masquerade."

"The ball and two other invitations."

"Very well, the ball and two of your gentlemen's pursuits. You can take him hunting or whatever." If Leo got shot, her tone implied, that would add to her entertainment. "I do not wish that person in my home."

"Well, I sure as Hades am not looking forward to turning the Meadows into a Marriage Mart."

The viscountess bit off a thread with her teeth. "Then you should have done your duty and taken a bride years ago. Which reminds me, if you are not going to marry the Westlake girl, what do you mean by still hanging about her skirts? The servants are talking."

"We are old friends. It would cause more gossip if I suddenly stopped visiting. I merely go for tea." And kisses. He'd kissed Ada good-bye again, and she had melted in his arms, again. This kiss hadn't been as cataclysmic as the first, not with old Cobble waiting to hand over his hat, but she hadn't boxed his ears. That was something he could cling to, if he could not cling to Ada. Rumors of those kisses would tangle his mother's yarns for sure.

Lady Ashmead put down the cloth she was currently working on, another seat cushion. "You aren't calling on that widow of Sir Rodney's, are you?"

"Good grief, no."

"Heaven be praised for small blessings." She went back to her needlework, then paused once more. "Egad, it's not the attics-to-let sister you go to see, is it?"

"Tess is merely eccentric, Mother, in an artistic way. When I go, I visit with the entire household." When he could not get Ada alone.

"Then stop. People are talking and it will hurt Ada's chances."

"Ada's chances of what, pray tell?"

"Her chances of not leading apes in hell, you ignoramus. Ada won't have any reputation left if people start whispering that you two are having an affair instead of a wedding."

The next person who suggested such a thing had better be prepared to meet his maker.

As if the day wasn't bad enough, Chas had to spend the evening crisscrossing the countryside, looking for the local riding officer. In the rain. His Ada thought she'd return the unpaid customs taxes to the excise men in the morning.

Chapter Eleven

Ada's day had gone very well, she reflected as she readied for bed. She'd received her second proposal in a sennight, and Chas was jealous.

A lady did not boast of her conquests, not even to herself as she brushed her hair, but Ada could not help being pleased. Reverend Tothy had offered because she would be a worthy wife, not because he had known her forever, or because he felt sorry for her. The vicar thought of her as a possible helpmate, a potential partner in his life's work, which was not to be scoffed at. Ada liked being needed, enjoyed keeping busy. She would never accept Mr. Tothy, of course, for she could not relish the idea of sharing his boring sermons, much less his bed, but it was satisfying to be asked.

She had told him she'd think about her answer, but only to ease her conscience, that she had not rejected a respectable offer out of hand. If Ada were willing to accept a marriage of convenience, however, she could have wed Chas two years ago, which would have been infinitely more convenient, from a practical viewpoint. Ada paused in her brushing to consider if one of her recommendations to the vicar might just be her ability to stretch a shilling. Well, she could have done more for the parish, too, as the wife of its leading landowner, than married to its man of the cloth.

She would tell him on Sunday, Ada decided, that she was honored by his proposal, but she felt she had to refuse. With regrets. She would be certain to add her regrets. Her family needed her more at home right now, she would tell him, which he had to understand. There was no way Tess could fit in the tiny manse, if Mr. Tothy were willing to invite her, and Ada would not leave her sister to Jane's untender mercies. Mostly, she would tell him, she was not willing to give her hand where her heart could not follow. He might chide her for holding onto silly schoolgirlish dreams the way Jane had, but the vicar would never shout at her or slam doors, since neither his heart nor his pride was involved. Ada did not have to worry about bruising any masculine feelings, which naturally reminded her of Chas.

He had been jealous, she knew it. First of Leo Tobin, then of the vicar, and jealousy was not a bad thing, Ada considered, not in someone who was used to thinking of her as just another playmate. Of course, the notion of Viscount Ashmead entertaining a house full of well-bred, well-dowered, and willing young females was not sitting so easily on Ada's plate, either, but if she could suffer that unpalatable prospect, his lordship could resent Reverend Tothy.

How did she know he was jealous? A mere friend would be happy that Ada had received an honorable offer. A family confidant might even have urged her to consider the vicar's suit, since respectable swains were not thick on the ground around Lillington, and spinsterhood loomed. An old chum might have laughed with her at the absurdity of the hoydenish Miss Ada Westlake turning into a pillar of the community.

Chas had growled. Yes, it was a distinct growl. The memory warmed Ada even as her bedroom grew cold as the fire died down. Still, she dawdled over braiding her hair, missing half the flyaway curls anyway, letting an even warmer recollection stave off the chill. He'd kissed her good-bye. He didn't have to, was not supposed to, should not have repeated the previous day's folly, but Chas had kissed her again. The ground did not move this time, but neither was it a fond, brotherly salute, not by half. Ada trembled, and not from the cold. If kisses were roses, she'd tuck this one away under her pillow.

What was he about, then? Chas could never be so ungentlemanly as to entertain rakish notions, could he? No, Ada refused to think that his intentions were anything less than honorable, no matter what Jane said about his repeated visits. Ada would just have to wait to see what tomorrow brought; a growl and a kiss were enough for today.

The rest of the day, after Chas left, had also been a pleasure; Jane had kept to her rooms. So *aux anges* at the thought of the invitations to come from Lady Ashmead's house party, Rodney's widow had spent the rest of the afternoon and evening closeted with her maid, unpacking all of the trunks from the attic to see which gowns could be refashioned in the current modes, which fabric could be unpicked to make new frocks. She'd already been to the Misses Hannefords' lending library for the latest editions of every ladies' fashion magazine the sisters carried, and studied them over a meager dinner on a tray in her bedroom. She was not going to look a dowd in front of the viscount's tonnish guests, whatever it took, including losing a pound, or ten.

Jane had also sent her uncle Filbert off in the carriage to fetch Cousin Algernon home from school. Ada found out when it was too late to recall Mr. Johnstone. What did an education matter, Jane demanded, when so many heiresses would be so close to hand? From the amount of studying the dunderhead ever did, likely nothing, Ada had to agree. Algie was only in school at Ada's insistence and by Chas's influence anyway, after he'd wounded a grazing horse, hunting for hares. The clunch needed spectacles, not a wife.

Still, dinner was a delight with Ada and Tess alone for once. Ada had never seen her sister happier, buoyed by Leo Tobin's interest in her opera. Of course the opera was now a book to be copiously illustrated, whetting the public's appetite for seeing the story set to music. They'd have twice the sales that way, Tess predicted. Leo, it seemed, agreed, although Ada had hardly heard him utter a word. The ship captain was going to take Tess aboard one of his boats on the morrow so she could sketch the settings, with a maid along for propriety's sake, Tess added, at Leo's suggestion.

Did Ada think that Lady Ashmead might like Leo and her to do a reading from the story for her company? Tess wondered. Ada thought Lady Ashmead would rather see her husband's dead body exhumed and eaten by crows.

Jane might be correct, Ada reflected as she untied her dressing gown, that Leo Tobin had quaffed too much of his cargo. Or else, as Ada supposed, being Chas's half-brother only gave him half Chas's intelligence. Either way, the man seemed smitten with Tess. As for Tess, she declared that she would not accept any invitations to the Meadows if Leo were not also invited.

Ada doubted if Lady Ashmead would be devastated by that news. The last time they had attended an evening gathering hosted by Chas's mother, Tess had danced the waltz. Lady Ashmead had never forgiven her, not because the viscountess was such a high-stickler, and Tess had never received the nod from any of the Almack's hostesses before performing the daring dance, which was an absurdity, considering Tess's advanced age. No, what had sent Chas's mother into paroxysms was that Tess hadn't waltzed at a ball; she'd danced at a musicale, in front of the hired orchestra and fifty seated guests. Without a partner.

Chas would see that Tess received invitations, nonetheless. Leo might be another matter. Ada yawned. She'd worry about that another day, too.

Before getting into bed, she knelt on the stool alongside, to say her prayers. "Thank you, Lord, for a lovely day," she began, wondering if it were quite proper to thank the Almighty for Chas's kiss. She decided to keep that to herself, thanking God for the health and prosperity of her household instead.

"And thank you, Lord, and Rodney too, if you made it to Heaven, for letting me have a day's rest from Jane's nattering about the money. She feels that since it was found on Westlake property, it belongs to all of us equally, but I cannot agree. Lord, if you meant it as a gift from heaven, I really wish you had sent it on a bolt of lightning or something, so we would be sure, not left it in a tree. Please guide me to do the right thing with it."

The money was safely locked in her father's old desk, but it still worried Ada. She simply could not be comfortable claiming someone else's fortune, or smuggling profits. She was also bothered by the niggling urge to take some of the money and buy pretty gowns for her and Tess to wear at the upcoming social gatherings. She'd get rid of the money tomorrow, before she succumbed to such a base temptation.

"Please keep me from giving in, at least until I reach the Customs office. Oh, and do watch over Emery, Lord, and keep him safe, with all of his friends and fellows in the Army. If it is not too much, can I ask you to look after Chas too? He really should not be getting into tavern brawls, you know."

Ada climbed into bed and snuggled under the covers. Then she remembered what old Cobble had said when he handed her a candle to light her way to bed, how Chas's dog had followed him to Westlake Hall as usual, but the dog hadn't stayed in the stables. Instead, the hound had gone gamboling, to put it politely, with one of the shepherds' herd dogs, and not for the first time, either. Ada did not like dogs, not after inadvertently catching the tail end of a fox hunt, but she knew how much the animal meant to Chas. She sighed, got out of bed, and knelt on the stool again. "Lord, could you please not let Chas find out his dog Tally is a trollop?"

The riding officer was a smooth-cheeked, pale-eyed young man, whose nervous stammer made Leo Tobin into a Marc Antony. He was assigned to Lillington because his mother's bosom bow's niece by marriage was a second cousin to Lady Ashmead. They wanted a nice, safe place for Lieutenant Quintin Nye to serve his country, at least until an uncle died and named him heir. Lady Ashmead had effortlessly seen the deed done: she'd handed the letter to her son Charles.

The lieutenant was given a horse, a cottage, an office, the occasional invitation to dine when Lady Ashmead's numbers were not even, and an overall directive: under no circumstances was he to be looking for smugglers. Occasionally a town drunk or a capsized French fisherman would be tossed his way so he could appear competent to his superiors. Otherwise, assured by Lord Ashmead that he was aiding the war effort, Quintin was to be zealous in pursuit of looking busy.

Last evening, however, the viscount had tracked Quintin down at an inn near Dover, where he was checking the excise stamps on the brandy bottles for forgeries. Ashmead had purchased one, to test its authenticity, he said, and beckoned the lieutenant to follow him to a private parlor. There, his orders had been more specific. Quintin was to be on the lookout for a missing French informant named Prelieu, he was to stay away from the coastline next Wednesday night, and he was to refuse to accept money from Miss Ada Westlake.

"N-no, m-ma'am. Th-that can't be smuggling m-money b-because we d-don't have any smugglers." The lieutenant's face was red and his fingers trembled as he shoved the pouch back across his desk toward Ada.

"We don't?" She could not help glancing out the window where Tess and Leo were sitting on a bench waiting for her, discussing the setting for the next chapter's illustrations. At least Tess was conversing; Leo was listening. Lieutenant Nye followed her gaze and waved to Leo. The riding officer waved to Leo?

"Oh, uh, M-Mr. Tobin? Sh-shipper, d-don't you know. In trade."

At her look of disbelief, Quintin tugged at his too-tight shirt collar. "G-great p-patriot, Mr. Tobin."

The young man's brainbox had to be as empty as Ada's bank account. Still, she was not about to tell the lieutenant what the entire neighborhood knew, not when Leo had just fetched Tess a sack of peppermints from the apothecary, her favorites.

Lieutenant Nye had been given permission to tell Ada the truth, since Chas knew she'd never let the matter rest, and poor Quintin was not up to her weight. "N-no one's supposed to know, b-but seeing as how M-Miss Westlake is h-holding his hand, I can tell you that M-Mr. Tobin is a regular hero, using his ships to gather information to d-defeat Napoleon."

That was why, the young officer went on to explain, losing his stammer in his enthusiasm, he could not take her found money to headquarters as illegal profits from the smuggling trade. If there was a profit, then there were smugglers, and if there were smugglers, he'd ought to be capturing them. If he didn't arrest anyone, he said with another glance out the window to where Leo now had his arm around Tess, looking over her shoulder at a drawing in her lap, he'd lose his post. But if he did arrest anyone—Leo was nibbling on Tess's ear!—then Lord Ashmead would have his hide, to say nothing of his horse and his cottage.

"Th-therefore, m-ma'am, there are no smugglers. You m-might as well keep the m-money."

Chas had left one final directive with his young subaltern: Do not, under pain of dismissal, dismemberment, and/or decapitation, propose marriage to Miss Ada. But there she was, the pretty little lady, looking adorably confused, holding a heavy sack of the ready and rhino.

So he asked if she'd save him a dance at Lady Ashmead's ball. The viscount couldn't call him out over one country dance, could he?

Chapter Twelve

"Did you know, Tess, about Mr. Tobin?"

They were waiting for Leo to return from the livery where he'd left his carriage. Ada was happy she had her fur muff to ward off the day's chill. Of course she had the confounded coins in there too, but that was not her immediate concern. "Did you know all along he was not a criminal?"

"A criminal? My Sebastian? How could he be? One look into those wide eyes shows you what a gentle man he is. The eyes are the window to the soul, you know, and Sebastian's soul is noble, unblemished by base greed and ambition." Her voice rang out with passion; a delivery boy stopped to stare. "He is brave and true, with boundless courage to fight the forces of evil. He is wise and considerate of those in his care, a perfect crusader, the flower of chivalry, true to his cause."

"I thought Sebastian was a pirate."

"A pirate with exemplary character, the essence of nobility, the very embodiment of manly virtue."

"Yes, dear, I am sure Sebastian is all of those things, but I was speaking of Mr. Tobin."

"So was I."

"Then you knew he was helping Lord Ashmead gather intelligence for the War Office?"

"Of course. He told me. Not that I did not recognize his intrinsic goodness and strength of purpose on my own, mind. Don't tell me you suspected Leo of nefarious doings? Ada, Ada, how can you be so blind?"

"Blind? I'd have to be deaf and dumb, besides, to miss all the rumors, all his trappings of wealth."

"Ah, but you see only with your eyes, hear only with your ears. Where is your instinct, your intuitive recognition of true worth? Am I the only one in the family to transcend the experiential boundaries, to grasp a person's aura?"

Tess might be the only person in the world, for all Ada knew. Leo pulled up with the carriage and Ada saw an expensively dressed . . . smuggler.

Her sister tsk-ed as she stepped into the coach. "Ada, you have to start letting your heart guide you, not your head. That's the only way to find true happiness."

So after luncheon, when Tess and Leo went off to visit his ship, Ada let her heart guide her—straight to the Meadows.

There was nothing odd about Ada's calling on the viscountess, since she often stopped in to pay her respects, admire the current needlework project, help sort yarns, and listen to her ladyship rant about undutiful children. She had wondered if Chas's mother might be furious at her over her latest and last refusal to wed the woman's son, but Lady Ashmead was too excited about planning her gathering—and her son's betrothal to some female more deserving of the Ashmead name—to resent Ada.

Lady Ashmead, in fact, was delighted to see her young neighbor, immediately putting Ada to work addressing invitations to the masquerade ball. Tess would be in alt at the chance to wear a costume, Ada knew, especially since Mr. Leo Tobin's name was one of those on the list to be inscribed.

While Ada worked, Lady Ashmead continued on with her sewing. She was embroidering the Ashmead coat of arms on a gold tunic, for she intended her son to be dressed as a knight for the masquerade. A fine disguise, Ada agreed. No one would know who he was.

"Mind your sauce, girl. Ashmead will be dignified, as befits his position. You, I suppose, will dress as a Gypsy." Her wrinkled nose seemed to suggest that Ada's everyday appearance was not much better.

Since a Gypsy was exactly what Ada had been thinking of when she heard about the masked ball, she bit her lip, which was usually the best strategy for dealing with Chas's mother.

Satisfied she had both quelled any insolence and delivered a snub, Lady Ashmead cheerfully went on to describe the house party, and how much work it entailed. Ada had seen all of the servants scurrying back and forth with rags and mops, buckets and brooms. She had no doubt they were indeed working hard.

Most of the guests would only be coming to the Meadows for the weekend of the ball, still a fortnight away, but a few would arrive within days.

"And you cannot believe the effort it is all taking," Lady Ashmead said from her comfortable chair near the window while Ada sharpened yet another quill and stretched her cramped fingers. "But I am not complaining, mind. It is a mother's duty, after all, to do what she must to see to her children's welfare, yes, even at the cost of her own health. A son's happiness comes first."

Ada didn't think Chas was happy about having his house full of idle party-goers, but she knew better than to contradict his mother, who was already going on: "Not that you would understand, missy, not being a mother. At the rate you are going, you might never be one. Your poor mother must be grieving in her grave. One son dead with no heirs, one son endangering the whole line by playing soldier, one daughter with more hair than wit, and the other one turning down—But no more on that score. I know when to hold my tongue."

Lady Ashmead held her tongue for as long as it took to lick a new strand of floss before threading it through the needle. Then she went on about the travails she suffered, the loneliness of having her ungrateful daughters move away, her disloyal son and lazy servants. The price of corn and the Prince's profligacy were in there someplace too, but Ada had stopped listening.

At last, done writing out the addresses, Ada made her escape. On her way out, she casually asked the butler, whom she'd known nearly as long as her own servants, if the master was in his office. The butler just as casually winked and nodded.

Chas was in his office, all right, sniffling and coughing from last night's wet ride to find Quintin Nye, who took his job of not finding smugglers seriously indeed. As usual these days, Chas was thinking of Ada instead of adding his columns of figures. He was wondering what excuse he could give for calling on his neighbors three days in a row, without ruining Ada's reputation. A pox on pawky proprieties!

He even had the unworthy thought, undoubtedly due to his stuffy head scattering his wits, that if Ada's virtue was compromised by his actions, she had no other choice but to marry him. It could work . . .

No, ruining Ada was as reprehensible as Leo's suggestion of running off with her to Gretna. Besides, she would never forgive him for forcing her hand. Then, too, he had no guarantee that his persnickety, perplexing peahen would not choose to stay ruined, rather than wed against her will.

He sighed and blew his nose. This courtship business was as bad as the ague.

Tally barked in agreement. No, the dog barked because Ada was coming into the room unannounced, as if his lordship's wistfulness had conjured her out of the air. Chas stood behind his desk as she approached. She sidestepped the dog, as usual, with a brief, insincere "Good doggie," and came close enough to pound her fist on the cherry wood surface. He sat down. No figment of a fevered brain, this, just Ada in her attitudes. He sighed again.

"Why didn't you tell me Leo was not a smuggler?"

"Good day to you too, my dear. May I say you look a treat with roses in your cheeks?" She did, too, and he loved the way her eyes flashed with spirit and her curls tumbled around her ears.

"Hello, Chas. You look terrible, even worse than yesterday, if possible. What happened?"

"Just the sniffles. You were saying?"

"Oh, yes. I was wondering why you never told me that Leo, who you never told me was your half-brother, either, was not a smuggler. I feel the veriest fool."

"But he is." Chas poured them each a glass of wine from the decanter on the corner of the desk. "I swear to you that the bottle this came from bore no customs stamps."

"He is more than a smuggler, though, isn't he?" She sat opposite the desk and sipped at the wine.

"A great deal more. Basically, now that his face is too well known in France for him to be safe there, he runs a network of spies and intelligence-gatherers. His sources have been amazingly accurate, and incredibly helpful to the war effort. He also makes sure that the information that flows in the other direction is vague or incorrect."

"And you?"

"I help finance the venture. The War Office would not let me take part, for if I were captured there'd be hell to pay, to say nothing of an exorbitant ransom. They let me coordinate the operation at this end, playing courier and such, but mostly I get to pay the informants."

"Then Leo really is some kind of hero, and not just in Tess's imagination?"

"As soon as the war is over, his name will be cleared. Till then, though, make no mistake, he is a smuggler, and makes a tidy profit by the trade, too. So do the local men, some of whose families would be going hungry now, due to the blockade. I know the thought of putting money in French coffers rankles—I have friends in the Army, too—but there seemed no other way of ending the war more quickly."

"Then the money I found really wasn't left by the free traders?"

"I—" He blew his nose again in one of his myriad monogrammed handkerchiefs. "I assure you, no self-respecting smuggler would leave a treasure trove in a tree. Devil take it, Ada, why don't you just spend the cursed money already and be done with it? You are driving me—That is, you are driving yourself to distraction over a trifle."

She swirled the wine in its priceless crystal glass. "Only Golden Ball would call a small fortune like that a trifle."

"Then it can pay some of your immediate debts and leave enough to buy something pretty for yourself."

"Why?"

Why? Because Chas couldn't buy it for her, not under the rules of polite society. "Because you deserve it, working so hard for everyone else. How long has it been since you had a new gown, one you did not have to stitch up yourself?"

Ada looked down at her perfectly serviceable dark blue dress. Now he was criticizing her clothes, too? "Oh?"

"Lud, there is nothing wrong with your frock." Nothing except she'd appear the dowd next to the London Diamonds his mother was inviting. Chas couldn't have cared less. In fact, he'd give his good right arm to see Ada in less, a whole lot less, but he knew she would be conscious of the disparity between her wardrobe and that of his house guests. "I just thought you might like something new."

Of course she would. What woman wouldn't? Ada would adore a gown made from something in one of Jane's fashion magazines, pink, with three rows of flounces. Unfortunately, Ada could not afford a feather for her hair, much less a flounce. With invitations to the Meadows, the Westlakes ought to reciprocate with some kind of entertainment for Lady Ashmead's guests, besides, if Ada could find the funds—in her own accounts, not in someone else's sack. If someone, someone she would not name, thought perhaps she would accept his charity, he could think again.

"I cannot, Chas," she told him. "It wouldn't feel right, and Tess says we should let our feelings lead the way."

"You are taking advice from your sister? The sister who ruined her London Season by singing an aria at the opera, from Princess Esterhazy's box?"

Chas insisted on riding beside Ada's pony cart on her way home, despite his running nose and watering eyes, and despite his mother's frowns, using the early autumn darkness as an excuse. Ada insisted he come inside for some hot tea before the return trip.

Jane sweetly apologized—to the viscount, not Ada—for having taken over the parlor for her dressmaking, since the light was better than in her bedroom. She had every table and chair covered, taking the lace from this gown and the ribbons from that one, to make one elegant, *au courant* evening gown. Jane was going to make an impression on Lady Ashmead's gentleman guests if it killed her. Living the rest of her life as a poor widow certainly would, otherwise.

When Ada informed her that the ball was to be a masquerade, Jane would have had a fainting spell, except there was no available surface except the floor. She shrieked instead. Chas winced.

"No, I shall wear this gown, with this bodice, and this overskirt and this trim, by thunder. I absolutely refuse to wear some insipid shepherdess costume."

Since that was Ada's second choice of outfit for the masked ball, she winced.

"I shall wear a domino over my gown, that's what I'll do. Ladies and gentlemen both wear them all the time when they don't wish to act like some foolish characters in a play. Isn't that right, Ashmead?"

He nodded, but Ada asked, "Do you have a domino, Jane?" She'd never seen her sister-in-law with one.

"No, we'll simply have to purchase one. Blue, I think, to match my eyes."

"I'm sorry, Jane," Ada said, with an embarrassed glance

toward Chas, "but you know we cannot afford the expense right now."

Jane got ready to scream the house down, but her eyes narrowed instead, focusing on the suspiciously lumpy fur muff Ada hadn't found a place to set down. "What about that money you found that you've been hoarding? I insist on my fair share of it!"

"Oh, this?" Ada clutched the muff more firmly to her chest. "I am bringing it to the magistrate tomorrow."

Viscount Ashmead groaned.

"You had a better idea?" she asked sweetly.

"I . . . I . . ."

"You really ought to be home in bed with a hot posset, Chas."

"Come on, Tally, old girl. It's going to be another long night."

Chapter Thirteen

Ada passed another sleepless night. Strange, she thought, how one night she could not fall asleep because Chas had kissed her. The next night she could not, because he had not. She supposed his lack of a farewell kiss could be ascribed to congestion, or abiding by convention. Or the conviction that Ada's kisses were unsatisfactory.

What if he had not been affected by that storm of emotion she felt when their lips met, when his arms went around her, when he pressed her against his hard chest? Had he kissed her once to make sure they wouldn't suit and the second time to be certain? What if, as Jane kept hinting, Chas was harboring dishonorable intentions toward her, now that his honorable offer had been summarily rejected? Were such kisses the stepping stones along the primrose path, and he'd reconsidered? Worst, had Chas lost interest in her now that his mother was dangling society's darlings in front of him?

No, Ada would not dwell on such depressing thoughts.

She brightened. What if he were truly ill? Why, then she'd have an excuse to go visit him later, after her errands were completed.

She hurried through her morning toilette, donning her oldest dress and gulping her morning chocolate and a sweet roll, before meeting Tess in the attics. They were going to see what they could find in their mother's old trunks that might be usable for costumes. Tess was determined to appear as the sea goddess from her drama, to whet the guests' appetite for the forthcoming publication. Advance publicity, she explained to Ada. If the house party was interested, perhaps Lady Ashmead would consider having a reading from the book as well.

Tess had not yet convinced Leo to dress as Sebastian, the pirate, for he wished to appear before Lady Ashmead in his finest evening ensemble, not half-naked with a gold hoop in his ear and a curved sword at his side. The question was not whether Tess could talk him into the pirate's costume; it was whether she could locate a stuffed parrot to sit on his shoulder.

Ada absolutely refused to be the evil kraken, dragging its serpent's tail through the quadrille.

"What about the princess, then? Sebastian saves her from the monster, and is rewarded by her father the king. Of course he loves the sea goddess, and I have not decided what happens to Princess Pretty, but I am sure she finds True Love and a happy ending."

Ada fancied the idea of being dressed as a lady from the days of chivalry, if they could find anything resembling a wimple, farthingale, or stomacher. Surely the sisters could unearth something they could make into an embroidered overdress, even if they had to use the table runner Lady Ashmead had presented to them last Christmas. The fact that Chas was to be garbed as a knight of old had nothing whatsoever to do with Ada's decision. Tess's epic needed all the publicity it could get.

Having taken trunks down from the attic, Ada proceeded to carry a few boxes up. With Jane's cousin Algernon due home any moment, Ada wanted to hide whatever weapons and ammunition she could. Mr. Johnstone, it seemed, had taken Rodney's hunting rifle, but Ada stashed away the dueling pistols, the fowling piece, the butler's old blunderbuss, and the extra shot. She could always say she sold them, to pay for the damages Cousin Algie was sure to incur. If anyone complained about the house being unprotected, too bad. Ada felt safer with the guns out of Algie's hands.

Next she inventoried the nearly bare linen closets with Mrs. Cobble, the butler's wife who was acting as both cook and housekeeper, spoke to one of her herdsmen about winter forage, and to a tenant farmer about his leaking roof. She promised to try to find funds for them all.

Finally she was ready to set out for Squire Hocking's, with her sack of gold and silver, enough for most, if not all, her immediate needs, even the green gauze Tess required for her trailing seaweed. They'd just have to use paints, and hope for a rain-free evening, for Ada could not consider the money as theirs. She stuffed it back into her muff, thinking of it more like the apple in Eden than bounty from her orchard. "And lead me not into temptation," she hurriedly prayed, because the money had to belong to someone else.

The magistrate disagreed.

Squire Hocking's family had held the justice position for the area forever. The Lords Ashmead were too often out of the county, and preferred letting a local man handle local matters. The Westlake baronetcy was much newer.

Cyrus Hocking, the latest holder of Hocking Manor, was a reluctant officer of the law. Instead of being a hale and hearty, heavy-drinking, hunt-loving countryman, Cyrus Hocking was tall and thin, somewhat stooped, with thinning hair. He presided over the courts reluctantly, much preferring his greenhouses, which was where Ada found him. Squire was, in fact, a botanist by bent, a farmer only by fate, and magistrate by misfortune, his elder brother having succumbed to a wasting disease. In addition to the estates and duties, Cyrus had also inherited his brother's wife and three daughters. Added to his own five hopeful, and hopelessly undisciplined children, the manor was overrun. Ada preferred the glass houses, too.

She always liked the smell, the warmth, the weak autumn sun streaming through the clear ceiling. Unlike Squire's wife, who was eternally increasing, Ada was endlessly fascinated by the odd plants and exquisite flowers to be found in the steamy, jungle-like enclosures. Hocking always appreciated her interest, and often advised Ada about crops for the kitchen garden and ornamentals for the landscaping. He was less helpful about the money.

"How long did you say you have had the money in your possession since discovering the purse?" He was snipping dead flowers off a trailing vine.

"Less than a week" was her answer as she followed him down the rows of plants on shelves and benches. Others were hanging from hooks in the rafters, and larger specimens were in tubs of their own, on the ground. Ada tried to keep her skirts off the floor at first, but quickly gave up.

"It must be in the books, of course." Squire waved a trowel-filled hand toward the house and his library of legal tomes. "Everything else is. But I cannot quite recall what the exact ruling is. Thirty days? That sounds about right. Yes, if no one claims the purse in thirty days, you may consider it yours. Finders keepers, don't you know."

Then Hocking recalled his visitor of last evening. Fine man, Viscount Ashmead, interested in orchids, he was. Not terribly knowledgeable, but willing to be advised, and there was nothing Squire liked better than talking about his orchids. Why, he could go on for hours, and often did, when he had the rare willing listener like Ashmead or Miss Ada. What had Ashmead called about, before they got on to cymbidiums? "Oh, but you said the money was found on your property, didn't you?"

"Yes, in my orchard."

"Well, then, since it was on your own grounds, I would say that five to ten days is ample enough to wait before declaring it yours, since whoever put it there was trespassing in the first place."

"Do you mean that if your bull wanders onto my property and stays for five days I can keep him?" Squire was a notoriously negligent landowner, and they had argued about his straying beef before, until Ada realized what a good, free stud the bull was.

"No, no, not at all." Squire stuck his finger into a pot of soil, checking the moisture. "There are other rules for livestock. The law is very specific there."

"Where do you think it came from?"

"The law? Some feudal lord who was trying to keep peace at his borders, I suppose, and fancied himself a Solomon."

"No, the money."

"Well, if it were lying on the ground, I would say that someone lost it. But in a tree? I daresay the hedgehogs did not carry it up there, and not even I have been able to make money grow on trees. Heh heh."

"Someone put it there, of course, but have you no idea who it could have been? No highwaymen plying their trade? No bank robberies?" Ada was beginning to wish she had not hidden the pistols, after all.

"Now, now, my dear, don't get yourself in a swivet. We don't have that kind of crime in this neighborhood, thank goodness, or I would never get any of my repotting done. The occasional squabble, a pilfered hen, that kind of thing is what I hear. No, your bounty must have been left by some passerby with reasons we will never know, like why this flower sometimes has pink blossoms and sometimes lavender."

"So you think I should just keep it then, not advertise for its rightful owner or anything?"

"What, and have every beggar in England on your doorstep, claiming to have lost a leather purse?" Squire heh-heh-ed again, then put down his trowel and his shears. "Do you want to know what I would do with this prize, my dear?"

At her nod, he took Ada's hand and led her to a stone bench. Luckily she was still wearing her leather driving gloves, for his hands were filthy from the soil. She noticed when she pointedly looked down, signaling him to release her hand. He did not, too rapt in his own thoughts. "If I had a fortune handed to me out of the blue," he began, all dreamy-eyed, "I think I would run away."

Ada tugged on her hand. He patted it with his free one.

"Yes, I would leave England, take ship for a tropical island somewhere, where orchids grew wild and colorful birds sang overhead and no one wore neckcloths."

"But your lands, the estate?" Ada waved her other hand at the manor house behind them, the expanse of the glass enclosure. She could not believe anyone would turn his back on his heritage, not even in jest.

"I have sons to carry on. One of the dolts seems to enjoy counting cows and cabbages. Let him have the lands and the income, and the responsibilities that go with them. I would have sunshine and soft rain, flowers that bloom once in a lifetime, blossoms as big as dinner plates, the sound of water lapping on sandy shores."

The sound of children's high-pitched voices came to them, even through the layers of glass. "Your sons are not half grown, sir. Would you leave them to fend for themselves, then, along with your fatherless nieces?"

"Faith, they'd have trustees and stewards to guide them. How do you think I learned enough after my brother died? I was not trained to this life, don't you know, the way he was. And the children would have their mothers, too, of course."

"Heavens, you wouldn't take your wife?"

Squire Hocking looked at Ada as if she were an aphid on his roses. "I said I was running away. What is the point of taking everything with you? That is moving, not escaping."

Then he patted her hand again, which was beginning to worry Ada, and suddenly those children's voices seemed to come from far away. She tried to make light of Squire's fantasy. "Ah, but you would miss the conveniences we take for granted, like enclosed stoves and oil lamps. I daresay tropical isles have no newspaper deliveries, either. You would miss the companionship of your friends and family." Ada knew she would, no matter how lovely the locale.

Hocking shook his head, limp strands of hair separating to reveal an even greater expanse of forehead. "You do not understand." He stared ahead again, not seeing Ada, she assumed, except his fingers started to stroke her hand. She was doubly thankful for her gloves. "I would not be alone."

No, Ada thought, not the scholarly squire! Never. She must have misunderstood, and he intended to take a servant or two on his purely hypothetical, she prayed, jaunt. Her new interpretation was comforting, except that Ada could feel the heat of Squire's dirty hand even through the leather. She pulled harder.

"A courageous young woman who appreciates growing things, a lovely lady who sees the beauty in nature, that's who I would take along, my dear Ada, if a fortune suddenly fell into my hands."

He could *not* be suggesting what Ada thought he was suggesting, but she did not want to stay around to find out. Not by half. She reclaimed her hand, her feet, her muff, and, too late, her wits. While Cyrus Hocking was still begging his ladybird to take wing with him, the bird was flown.

"Run, Lulu, run as fast as your old legs will carry you and the cart. Run, girl. I need a bath!"

She needed a keeper, Ada told herself, furious at her own idiocy. People laughed at Tess for her eccentricities, but Ada was the one who ought to be locked away for her own good. Addled Ada, indeed. How Chas would gloat at her latest contretemps—if she ever told him, which she never would. How many times had he warned her she could not keep traipsing blithely around the countryside without a chaperone, a companion, a groom, or a maid, without her reputation suffering? Country manners were not so exacting as those in London, he'd often reminded her, but she could expose herself to insults, even danger. Hah!

What about assault with a deadly watering can? Ada wished she'd taken Tess, or Mrs. Cobble. Confound it, she wished she'd taken her brother's pistol!

Here she was, tooling around the countryside, granted not three miles away from her home, with a bag of money. What kind of fool was she anyway? The worst kind, the kind who deserved to have her hand fondled by a flower-fancying philanderer, and worse.

Men were known to kill for less coin than she carried in her muff, so Ada supposed she was lucky to have suffered no more than a horrid embarrassment on its account. It was evil, that money, overriding men's principles. Since she'd found it, all the gentlemen of her acquaintance had gone queer as dick's hatband, with their proposals and propositions and promised dances. Chas, who did not need the money, was the only one who had not made her some kind of offer, but he'd taken to kissing her instead. Evil indeed.

If that blasted bag had pillars of the community acting like mooncalves, Ada could not imagine what it would do to a common man.

There were none more common than Filbert Johnstone and his son Algernon.

Chapter Fourteen

Ada was glad to be home, even if Jane's relations had returned before her. They were already in the library, discussing the money, her money. Well, if it was not hers, Ada believed, at least the treasure was hers to dispose of.

Jane leaned forward eagerly, showing more than her usual cleavage after refurbishing another gown by removing its lace insert. "So, did Squire Hocking say we could spend it? I am sure that old windbags agreed with me."

That Ada would be better off on a deserted island with a bellows-to-mend botanist? Perhaps. "He did not say that in so many words. There are time constraints, you see, during which the original owner should be allowed to claim his property." She would not tell them that one span Squire had set was nearly elapsed.

"Bosh, I say."

Uncle Filbert was stuffed into a satin-striped waistcoat this afternoon, puce alternating with pea green, with yellow Cossack trousers. He looked like a balloon ready for ascension, to Ada's weary eyes. "Whoosh," she wished to say, wafting him back to his own rooms in Town, if the lease had not been broken for lack of payment.

"Bosh and botheration, what? Possession is nine-tenths of the law. Did not your county lumpkin lawyer tell you that, missy?" Having heard an hour of complaints from his teary-eyed, domino-desiring niece, Filbert was not in good curl. He was certain Jane would have wheedled at least a golden boy out of Ada while he was gone.

"Squire Hocking never read for the bar, and he did not have time to consult his legal encyclopedias, but he was very clear on the matter." About as clear as the dirt under his fingernails, Ada thought to herself. She locked the leather sack in her father's old desk.

"No one is going to claim misappropriated funds. That's what it has to be, what? So there's no reason to wait the whole time. How long did you say before the blunt is officially ours?"

Ours? Ada carefully tucked the key, on its ribbon cord, back under the high neck of her gown without answering, which did not stop Filbert from huffing, "Even a slim bit of the ready now could make life a lot easier all around, what?"

If he meant a sovereign would silence Jane's grievances against Ada's cheeseparing, he might be correct, for a time. If Filbert Johnstone thought Ada would spend a farthing on his foppish self, he was far wrong. Furthermore, Ada did not like the way the old coxcomb's puffy eyes shifted from the locked drawer to Jane's elaborate coiffure . . . to Jane's hairpins, to be exact. She would have to move the leather pouch later, to a safer locale, like the pillow under her head. Not even Uncle Filbert would dare look there. Ada supposed she ought to be glad that he hadn't offered for her.

Algernon, meanwhile, was all for searching the orchard for more treasure. Ada was perfectly willing to let the slowtop spend his days, and his nights, too, for all she cared, out of the house and out of her sight. Unfortunately, he meant to search with an ax.

Worst of all, in Ada's view, Jane's relatives were rude to Leo when he and Tess returned from their visit to his ship. Tess looked all windblown and excited, gaily describing the captain's quarters and her plans for a new chapter, or scene, or song. Ada was losing track of the epic, but not of Tess's happiness. Leo stood quietly at her side, as usual, looking like a rough-hewn god, but he too wore a wide grin.

Filbert would not leave, not with tea about to be served, but he dragged Algie to the other side of the room when the youngster's mouth fell open at the sight of Leo's broad shoulders and swarthy complexion. "But I wanted to ask him how many men he's killed," Algernon whined.

From the far end of the room, where he was pretending to be asking about his son's studies, Filbert took out his quizzing glass to survey the impressively built smuggler in his elegant ensemble. He tugged at his own flamboyant waistcoat and said, loudly enough to reach those on the sofa, "Contrary to what you might hear, my lad, clothes do not make the man. Breeding will always tell."

If so, Ada thought, it was telling her that a viscount's by-blow was worth three of Filbert. She wanted to yell out that Leo was a hero, a patriot who was doing more for the country than Johnstone ever had, or would. Of course, she could not, not without betraying a confidence. She wanted to shout to the dastard that the bastard was making her sister happy at last, and Ada would love him for such kindness if he had horns and a tail. She could not say that either, of course, not without mortifying Tess and Leo both, so she did better: she invited Leo to dine with them. And made sure he was seated at the head of the table opposite Jane.

After dinner, Tess and Leo put their heads together at the pianoforte, going over the music for the opera. Tess played and sang, pausing whenever a new thought occurred to her. Leo turned the pages and made corrections on the score, when he could drag his eyes away from the auburn-haired beauty at his side. Ada was reading a book and Uncle Filbert was sleeping behind his newspaper until Jane tossed down her cards, declaring that she wouldn't play with Algernon any longer for he cheated, which meant that Jane was losing. Petulant at being ignored by the only available man in the room, even if he was a baseborn freebooter, Jane started in on Ada again: the curtains were faded, the rugs were stained, the chairs were threadbare, to say nothing of the meager meals that were served. How, then, Jane demanded, was she expected to entertain Lady Ashmead's lofty company?

Not with a card party, that was for sure. Luckily Ada was not expected to provide an answer.

"And why should I have to look like I am paddling up River Tick, in an outdated wardrobe?"

Perhaps because she'd helped sink the family's ship, and the tide kept rising. Again, Ada had no chance to express her sentiments.

"Why, by all that's holy, must we let the world think we are paupers when you have a fortune in coins locked away? Rodney never denied us anything"—which was a great deal of the problem—"so why must you?"

"Here, here, cuz. You tell her. You're mistress here, ain't you? Dowager Lady Westlake and all."

Jane slapped Algernon's hand away from the dish of comfits. She was not old enough to be dowager anything, and needed no reminder that Emery had left his sisters in charge of Westlake Hall, his younger sister in particular! "I am not a dowager until Emery returns and takes a bride, you dolt." She turned back to the evening's target: "Speaking of Emery, I am certain he will be furious to have Westlake Hall become known for its lack of hospitality, when we have the means at hand to throw a party to rival Ashmead's. Or have you finally realized that you'll never attract another eligible gentleman, so you don't mean to try? Just because you are used to whistling fortunes down the wind, Miss True-Love-or-Nothing, is no reason for the rest of us to suffer."

"She sold the pistols, too, cuz."

"Will you stubble it, Algie? I am speaking to Ada."

"Here now, no cause to rip up at the boy, I say, not when it's Ada who is holding out on us." Filbert couldn't sleep, so he decided he might as well add his complaints. "She keeps the place so understaffed my valet is threatening to quit if he has to haul the hot water himself. That brass could hire an army of servants, I swear."

"Hah! What is your lazy servant compared to my blue domino?"

"Or the pistols."

"We ought to have a proper butler if those London swells are coming."

"We ought to have a new chandelier."

"And ammunition."

Ada had heard enough. "Stop, all of you. Just listen to yourselves, bickering like children over a treat that no one promised you. Once and for all, the money is not ours! Not yours, not mine, and I would rather give it to those who are truly poor than listen to any more of your carping."

"What do you mean, she's going to give it all away?"

Leo shook his head. "Miss Ada wouldn't say where or when, but Tess swears she'll do it, she was that mad at the fishwife and her kin."

"Hell." They were out in the stables again, and Chas was blowing his nose, again. Dragged out of bed to hear Leo's message, he was half asleep, and half ready to go confess, again. Deuce take it, he couldn't think, and there was his half-brother, leaning against an upright beam, merry as a grig at Chas's discomfort. "And to hell with you, too."

Leo laughed. "I came to tell you, didn't I?"

"I thought you had information about Prelieu, dash it."

"No, unfortunately. Only what Tess and I thought you ought to know."

"Tess, is it?" Chas sank down onto a pile of clean straw, Tally at his side. "It seems the two of you have grown uncommonly close, doesn't it?"

A moment passed before Leo quietly asked, "Are you asking my intentions, Charlie?"

"Tess is a lady. I am like a brother to her."

"Aye, and to the sister, too, from what I gather. Until you can manage your own affairs, you have no call to be prying into mine."

"We will leave my affairs out of this, thank you. Ada can look after herself. Tess is . . . different."

"Special, you mean."

Chas nodded. "She is that. But what I meant was that Ada is used to taking care of things; Tess lives in her own world, by her own rules."

"I intend to make it my world, if she'll let me in. I mean to do the thing right, though, give her time to make sure that's what she wants, then ask her brother if I can pay my addresses." A moment went by before Leo added, "It is not an easy thing, asking a lady to step down."

"Gammon. Show her the house you're having built. It will be the finest in the area. Make sure you show Tess the indoor plumbing."

"I am not talking about the financial aspects, and you know it. How can I ask her to marry a man with a soiled name?"

"Your name will be cleared, dash it. You won't always be a smuggler."

"No, but I will always be illegitimate."

"You will always be the son of Rose and Sam Tobin, decent, God-fearing folk who loved you."

Leo sighed. "The gossip will never go away, though, and you know it. How can it, when it is the truth? Tess ought to have a prince, not a—"

"Wealthy man who adores her? Not a successful merchant who can afford to let her dabble in whatever arts she wishes and never take her place in the everyday world? Not a moonstruck muttonhead who might be the only person in the world besides her loving sister who thinks Tess is a genius? Hell, you two deserve each other."

"But those others will try their best to turn her against me, sure as Hades, that shrewish sister-in-law, the toplofty old fop, and that fribble of a cousin."

"Spotty-faced sprig with no chin and less brains?"

"Aye. Algernon."

Chas sat up, one hand on his dog. "Did you hear that,

Tally? The Johnstone cub is back. Stay out of the woods. And the fields." The dog licked his hand and went back to sleep. "They're all parasites, so it doesn't matter what they think. If they knew how deep your pockets were, they'd be throwing the girl at your head."

"I suppose." Leo straightened up, ready to leave.

Too tired to move, Chas asked, "What are you going to do?"

"What I would do if I was rowing a boat ashore in enemy waters: wait and see. It's early days yet." Leo reached a hand down to lift his half-brother. "What are you going to do?"

"About the money?" The viscount's head ached, he felt feverish, and his dog was getting fat. "Lud knows."

"About Ada."

"Lud knows."

Ada couldn't sleep again. This time she told herself it was because of the lumps under her pillow; her sleeplessness had nothing whatsoever to do with jealousy of own sister's happiness. Tess loved her sea captain, she'd confided when she came to wish Ada a good night, and she thought he might even love her back.

"He hasn't spoken yet, of course."

Ada nodded. "Quite right. You've hardly known each other a sennight. You have to be sure about these things."

Tess put her hand over her heart. "I am sure."

Tess might be certain of her own feelings, but she was worried that her reputation, her other interests, her devotion to the creative arts, might alienate Leo.

"Oh, no, Tess. He seems to admire your work, and he is encouraging you to complete the illustrations and the score. Why, he even agreed to sit for the paintings."

"But what if Sebastian is not a success? Then all the talk will be true, that I have a breeze blowing through my cockloft. I know that's what people say, Ada, people who don't feel things as I do."

"That's their loss, dearest. If Sebastian—If Leo loves you, nothing else will matter. Would you like him any less if his shipping business failed?"

"Of course not. But I never thought to marry, you know. I never thought my reputation mattered, so I went my own way. Is it too late, do you think?"

Ada told her sister it was never too late. Now, alone in the dark with her lumpy pillow and thoughts of Chas, she prayed her words were true.

Chapter Fifteen

The first of Lady Ashmead's guests arrived the next day, early by design. The design was lovely. Lady Esther Wrentham, daughter of the Earl of Ravenshaw, was a regular china doll of a young miss, petite and perfect with blond ringlets, wide blue eyes, and nary a blemish. There was nary an ounce of intelligence in that pretty package, either.

"Mother, she lisps!"

Lady Esther was resting after her arduous journey into Kent, a journey made longer and more tedious by the frequent stops. The delays were necessitated by rain, the lady's travel sickness, her duenna's dyspepsia, and a damaged wheel on the baggage coach. This cumbersome carriage contained the lady's wardrobe, abigail, and assorted knickknacks without which, the lady lisped, she would feel too, too homethick.

One of those knickknacks happened to be a cat. Not a china cat to match Lady Esther's porcelain beauty, but an ugly old striped tom that was spoiled, surly, and sprayed the front step to mark his territory. Thweet William, it was announced, had to have free reign of the house, for he would shred the bedroom upholstery if confined. Since Lady Ashmead had directed the servants to give her prospective replacement the best guest chamber, the one with the family shield elaborately pieced and appliqued on the bed-hangings by Lady Ashmead herself, Thweety was not confined. Tally, Chas's dog that he'd rescued from a watery grave as a pup, who followed him everywhere, whose comfort and contentment consisted of sleeping with her head resting on Chas's foot, Tally was consigned to the stables. The grooms all made much of her, handing her tidbits so she would not throw her head back in her lonely baying howl. Chas sneaked her into his bedroom at night, of course, and his office when he could shut the door, and took her along in his curricle when he drove around the estate. His own pet's banishment for a curmudgeonly cat still rankled, though not as much as the scratch marks on the back of Chas's hand rankled, from when he'd tried to make friends with the beast.

"You said you would be polite to my company," was all the sympathy he got from his mother.

"I did not say I would toss my dog out in the cold for her."

Lady Ashmead did not bother looking up from her needlework. "Dogs do not belong in the house."

"Cats do? Wait until Thweety plays havoc with your yarns."

Lady Ashmead closed the lid on her workbasket, and on the topic. "Lady Esther seems a prettily behaved chit."

Good behavior did not involve turning one's host's household upside down. Chas did concede that she made a pretty curtsy.

"Nor can you find anything to complain of in her looks, I would wager."

Of course he could; she did not have freckles. Out loud, Chas said, "She is short."

"They called her a Pocket Venus in Bath."

"Who wants a woman in his pocket? The chit barely comes to my shoulder. Why, helping her down from the carriage, I was afraid I might break her bones, she appears so fragile."

"I daresay she will prove sturdy enough to bear sons."

"Thons. She will bear thons, Mother."

Lady Ashmead's eyes narrowed. "Are you belittling a gently bred female because of a handicap? I thought I raised you better than that."

"You did not raise me, Mother, Nanny Kitching did. And that lisp is no affliction; it is an affectation, though why the deuce any chit thinks men might find it attractive is beyond me. Your little lady does not need any artifice to make her appear younger. I swear if the chit were any more childlike I would offer her a glass of milk instead of sherry."

"Give over, Charles. You said you did not want any brittle polished beauties. Lady Esther is a lovely girl, with an even lovelier dowry. She will grow on you."

"Whiskers grow on me, ma'am. I shave them off."

"Give the lady a chance, Charles. Get to know her. You owe me that much."

So he took Lady Esther thight-theeing.

His curricle was handsome, but could he not drive so fast, please.

The lane was lovely.

The weather was clement.

The fishing village was picturesque.

The home farm was orderly.

The viscount was exhausted from trying to make conversation. The chit had less to say than the stable boy he was forced to carry up behind them as tiger, for propriety's sake. Young Ned, at least, whistled when his lordship feathered his corners. Lady Esther silently clutched the side rail.

She had taken half an hour to don half her wardrobe, it seemed, dressing as though they were exploring the frozen tundra instead of the nearby farms. Her hired bear leader, a Mrs. Morton, came out to make sure the chit had her fur-lined mantle, a blanket tucked around her knees, hot bricks at her feet. Meanwhile, his horses had been kept waiting in the cool air. Chas could not even tell if the woman—he had to keep reminding himself not to call her a girl—was enjoying herself now, for she kept her face averted, what he could see around the fur-lined hood, anyway. Was she so shy, then, afraid of him? Perhaps the sight of his scraped face offended her. Or else, oh lud, she was going to be ill!

"I know, why don't we pay a call at the closest neighbors?

Get down and stretch a bit, have a cup of hot tea? Sir Emery is with the Army, but you will enjoy meeting his sisters, Miss Westlake and Miss Ada Westlake, and his widowed sister-in-law, Jane. They are some few years older than you"—zounds, even young Ned was older than Lady Esther—"but you will appreciate knowing other ladies in the neighborhood, I am sure." Chas was not sure if her father would appreciate his well-dowered duckling being introduced to the likes of Algie Johnstone, but he'd worry about that later.

Lady Esther nodded, so Chas turned the carriage in the direction of Westlake Hall. Then he recalled that while such a sheltered miss might have come upon spindle-shanked and skitter-witted schoolboys before, chances were Lady Esther had never met anyone like Tess.

"Tess, that is, Miss Westlake, for she is the elder, is an artist of some repute." Chas did not say that Tess was reputed to be rowing her boat with one oar.

"I paint in watercolors."

"Do you? I am sure you and Tess will have a great deal in common, then." His dog had more in common with Tess; Tally was a better conversationalist. It was Ada he was counting on, at any rate, to welcome Lady Esther to the neighborhood. Ada might be as prickly as a cactus and as stubborn as a mule, but she was never at a loss for words.

Ada was not in sight, though, nor was Jane or her dirty-dish dependents. Tess was in the front parlor, painting. Leo was in the front parlor, posing.

Chas supposed he couldn't blame Lady Esther. If he saw a half-naked man with a dagger clutched between his teeth and a scimitar in his hands, he might have panicked also. He doubted he would have cast up his accounts at the bare-chested berserker's feet, but it did the trick. Leo dropped the weapons and grabbed for his shirt, while Tess went to Lady Esther's assistance. Chas was too busy laughing to help any of them, which earned him the enmity of all three.

Once the earl's daughter was restored, revivified, and reassured, Chas asked after the other members of the household.

"As if you care where Jane or Algernon have taken themselves," Tess said, still angry at him for interrupting her artwork with an ailing heiress, then acting like a looby when the poor puss announced she was going to be thick.

It was Leo who told him, "Ada's out, gone to the orphanage near Folkstone."

"The devil you say! Is she going to . . . ?"

Leo shrugged. "I don't know if she took the money. She did take the gardener with her."

Why, to help the orphans plant potatoes? Chas had to go. There was no telling what Ada would do at the orphanage, not with Prelieu's purse in her hands. Chas was as generous as the next man, more so than many, and he believed his mother was even one of the orphanage's benefactors, but that particular money was Ada's now, and he meant to keep it hers. Unfortunately, little Lady Esther was expecting him to play her escort for the rest of the afternoon.

"I, ah, don't suppose you'd like to see our local foundling home, would you?" he asked her. "My mother helps oversee the orphanage, and a problem has arisen that I really should address."

Now it was Leo's turn to grin, and Tess snickered. "Taking the lady to all the scenic spots, are you, Charlie? Waterfalls, churches, children's hospitals . . ."

"Many great ladies do hours of charitable works," Chas reminded her, impatient to be gone.

"Ada and I have been knitting hats and mittens all fall for the orphans' Christmas. Lady Esther can help us with that."

Knitting? Lady Esther had thought that only the lower orders knitted. She had as much interest in learning how as she did in visiting an orphanage. Dirty, smelly places, they were, filled with ragged children. Why, she'd rather encounter another naked, sword-wielding savage, especially one with broad shoulders and a nice smile, who was not being proposed as a prospective husband.

Chas was about to suggest that Leo see Lady Esther back to the Meadows, with the groom present, of course, when he caught the girl's speculative look at his handsome half-brother. The Earl of Ravenshaw would have his head for certain, if Tess didn't.

"I'll drop you off back at the Meadows, then, miss. My mother will be glad of the company." That was her excuse for inviting the hare-brained heiress; let her try to entertain the chit.

"No, I shall go with you, my lord. I am sure I know my Christian duty as well as any lady." Esther also knew Lord Ashmead had been as close to being engaged to Miss Ada Westlake as possible without a formal announcement. His own mama had told her, and Mrs. Morton had confirmed the fact, from the servants' gossip. The man might be ill-tempered and intimidating, he might even have laughed at her, but he had a title. The unwed dukes were ancient or infants, and earls were scarcer than hen's teeth. All the marquises she knew of were married, and Papa insisted on a title, which left this highly valued viscount. Lady Esther was not going to lose her chance at snabbling up the most eligible *parti* on the marriage market, not with her father threatening to contract a marriage for her with a foreign prince who did not even speak English. She was not, therefore, going to let her viscount encounter Miss Ada Westlake on his own if she could help it.

"No, my dear, the trip is too far, and too cold," Chas said as he handed her into his curricle and tucked the lap robe around her. "You might be sorely affected by the sights there, too."

He almost dropped the reins when the ninnyhammer next to him, who had not said boo to a butterfly, announced, "I am going with you. Thpring 'em."

Chapter Sixteen

On Ada's previous visits to the Lillington-Folkestone Foundling Home, the children had been lined up, freshly scrubbed, smiling sweetly at their benefactress. Lady Ashmead had handed each orphan a hat, scarf, and mittens at Christmas, new shirts and aprons at Easter, all knitted and sewn by the ladies of the area. Lady Ashmead then presented a check to the superintendent and his wife, the Kirkendals, who bowed and curtsied while the children chorused, "Thank you, Lady Ashmead, and God bless you."

Ada supposed the check went a lot further than her puny, lumpy efforts, but writing a check—or having one's son do so—seemed a lot easier to her. When Ada could, she put a ha'penny in each sock or mitten. When she couldn't, she put in a peppermint candy.

Today she had nothing but a troublesome sack of money she was determined to get out of her house and put to good use. No one was going to claim it, she acknowledged, except sneakthiefs like the chandler's boy, who tried to tell her that he'd lost his father's deposit money on his way to the bank. In an apple tree? She sent him away with a flea in his ear, telling him—and everyone she knew would get wind of the tale—that the money was being held by her man of business pending its rightful owner's return. Ada was beginning to fear that her house would be broken into next, if word of her windfall passed beyond the boundaries of her own neighbors.

The money ought to be in a safer place, and would be, after today.

With Garden George asleep in the back of Lulu's cart, Ada drove between the gates of the orphanage. A group of children were huddled together in the side yard, and another five or so were bunched near a hedge, out of the cold wind. Ada wondered why they were not at lessons or chores, unless the Kirkendals had progressive ideas about fresh air during free times. Ada believed in the benefits of healthy exercise herself—wasn't she always urging Jane off the sofa and out to pick berries or gather lavender?—but not on such a cold day. In addition, she saw no brightly colored caps or mittens. Ada's efforts were done in plain boiled wool, but Tess always found scraps of red and yellow, orange and green. The children looked cold and miserable, dirty and disheveled, in fact, with nary a single cheerful smile among them.

Two of the older boys got into a fight over who would hold Lulu's reins, as if the old mare was going to bolt, and started pushing and punching at each other, exchanging blows and foul epithets.

"Here now, lads, none of that," Garden George stirred himself to say. "Not in front of a lady."

"Or the younger children," Ada added, stepping between the combatants, earning a handful of dirt tossed in her face. "Why, you bl—"

"Not in front of the children, missy." George went to Lulu's head and spit tobacco juice on the ground. The boys disappeared.

"Where is Mrs. Kirkendal?" Ada asked a shivering girl near the front door.

"Gone."

"I can see she is gone, the way there is no supervision out here. When will she be back?"

The girl hunched thin shoulders under a thin scarf, not one of the thick woolen ones Ada had so painstakingly knitted. "Never, I s'pose. I wouldn't come back neither."

Ada was getting a very bad feeling about this. "What about Mr. Kirkendal?" She preferred dealing with the matron, who always offered Lady Ashmead's lackeys poppy seed cake, but she could talk to Mr. Kirkendal just as easily.

"Himself's in there."

Ada was relieved, until the girl said, "But he can't talk to you."

"What, is he sick?"

The child just shrugged.

"What about the other staff? That nice young teacher, Mr.— What was his name?"

"Gone."

That was definitely not his name, nor what Ada wished to hear. "Mr. Barnell, that was it."

"Gone. Run off with herself. And the funds."

Oh, dear. Ada clutched her fur muff and its contents closer. Perhaps the money was heaven-sent after all, to help these poor unfortunate children at their time of need.

"Well, I shall just have to speak to Mr. Kirkendal, no matter how he is feeling. We cannot let this situation continue, can we?"

The girl shrugged again and turned away, expressing her opinion of the outcome of Ada's efforts. "Wait, dear," Ada called to the pinch-faced girl. "Why are none of you wearing your warm hats and mittens?"

The girl jerked her bare, nearly blue thumb in the direction of the door. "Himself sold them. For laudanum."

"For the pain?"

"For the laudanum."

Ada asked Garden George to come inside with her. He was old, but he could still wield a pitchfork. Regrettably, Ada hadn't thought to tell him to bring one.

Walking through the empty house, Ada wished she'd asked how long Mrs. Kirkendal had been gone. Ages, it appeared, from the dust and the dirt. Ada could see where paintings had been taken off the walls to be sold, and carpets lifted from the floors. If this was the state of the public rooms, she dreaded to think what the children's dormitories must look like, or the kitchens. Mr. Kirkendal might have had a hard time finding someone to take over his wife's many duties, especially without funds, but this was beyond the pale. All he had to do was apply to Lady Ashmead, who would see that Chas set matters right, and so Ada intended to tell the man, as soon as she found him.

Mr. Kirkendal was in the establishment's office, but he was beyond badgering. His head lolled back on his neck and a trail of drool hung from his mouth. He smelled, besides, and his linen was soiled. When Ada nudged him with her boot, he opened glassy, unfocused eyes. He reached for a cup filled with a murky liquid, but Ada pushed it farther across the littered desk, out of his reach.

"Get up, sirrah, and tell me what you have done with the children's mittens!"

"Mittens?"

It sounded insignificant to Ada too, but she was so angry she couldn't think. All she knew was that she'd believed her meager efforts, whose cost in time and money she had begrudged, were doing the children some good. Guilt ate at her, that innocent babes, with no one to look after their interests, were suffering while she was arguing with her sister-in-law over a blue domino for a ball. "Yes, mittens and . . . and everything else you stole from them."

" 'Twas m'wife who cleaned the bank accounts," Kirkendal whined. "M'wife and that blasted Barnell."

"That was some time ago. What have you done about it since? The children are cold and I daresay hungry." Ada kicked his foot again when it looked like he was about to nod off once more. "What have you done about it, I said?"

"I . . . I . . ."

"You did not go to the trustees, did you?"

Hunching lower in his seat, the head of the orphanage admitted, "Couldn't. The books wouldn't have stood examining, even before the faithless witch left. They'd have had me transported, likely."

"What about Lady Ashmead, your patroness?"

Kirkendal shivered. "She'd have had me hung. Likely saying it was no wonder m'wife left me, while she watched."

Ada seldom agreed with Lady Ashmead, but now was one of those times. "She'd have been right. You are a sad excuse for a man, robbing from orphans. It's no wonder you are trying to kill yourself with these noxious potions."

"You don't understand. It was m'wife who managed everything, the books, the shopping, the children, toadying up to Lady Ashmead. I couldn't . . . I couldn't do it on my own." He dabbed at his eyes with a grayish handkerchief, then looked at her more closely, hope dawning across his unwashed, unshaven face. "But you are here now, Miss Ada. Always been good to the children, you have. You'll help me, won't you?" he begged. At her frown of distaste, he added, "We can get the older girls to help fix the place up."

"What, do you think a dust mop is going to solve your problems?"

"I heard in the village about the money you found. You can pay off the merchants so we can get food and firewood delivered. We'll come about, ma'am, with just a little help from your kind heart."

"You think I would give a shilling to a . . . a . . ."

"An opium eater," George put in from the doorway.

"To a man who hides in a vial of forgetfulness? You would only use it for your needs, letting the children go on suffering." She turned in disgust. "I will leave it up to Lord Ashmead to find punishment befitting your misdeeds—after he sees to the children's welfare, that is."

Kirkendal grabbed at her arm so she could not leave. "Don't tell him, miss. Don't tell him. He might kill me."

George was making his slow way across the room when a very welcome voice came from the doorway: "If you don't take your hands off the lady this instant, he will kill you for sure."

Kirkendal's hands fell to his sides, and he started blubbering.

Ada had never been so glad to see Chas in her life. Freed, she ran to him, and his arm went around her, but his eyes never left Kirkendal. If the man made one suspicious move toward Ada or a weapon in the desk, Lord Ashmead's stance seemed to say, he'd be maggot bait by morning.

"His wife ran off with the bank account and the instructor," Ada started to explain. "He was afraid to come to you for fear of losing his position, because previous irregularities would have come to light."

"His position? The dastard ought to fear losing his head, letting this place go to wrack and ruin without consulting the trustees."

"Then he sold what he could to pay for his own need for laudanum."

Chas was appalled by what little he had seen, furious that Ada had been exposed to such depravity. "If you could not face your sins, the least you could have done was blown your brains out like a man, instead of turning to morphia. The children would have been better off."

"Medicine," Kirkendal pleaded. "It's medicine, I swear."

"He sold the children's clothes, and blankets, too, I fear. They'd have been wrapped in them outside, otherwise."

"The blighter sold four of the older boys," George put in, "to the mines up north, according to one of the other lads."

Livid, Chas grabbed Kirkendal by the collar and shook him. "You took the children in your care and handed them virtual death sentences, to support your own filthy habit?" He dragged Kirkendal to the door, then outside, past the wide-eyed children and down the path to the gate. The viscount gave the other man a final rattle before tossing him into the roadway. "If I ever see you again, I won't bother bringing charges before the magistrate. I'll have you put on a ship for New Zealand before the next sunrise."

Ashmead's tiger cheered from where he stood at the horses' heads near the gate, but Lady Esther, still seated on the curricle's bench, cried out in dismay and hid her face.

Ignoring her, Chas turned to Ada, who had naturally followed him out of the building rather than avoiding the sight of fisticuffs, as a proper female would have done. "You are all right, aren't you? That poltroon did not hurt you?"

"Not at all, except for turning my stomach. But you will do something about the children, won't you?"

He raised an eyebrow. "What, did you think I would turn my back on a bunch of starving orphans?"

"Of course not, but you have other commitments." Ada turned to look at the lady in his curricle, who was now whimpering into her handkerchief. With the expensive, ermine-lined hood pulled up, all Ada could see were a few golden curls and a rosy cheek. "You should not leave your guest out in the cold, but the inside of the orphanage is no fit place for a lady either."

"Hell and thunderation." Chas glowered at the offending building, then realized he was only frightening the children further, to say nothing of Lady Esther. She, at least, knew where her next meal was coming from. The children were cowering together as far from him as they could get, not trusting his temper any more than they'd trusted Kirkendal. Ada, though, gazed at him as if he could snap his fingers and make a miracle happen in this dingy yard. Frustrated that he couldn't, Chas cursed again. "There is not much I can do from here in any case. I'll have to return to the Meadows to order out the wagons. We can provide food and blankets, but I'll have to send someone to the village and the farms to see if we can locate warm clothing. Will you and George wait here, meanwhile, to see that the dastard doesn't come back to sell anything else?"

"Of course. And I will reassure the children that they have nothing more to fear."

"Good. I'll go raid the kitchens—Mother and her company can take pot luck for a bit—and I will return with some of the staff. She hired hordes of extra servants for the house party so I know we can spare as many as it takes, until I can find a permanent solution to this mess."

"Don't forget wood for fires, towels so the children can wash, and whatever medicines your housekeeper thinks might be handy." Then Ada thrust her fur muff at him. "Here, this will help."

Chas looked back to where Lady Esther was wailing into her handkerchief. "No, thank you. She brought her own. Besides, you are going to be out here in the cold with the children until I can get back. You will need it more."

"I meant it for you, gudgeon."

"I have my leather driving gloves." The viscount was trying to count how many children were in the yard, how many coats and pairs of shoes he would have to find before he could consider thinking of his own comfort. "And I am not cold, just so angry I could tear those filthy Kirkendals apart in my hands."

"Silly, I am not offering you my hand warmer. It is the money I found. Use it for the children."

Now Chas turned to look at his old friend, whom he could trust to do the necessary for these ragamuffins while he was gone, and without an ounce of complaint. She certainly would not go off in hysterics or enact him a Cheltenham tragedy, not his Ada. Raising his hand to caress her cheek, he said, "Ada, you have the biggest heart of any woman I know, but this is my responsibility. I should have had my man checking on conditions here, not trusting Kirkendal's reports. I will make things right for these waifs, I swear. I cannot take your money to pay my debts."

"Just as I could never take yours for mine."

Chas wasn't certain of her meaning, but he suspected it

had something to do with that blasted leather purse. Now was not the time to discuss her intransigence or his insanity, however. He said, "I'll be back with help as soon as possible." Then he lovingly kissed her forehead.

Lady Esther was crying for real now. Lord Ashmead patted her hand once he had the horses headed for home. "Please do not cry, my dear, although your pity for the children speaks well for your gentle character. They will be fine by evening, I promise, with warm fires, hot food, and kind, decent people to look after them, people who will work harder to find them homes of their own."

Esther was not crying for the children; she was crying because she'd seen that tender passage between Ada and the viscount. Her father would have her wed to that German prince before the cat could shred another pair of Lord Ashmead's boots. She sobbed louder.

Chapter Seventeen

When you run out of firewood, it is acceptable to burn the fence posts. That rule must have been written somewhere, Ada hoped as she set Garden George to work with an ax he found near the empty log box. She was not going to leave those children out in the cold, which was warmer than the interior of the home.

Ada also discovered that there was food in the larder, only it was locked away for the Kirkendals' private use. George's ax was called for again.

With the help of Sarah, one of the older girls, Ada prepared a meal. It was an odd meal, to be sure, consisting of nuts, raisins, and fruit preserves spread on slices of cold ham, with a few dried kippers on the side. The children did not complain. Ada put the rest of the ham in a pot with whatever vegetables she could find, for soup for later. As soon as George got the kitchen fire going, there was steaming tea, and hot water for washing. Ada used Kirkendal's laundered shirts as face cloths and towels, since they appeared to be the only clean fabrics in the house. As she scrubbed ears and wiped hands, Ada tried to get a count of the orphans. Eighteen, she thought, although she might have counted a few twice, as they dragged pallets and pillows into the kitchen, to stay together in the warmth, and to watch her prepare biscuits.

When she asked why there were no babies, red-haired Sarah busied herself scrubbing a baking sheet for Ada to use. Babies died, she finally admitted, even when Mrs. Kirkendal had been around. They never had a wet nurse for them, or enough heat, and no medicine when they caught the contagions the other children managed to survive.

If those biscuits were leavened with tears, the children did not notice. The last of the jam was spread on top, and one gap-toothed towhead declared it the finest meal he'd had since his mum left him at the gates.

While they were cleaning up, and the contented children were gathered around George to hear his entirely fictitious accounts of Sir Emery's exploits on the Peninsula, Sarah asked Ada for a position at Westlake Hall. Studying Ada from under her lowered lashes, the girl proposed herself as an apprentice ladies' maid.

Ada had to laugh around the lump in her throat. "That bad, am I?" She knew she must look as bedraggled as the orphans, with her hair all undone and her gown covered with her culinary efforts and still damp in spots from the face-washings.

Blushing furiously, Sarah denied any implied criticism of her newfound idol. She had simply always wanted to learn to be a ladies' maid like her mother had been, before losing her virtue to her employer's husband and being tossed out like yesterday's trash to die in the poorhouse. Sarah would not make the same mistake, she swore.

"Of course you won't, dear, but I fear I am not the one to teach you about becoming an abigail."

"You could show me how a real lady goes on, though," Sarah persisted.

"That's very sweet, Sarah, but, you see, I am at *point non plus* myself." At the girl's confused look, Ada explained, "We are as poor as church mice ourselves at Westlake Hall. We can barely afford to pay the servants we have now."

Sarah's expression went from worshipful to woebegone in a flash. "We heard himself say you found a pot of money."

"Not a pot, and not mine to keep. I am truly sorry, Sarah, but I couldn't offer you more than a bed and board."

"That's better than what I been getting here. I accept."

Ada hadn't thought she'd offered, but how could she destroy the child's hopes? Sarah was fourteen and would have to leave the orphanage soon anyway, to go heaven knew where, without references. While here, she would be nothing but a caretaker for the younger children, with no chance to learn skills that might improve her lot in life. At least Ada could make sure the girl learned her letters. Tess could help with that.

Thinking of her sister reminded Ada of how much time Tess was spending with Leo, with nary a chaperone in sight, not even a maid. Then, too, with the parties sure to be held in the neighborhood for Lady Ashmead's guests, Tess and Ada could use some help with their clothes and hair.

"Very well, Miss Sarah. You can come to Westlake Hall."

"And my brother Robin? He's nobbut eleven, but he's big and strong. The governor would of sent him off to the mines, but I made Robby cough so they thought he was sickly. He's not, ma'am, I swear. He can fetch and carry, or help your old man. I saw how Mr. Garden couldn't carry all the logs."

"That's George, dear, and I do suppose he could use some help." Ada also supposed another retainer might stop Jane's family from carping about the lack of service at Westlake Hall. "Are you sure Robin would not mind running errands or carrying cans of hot water for baths?"

Sarah was incredulous. "Instead of toting coal in a cold, dark tunnel? Why, Robby'd pay you to let him, iffen we had the money."

In the end, four children went home with Ada, three of them red-haired. Two of the boys were to be trained up as footmen so they might find positions later and another, sturdier lad was to help George in the gardens. They all promised to study hard at their books, work hard at their chores, respect the elderly servants, and admire Tess's artwork. Ada would find the food to feed all the extra mouths somewhere.

The children and their meager belongings would not all fit in Lulu's cart with Ada and George, naturally. Ada waited until Chas had helped unload the wagons and carriages full of servants in Ashmead livery, then she asked him for help transporting her new recruits. As he watched his staff take competent control, Chas grinned at her, half joking and half in relief that she'd been able to accomplish so much before he got there. The children seemed happier, and certainly cleaner. Nor were they as heart-wrenchingly fearful. "I did wonder about leaving you here with the orphans. I am merely amazed that you are only taking four."

"I had to leave some for you, of course," she teased back.

He was smiling still. "I thought about it, naturally, taking the whole bunch of them back to the Meadows."

"I think I would have traded my place in heaven for a look at your mother's face if you had."

"She might even have returned to her house in Bath."

They both said "Too bad," at once, and laughed together like the good companions they used to be.

"Lud knows there is enough room at the old barracks of a place," Chas went on before he ruined this moment of understanding between them with his maudlin thoughts. "But they'll do better here, for now. I found a better solution, too. Do you remember the Holmdale family?"

"Weren't they one of your tenants, the ones with the enormous family?"

"Yes, but the children have all married and moved away, or joined the Army. Tom was finding it hard farming his acres without the boys, and Margaret misses having a full house, so they were thinking of opening an inn. I was able to convince them to stay, so Mr. and Mrs. Holmdale will move in here tomorrow to look after the children. One of their daughters and her husband might come teach. I said I would double their salary, so the place will be a merry one for the tykes."

"That sounds perfect!" Ada put it to her charges, but they all decided they'd rather go with her, earn their keep, prepare for their futures, so Chas sent them off in one of his carriages.

"You see, Miss Ada," Sarah said as she was handed into the elegant equipage by a liveried groom, "we're doing better already." George drove Lulu home, carrying the children's sacks of belongings.

As soon as they left, Chas helped Ada into his curricle, then took his seat beside her and sighed. "It's been a long day."

Ada added her own weary sigh, and she'd only had to cope with eighteen orphans and an opium addict. Chas had to deal with a hen-hearted heiress. "Did Lady Esther recover once you reached the Meadows?"

The viscount took his eyes off the horses long enough to take a good look at Ada. She was adorable to him, even more so than usual, unkempt and unconscious of her appearance, messy and bright, glowing with happiness at the changes they'd brought to children no one else cared about. He would have fallen in love with her at that minute, if he hadn't before.

"Chas?"

"What—? Oh, Lady Esther. She'll get over it."

"Of course she will, for an eligible gentleman like yourself." Seeing the viscount help unload boxes and barrels, bend down to child-level to promise to come again, no woman could resist Chas. Ada couldn't, for sure. She admired him more than ever after this afternoon . . . when he was escorting his prospective bride. From what she'd heard, from what Jane had heard, the earl's heiress sounded the perfect wife for Chas, being beautiful, wealthy, and well-bred, with a delicate lady's sensitive, caring nature. Lady Esther was not caring enough to stay and help the children, but caring for all that. Ada was beside him now, though, and did not want to ruin her time with Chas in thoughts of the eminently marriageable miss.

"What about Kirkendal?" she asked instead. "What will happen to him? I doubt he will get very far."

"I had the magistrate send the constables after Kirkendal's wife and her lover, since they were the ones who absconded with the bulk of the foundling home's funds. That way we might recover some of the blunt. I couldn't see any use prosecuting Kirkendal himself, that sorry excuse for a man, as long as he stays away from the orphanage. I doubt if Hocking will do anything at all, though."

"The squire is full of surprises," Ada said, remembering the botanist's sudden mindstorm.

"Oh? I always thought him a prosy old bore, more interested in his plants than the parish. I called on him while the grooms were loading the wagons, and Hocking seemed afraid of me, for some reason. Odd, don't you think, after I had a perfectly normal discussion with him just a few days ago?"

So did Ada, and look where it had nearly led, to a tropical tryst. "What did you two discuss?"

Chas waved his hand, not about to tell her that she and that star-crossed sack of silver were the topic. "Just legal business, boundaries and such. Then he went on about his orchids, as usual."

Ada knew the reason for Hocking's new horror, that she might have gone to Chas with the tale of Squire's far-flung fantasy. She bit her lip.

"Ineffectual old goat," Chas was going on. "I doubt he'd roust himself out of his hothouses enough to find his bed, much less embezzlers. At first I thought he was afraid I'd hold him to account for the mess at the orphanage since he is another of the trustees, but he had no idea what I was speaking about. He said he hadn't been next or nigh the place in months, and I believe him, or there would have been a flower or two around the gate. He never did put down that cactus though, as if I meant to run him through with his own pitchfork."

"Squire thought he could defend himself with a cactus?" She should have thought of that.

"I told you he was a clunch. I mean to call on the vicar tomorrow, at any rate, speaking of clunches. He ought to have kept tabs on the children, wouldn't you think?"

"At least he should have noticed if they'd been to Sunday services. What about your mother? She is on the board of directors also, isn't she?"

"I never held her blameless for thinking that a check was the end of her responsibilities. When she began to reproach me for returning her pet heiress as a watering pot and berating me for subjecting a lady to such a scene, I reminded her that someone had subjected those innocent children to worse. She had nothing to say, for once."

"Good for you." Ada always felt that Chas's mother did not respect him enough. Ada doubted that Lady Ashmead respected Lord Wellington enough.

"She was quiet for a good five minutes, until I commandeered her servants and confiscated half the pantry. Once she'd had recourse to her vinaigrette she did mention that you should begin anew on hats and mufflers. But you don't need to, Ada, truly. I put word out in the village that I would pay for knitted goods. Let the local women make some money too with their weaving and spinning."

"Oh, that reminds me, the money. We really need to talk about the money from the orchard, Chas."

"I won't take it, if that's what you are thinking. Do not insult me by offering it again."

"No, I was only going to ask if you would take it back—"

"Take it back? Then you know—?"

"To the Meadows, to keep it safe and out of harm's way." Out of temptation's way too, but she didn't say that. "If you have it no strangers will be battering on my door for loans. Why, my own tenant farmers are looking at me accusingly when I won't give them new roofs. As for Jane . . . Well, you can imagine."

"The devil. I never intended—That is, are you sure you won't take it, spend it, save it for your dowry?"

What use had she for a man who would only marry her for her money? "I am sure. You can give out that it was meant for that missing Frenchman of yours, Proulous, was it, but I found it by mistake when he did not arrive."

"It's Prelieu, and he is a blasted spy, not a squirrel. No one would believe we put an informer's payment in a tree."

"That's the best I have been able to come up with. You think of some other excuse for the pouch being in my orchard, then."

He couldn't, of course. "Very well, I will keep it safe, but only until you change your mind."

Which mind? Ada wondered. He couldn't be speaking about her rejection of his suit, not when he was squiring a buffleheaded little beauty. Chas had to mean the money. She was no charity case. "I will never change my mind."

"Never say never, love, for I'll keep trying to change it for you."

"The money?"

"To hell with the money."

Chas pulled the horses to a halt, and pulled Ada into his arms. He kissed her, right there in his curricle.

Ada wasn't chilled anymore, at least. Shaken, breathless, and brainless, but not cold, oh, no. "What was that for?" she asked when he finally set the horses back in motion and her heart resumed its own functioning.

"For being such a Trojan with the children. For not throwing spasms. For being the most beautiful woman I know."

Ada sighed. He was right. To hell with the money.

Chapter Eighteen

"Don't expect my maid to share a room with any flea-ridden foundling," Jane predictably squawked. "Hapgood will give her notice and I will be alone in this lunatic asylum, right when I need to look my best." She waved the invitation to Lady Ashmead's masquerade under Ada's nose, as if Ada did not recognize her own handwriting. "Who knows who might be attending?"

Ada and Chas both had a fairly good idea of the guest list, but neither bothered answering, trying to reassure the children that, yes, they were welcome here and, no, the mean lady could not turn them into toads.

Tess and Leo returned from her studio then, and Ada could not convince herself that Tess's reddened lips must have paint on them. The sooner she established little Sarah as Tess's watchdog the better. When she explained about the conditions at the orphanage, and her plans to train these children for respectable careers in service, Tess was thrilled, especially with Sarah and her brother Robin and their bright red hair. "Sea sprites! That's just what the illustrations have been missing! Can any of you darlings sing?"

All four of the children hesitantly raised their hands, and Tess clapped hers. "This is the best, the very best birthday present you could have brought me, Ada." She kissed Ada and Chas, then Leo, then all four of the children in turn, then Leo again.

Chas cleared his throat, but it was Ada who said, "Your birthday is not until April, Tess."

Tess fluttered a paint-smeared cloth. "You really must endeavor to nurture your spirit of creativity, dearest. We'll work on that another time. For now, let us get these cherubs settled. Sarah can have the pallet in my dressing room, where she won't have to put up with hoity-toity Hapgood."

The children were smiling again, already adoring the whimsical Miss Westlake. Miss Tess could not compare in their estimation to Miss Ada, of course, but she seemed a right 'un, putting the shrill-voiced lady in her place.

Robin and one of the other boys were to have a room together below stairs near the kitchen, where Cobble and his wife could keep an eye on them. The room was not very large, but the boys considered it a stroke of good fortune that only two of them had to share the bed.

The third boy wanted to share the unused groom's quarters above the stables with George, if he could henceforth be known as Garden Martin, since he'd never had two names before. Martin liked horses, he liked yard work, mostly he liked Garden George's stories and his prowess with an ax.

"That's settled then," Ada was happy to note as the children followed Mrs. Cobble to the kitchens for a tour and a snack. Jane was already resigned to the new additions, since she would not have to deal with them, and they were not taking money out of the Westlake coffers. She did wonder aloud if pageboys were still in fashion, and if she could get nipfarthing Ada to purchase livery for them. "No," Ada told her, "and no to you too, Algernon." She could not like the way Algie had been eyeing young Sarah, licking his thin lips. "If you so much as look at her sideways, I will have you gelded like a bull calf, see if I don't."

His eyes widened, but he instantly took them off Sarah. "You cannot do that, Ada. Tell her she can't, Cousin Jane. Pater?"

His father harumphed. Filbert wouldn't put anything past

the farouche female. "Nonsense, my boy. Come along, I promised you a game of billiards, didn't I? Care to join us, Ashmead?"

Chas noted that Johnstone hadn't invited Leo Tobin to play. "No, I still have much to do this day, between the foundling home and the house party and the usual estate business." And the scheduled smuggling run. If Prelieu was ever going to make it to England, tonight was the night. "I'll be taking my leave, then. Did you still want me to take that parcel for you, Ada?"

Chas directed the hint toward Jane, who would have the whereabouts of Ada's windfall broadcast throughout the neighborhood by morning. No one would be battening on her after that, no one but her own usual dirty dish connections.

Ada, however, made sure she passed the money pouch over to Chas while Filbert Johnstone and his son were still in the room. She did not trust those two as far as she could throw them. Since she could not throw them out of Westlake Hall, the money was safer in the vault at the Meadows.

It was Filbert's turn to lick his lips while he watched the fortune change hands, and Jane pounded at the pillow on the sofa in her disappointment, dislodging the all-important invitation and some other papers in her lap.

"Oh, by the way, something came for you in the post this morning, Ada. I didn't recognize the hand. Likely another dunning letter."

Ada supposed she should be pleased Jane hadn't tossed her correspondence away. As she took the folded sheet and noted the quality of the paper, the unknown handwriting, the unfamiliar seal, she agreed it could only have come from another gambling associate of Rodney's, demanding payment on her brother's vowels. Ada almost wished Jane had thrown the infernal thing out.

"It's from Lieutenant Brookstone, Emery's friend. Oh, dear Lord, no!"

Chas was at her side in an instant, guiding her to a chair.

"It cannot be that bad, Ada, for the letter would have come from his commanding officer, by messenger."

"No, you are right," Ada said, reading on. "Emery was wounded, the lieutenant writes. He is in the field hospital, and he may lose his arm." She was only vaguely aware that Tess had gasped and leaned into Leo's embrace for comfort, or that Chas had his arm around her own shoulders. With streaming eyes, she turned to him and cried, "Good heavens, those Army surgeons are butchers! And the conditions are so bad, an injured soldier is more likely to die of fever than of the wound."

"If Emery dies and we have to go into mourning again, I will never, ever forgive him," Jane declared, waving Lady Ashmead's invitation in the air. Everyone ignored her.

Chas took the letter out of Ada's hands and continued reading. "See here, the lieutenant says that Emery has not developed any undue fevers or swellings, so he remains hopeful. In fact, he writes, they are putting Emery on a troop ship for home."

"Thank God." Ada found a handkerchief in her hands, a beautifully embroidered one. "And thank you, Chas. I don't think I could have borne it if . . ."

Chas was reading the closing paragraph. "Unless there is a change in plans, he will be aboard the *Speculation*, arriving at Portsmouth in"—he checked the date at the top of the lieutenant's letter—"in less than a week from tomorrow."

"Portsmouth? That's at the opposite end of the kingdom!"

"Yes, but it is the naval station. Likely they are using a damaged ship to transport the wounded troops, so they put in at Portsmouth for repairs."

"But it is so far away." Ada was thinking of the carriages she would have to hire, all the nights at inns, the days before she reached her brother's side and could bring him home. The expense. She took the leather purse back from the viscount.

"Not so far," he said, calculating. "I will have Emery home before my mother's masquerade."

"You?"

"Of course. I can ride cross country, much faster than you could manage, even traveling post. I can hire coaches when I get there, and bring him back in comfort, in company of a physician, if needed."

"But . . . but your guests. You cannot leave when you are expected to play host to your mother's house party. Lady Esther . . ."

"Might be the reason he is so eager to leave." Tess took the letter from Chas to see if she could read more about Emery's condition from his friend's wording.

Ada nearly blushed for her sister's outspokenness, although secretly agreeing. "Your mother will have conniptions. Besides, you are needed here to set up the trust for the orphanage we discussed, and to deal with the Kirkendals if they are found."

"Gammon. Mother will fuss no matter what, and my solicitor can handle everything else—"

"No need," Leo interrupted. "I'll go."

All eyes turned to the usually untalkative smuggler, who was no member of the family, no old friend, not even a fellow gentleman. Jane's uncle made a rude noise, but he did not offer to go fetch Emery instead.

Leo straightened his waistcoat, a white one today, with gold threads through it. "I can make better time than any of you, sailing around. My new sloop can outrun any—That is, I'll be back in jig time. If I miss the masquerade, Lady Ashmead won't be brokenhearted, not by half."

"It might answer," Chas conceded. "With the autumn rains, making fast time on the roads might be difficult."

"What about the seas and bad weather, though?" Ada asked, picturing poor Emery wet and cold, tossed from side to side.

"Don't be a goose," Tess told her. "It's a ship, not a rowboat."

"Aye, and a sturdy one. And my first mate knows more about doctoring than any Army sawbones, if your brother takes a turn for the worse."

Tess nodded. "The worst thing for Emery would be a long ride in a drafty carriage over bumpy roads, with stays at indifferent inns at night, and who knows what for meals. I have seen the appointments of Leo's *Challenger*, and Emery will be comfortable, however long it takes. Besides, I will be along to nurse him."

Jane gasped and Ada shook her head. "I'm sorry, dear, for I would like to go along too, but you must see it wouldn't be at all the thing. Not even if you took young Sarah with you. Not aboard a smuggler's—that is, a shipper's—private boat."

"I do not see that at all. My brother needs me, so I am going."

"The devil you will, miss," Leo said.

Chas more gently added, "The last thing a sick man wants is a female fussing over him. Emery is a soldier, used to rough conditions. You are not."

Trying to make Tess see reason, however, was like asking the eyes of a potato to read a book. She raised her chin. "Emery does not know Leo. Our brother will want a familiar face near him."

"I always said she was beyond hope," Jane told the room at large, starting to blubber. "But this is beyond the pale. She'll bring scandal down on all of us this time, I just know it."

Algernon snickered.

Ada stood up for her sister, as always, frowning at both of them. "What you know, Jane, would not fill a thimble."

"Here now, no call to be talking to m'niece that way, Ada. Lady Westlake, and all that. Old enough to know what's best, what?"

Everyone glared at him, especially Jane, for the reference to her age.

Leo'd had enough of words. He was a man of action, used to making decisions, used to being obeyed. He was not used to pitched battles in drawing rooms, so he took Tess's hand and dragged her out of the room, down the hall to the breakfast parlor, where he slammed the door behind them.

"Well!" Jane said in a huff. "I see his manners are just as execrable as Tess's. They deserve each other."

Ada looked at Chas and smiled, despite her anxiety over Emery and Tess's reputation. "Yes, I think they just might."

"You are not going aboard my ship, lass, and that is final. I will not have you destroying your good name."

Tess was pacing the length of the room, her skirts swirling around her legs. "My good name? Hah! I will never be anything but the mad Miss Westlake. I may as well enjoy the notoriety."

Leo grabbed her arm and stopped her, making Tess face him. "Do you know what you are saying? Do you have any idea what will happen on that ship?"

"Do you? I am asking to be your mistress, you great gossoon."

"No."

"What, I am not good enough for the position?" Tess tried to pull away. "You'd rather have a tavern wench? You did not seem so reluctant in my studio earlier."

"No."

"No, you aren't reluctant, or no, I am not good enough?"

"No, I will not take you to bed without taking you to wife."

"Now who is being daft?" Tess pulled back again, but Leo held her in an iron grip. "You can have my company without donning leg shackles."

"No, I cannot. I would not dishonor you, or my sons, by letting them be born as bastards the way I was."

"There are ways of preventing children, I have read all about them. You do not want to marry me."

"No?"

"Of course not. The notion is ridiculous."

"I have wanted nothing else since I set eyes on you, lass."

"Spanish coin if ever I heard it. You can have any woman you want. Oh, not some high in the instep belle like Jane, but you wouldn't want her anyway. Just look at you though, so tall and handsome, such a success by your own efforts." Against her will, it seemed, Tess's hand stroked the gold threads of his waistcoat. "What have I got? A half-finished, half-baked opera. I have nothing to offer a man like you."

"No? You have your beautiful self, your talent, your imagination. If I could soar half as high as you I would be content. I think I can, in your arms and in your affection."

"What a lovely thing to say. If I had my pad and pencil, I would write it into the second act."

"You see, you've turned this old salt into a poet already. That's what I need from you, Miss Westlake, your hand and your heart."

"Truly? You really want to marry me? I cannot think of anything I would like more, not even seeing Sebastian published, for I do love you, Mr. Tobin."

Once again, Leo'd had a surfeit of words. He took Tess in his arms and proved how precious she was to him.

Some time later, Tess suggested they get a special license, so she could go along with him to Portsmouth.

"There's no time, lass. I intend to be off at dawn, for I wouldn't leave a dog in an Army hospital longer than I had to. I want to do the thing right, too, so we have nothing to be ashamed about later. I will fetch your brother home and ask his blessing. If he cannot accept a common man, a baseborn sailor, as fitting husband for you, then I will sail you away to Scotland."

"Is that a promise?"

"Aye."

"You won't change your mind?"

"No."

That was Leo's last word for another long while.

Chapter Nineteen

"Why do women sell themselves so cheaply?"

"What, have you been giving Molly a tumble over at Jake's? I thought you were done with that now that you were courting Tess."

"I don't mean selling their bodies. I do mean Tess, and Ada too. What is wrong with the women of that family that they hold such little value of themselves?"

Viscount Ashmead and his half-brother were lying on their stomachs atop a cliff, watching Leo's men unload the cargo from a skiff that had been rowed ashore. The larger boat waited just offshore, a shadow in the night. This was the last boatload to be hauled and no Frenchman had stepped onto dry land. The viscount watched through his spy glass and cursed.

Both men wore dark clothing tonight, no finery to glimmer in the moonlight, no stark white shirts and neckcloths to draw attention to their presence. Both were heavily armed, also, in case a renegade band of raiders tried to steal the booty. With a pistol in his hand, a knife in his boot, and a rifle at his side, the sight of Leo would have made Tess proud, Chas considered. Then again, if she had known about their activities, Tess would have wanted to come along. The danger was too great to consider giving her a hint of their night's work.

They were not armed against the government men, since Chas had personally made sure Lieutenant Nye was busy this evening. His mother was holding a card party to entertain what guests had arrived at the Meadows, and Chas had dragooned the young lieutenant to take his place, claiming he had to stand watch over the orphanage in case the Kirkendals came back. He thought of Quintin partnering Lady Esther at whist and had to smile, white teeth flashing in the night after all. Lud, if those two made a match of it, their children would never learn to speak, between the officer's nervous stammer and the lady's affected lisp.

Chas wished for Quintin Nye's sake—and for his own—that the china doll would look the lieutenant's way, but he doubted such a possibility. In fact, the chances of Prelieu swimming ashore were better than Ravenshaw recognizing the riding officer as a suitor for his daughter's hand. With such a fortune as she would have, the earl would hold out for a barony at least. Which partly answered Leo's question: "Women are commodities in this world, that's why they lack confidence."

Leo looked down at the barrels and boxes on the shore. "No one buys and sells females, not in this country anyway."

"Hah. They might not call it bondage, but women are bartered constantly. They are sold for titles, for fortunes, land, even for votes or political influence. The difference is they become wives, not slaves, but their husbands and fathers reap the profits. They gloss it over by calling them advantageous marriages. My sisters were not encouraged to dally with the dustman. They barely saw a gentleman without a title to his name. Why should my father consider a man who could not keep a wife in style? And why should a rich man not grow richer? Their dowries, not their pretty faces and pretty manners, let my sisters select from the eligibles. Even among the lower orders a woman is pursued for what she can bring to the marriage, what coins her father might dower her with, when she might inherit a bit of land, how many cows."

"A poor man cannot always afford to take a poor wife. And a woman would not give her hand to a man who could not feed her and her children. How would they live?"

"Precisely. In the Westlakes' circles, the situation is worse. They have no great, hallowed name to bring, no lofty connections to better a gentleman's place in life. Without the meager dowries Rodney gambled away, they have no bargaining position, and they know it. That is why they consider themselves inferior merchandise, of lesser value than the empty-headed Lady Esthers of the *ton.* A man with no fortune can marry a woman with one, but he can also go out and make something of himself, the way you did. A woman doesn't have those options. Too many doors are closed to them, which likely makes them either give up, or dig their heels in."

Leo shifted on the ground, considering. "Mayhaps things will get better once the brother comes home. Do you think he can turn their fortunes around?"

"I pray to God he can. He couldn't do worse than Rodney, at any rate. If nothing else, Emery would see the need to accept a loan from a neighbor. That reminds me, here." He handed over the well-traveled leather pouch. "It appears our friend Prelieu is not going to require this to live in London after all. You'll need it for the trip to get Emery."

Leo shoved the purse back. "Nay, I have more than enough of the ready. Asides, it is more my right to fund the cawker's rescue than yours, this time. More a part of the family, like."

Chas slapped his brother on the back. "I take it I am to wish you happy then? I suppose it was your silver tongue that talked Tess round. By Jupiter, I am pleased for you both, Leo."

Leo grinned back. "Not official yet. Not till the brother gives his blessing. I wouldn't come between the lady and her kin, not unless I had to."

"How could Emery not welcome you to the family with open arms? You are good for Tess, and you have a bright future ahead of you."

"But my past . . ."

Chas tossed the pouch in the air. "Is outweighed by your purse. It's the money, brother. It is always the money."

* * *

It was the money, Ada thought, always the money. Suddenly, with word of Emery's imminent return, the merchants were willing to extend her credit. How they thought a wounded soldier was to make the fields and farms turn a profit when she could not was a mystery to Ada, but she accepted the reprieve from the bank and the shopkeepers. She did not wish to think about what would happen if Emery's injuries proved worse, if he never made it back. Some American cousin, so far removed she could not count, would inherit the baronetcy and Westlake. He'd most likely petition the courts to break the entail, sell off the acreage and the house, and toss them all out in the snow. Tess and Ada would be living by their wits, which was not saying much, these days.

Looking on the brighter side, Ada's sister had become acceptable to the villagers too, now that she and Mr. Tobin were an accepted item. Nothing had been formally announced as yet, also pending Sir Emery's return, but local gossip had them hitched. The publisher in Dover was newly willing to consider Tess's epic, and the manager of a traveling actors' troupe asked if he could see a script. With the hint that the wealthy Mr. Tobin might finance his fiancée's foray into the arts, Tess had talent. A few days ago she was crack-brained; now she was creative.

Even Jane was finding it politic to be polite to her sister-in-law. She did not go so far as to pose for the book illustrations—Tess still needed a picture of the evil stepmother—but Jane did label one of the songs "pretty" now that it might be performed with Leo's backing, and might make a profit.

Only the viscount's mother could not be swayed by the promise of money. Of course not, Ada thought; Lady Ashmead was too fixed in her ways, and too wealthy.

"Your sister will never be welcomed in my home if she marries that person," the viscountess warned.

Tess hadn't been welcomed—only tolerated—since she'd staged a ballet in the water fountain at the Meadows a few years previously, while the bishop was visiting. Tess with her sheer, flowing gown immodestly plastered to her lithe body was a sight the bishop was not soon to forget, Ada supposed. Certainly Lady Ashmead hadn't.

Ada did not know how to answer the viscountess. If her sister was not welcome at the Meadows, how could Ada accept invitations there? Loyalty to her family would keep her away from the house she'd run tame in most of her life. Then again, she wouldn't have to untangle Lady Ashmead's embroidery threads anymore either.

Chas would not let Tess be ostracized. He'd wheedled an invitation to the masquerade for Leo, hadn't he? Anyway, Lady Ashmead promised to return to Bath when her son married. His wife could entertain whomever she pleased. Ada was not pleased to think of Chas's wife.

Perhaps Tess and Leo would move to London, especially if her play was actually to be performed. The approval of Lady Ashmead and her ilk would matter less there, where Tess could establish her own coterie of artists and writers. Leo could find his own circle of smugglers—shippers, she amended. Ada saw no reason Leo could not conduct his legitimate business from London as easily as from Lillington. She meant to talk to Chas about seeing that the smuggling stopped, even if Tess was eager to run the blockade. Especially since Tess was eager to run the blockade. Instead of London, Tess might convince Leo to sail her around the globe, perhaps finding that tropical Eden Squire Hocking had described.

Then Ada would be alone. Emery would take a wife, she supposed, eyeing the young ladies Lady Ashmead had arranged like so many bonbons on a dish, for her son's delectation. None were as beautiful as Lady Esther and none were as wealthy, but Emery might find a lesser heiress to wed. Many a gentleman had repaired his finances that way. Of course he'd have to like the girl. Ada was not about to permit her brother to sacrifice himself for the family with a girl who did not make him happy. Heavens, Ada could have been the sacrificee ages ago, wedding Chas for his money. Some sacrifice it would have been, she chided herself, admiring the fine furnishings in Lady Ashmead's sitting room, the attentive servants, the lavish refreshments. Of course she still believed that Chas would have been the one paying the forfeit.

Lady Ashmead was going on while Ada was woolgathering, and woolwinding. "Money is not everything, you know."

Which was precisely why she had not accepted Chas's offer, the one she had made him swear not to repeat.

"No, there's breeding. Breeding, do you hear?"

Two young ladies sitting nearby with their needlework started giggling; Ada did not think Lady Ashmead meant propagating the species.

"Fortunes can be won or lost; breeding never can. A man of distinction does not need gold to be a gentleman; conversely, no amount of wealth can make a man of low birth into one."

Ada looked around the room at the gentlemen who had been invited to even the numbers, so Lady Ashmead's house party did not resemble an auction of fillies at Tattersall's. They were well bred, every one. Lord This, Sir That. They were all dressed by the finest London tailors in studied elegance, shod by the same London bootmakers and shined to a fare-thee-well. They all carried an air of boredom along with their quizzing glasses and snuffboxes. Ada would take Leo any day.

Not that she'd have a choice, of course. These fine gentlemen had barely glanced at her since the introductions, taking in her average looks and unfashionable frock, labeling her a country nobody, beneath their notice. If she'd had a fortune, no doubt they'd be at her feet as they were at Lady Esther's, composing sonnets to her eyebrows.

Faugh. Ada's eyebrows were plain brown. Such insincere flummery ought to disgust any sensible female, which obviously eliminated the little heiress, who was cooing like a dove. At least Ada did not have to watch Chas join the ranks of pigeon handlers, for he was out on estate business, likely giving a bunch of ragged orphans rides on his horse. These fine, blue-blooded gentlemen in Lady Ashmead's parlor would do the same—when the River Styx froze over and the devil went ice skating.

How many of these fribbles would let an amateur sculptor make a cast of his face? And then not be able to remove the plaster? How many of them could admire art in eccentricity?

Then again, how many of them would give up their respectability to aid the war effort? No, money was not everything. Neither was parentage. A good heart was what mattered.

At least one of the Westlake sisters had made the right choice, for the right reasons.

Chapter Twenty

Ada liked Lady Esther. She had not expected to, not at all. The girl was too precious, too wealthy, and too obviously intended for Viscount Ashmead. And she was a widgeon. The earl's daughter was sweet, though, and when she was not hanging on Chas's sleeve, Ada could appreciate the female's finer qualities. She was pleasant to the other, less favored ladies at the Meadows, and flirted with whichever gentlemen happened to be in her sphere at the time. Why, she'd even batted her fanlike golden eyelashes at Algernon. No, Lady Esther must have had something in her angelic blue eyes, Ada decided. No woman could be that corkbrained.

Algie had nearly fallen at the Diamond's feet. He must have had something in his eye, too, for not even Algie could be idiot enough to think Lady Esther was interested in a spotty schoolboy with no title, fortune, or chin.

They were upstairs in Westlake's attics, in Tess's studios, to be exact, getting ready for Lady Ashmead's masquerade. Many of the house party guests had arrived without costumes of any kind, and the Meadows' storage trunks yielded only so many Queen Elizabeths and Diana the Huntresses. The local shops were no help, but Tess's workroom was filled with sequins and beads and feathers. Granted they were goose feathers, not egret or ostrich, but Tess was willing to dye them, to help the young ladies with their masks.

Tess and Ada had decided on this as the way to repay Lady Ashmead's hospitality, entertaining her ladyship's young female guests while Chas took the gentlemen out shooting. He did not invite Algernon.

Jane was in the parlor, conversing with the mamas and aunties and paid companions who chaperoned the marriageable misses everywhere, lest they fall into the clutches of rakes, rogues, or fortune hunters. Jane was pouring endless tea and gnashing her teeth that there were no rakes, rogues, or fortune hunters among the company. Her sap-skulled sisters-in-law had devised a party with no *partis.* The still-youthful widow had her eye on those Town Bucks and Beaux brought out for the viscountess's ball. At least she'd had her eye on their backs, as they rode off with Ashmead. Surely one of those gentlemen was in the market for a wife of wit and wisdom to share his wealth. The simpering little buds upstairs paled next to her mature bloom, or so Jane firmly believed. Now if only her chin and bosom were as firm.

As for her costume, Jane had her blue domino. She'd had to sell her diamond ear bobs to purchase the elegant item, but she considered it an investment in her future. Ada had considered it a betrayal.

"You still had your diamond earrings?" she'd shouted, having sold all of Tess's, her own, and their mother's heirloom jewelry long ago, to pay Rodney's gaming debts.

"I set them aside for a rainy day," Jane had declared, "and I aim to be the reigning Toast of Lady Ashmead's gathering."

A mask would defeat Jane's purpose, so she stayed below with the biddies. Who knew, one of them might have a son or a brother.

The younger women were happy to be away from the formal atmosphere of the Meadows, where they were constantly on exhibit and on their best behavior for the viscountess and her very eligible son. The other gentlemen were to be found in Town at the usual social events, but Lord Ashmead was known to be more difficult quarry to corner. Trapping him in his own lair was too good an opportunity for the young ladies' mothers to pass by.

The girls were happily sewing ribbons, lace, and fabric to their creations—once Algernon had been relieved of a Diana's bow and arrows—but what intrigued them most were Tess's drawings for her book. While they cut and stitched and glued, therefore, Tess told them the story of *Sebastian and the Sea Goddess*. They all cheered when Sebastian killed the evil kraken, and cried when he nobly let his friend, Generalissimo Markissimo, claim the hand of the princess. They stopped working altogether when Sebastian sailed into the realm of the Sea Goddess, who vengefully created a storm to swallow his entire ship. Sebastian boldly declared his love for the deity . . . only to drown! He and his men—and the faint-hearted Miss Arbuthnot who had swooned into the dish of sequins—were revived in the third act, to thunderous applause from the young ladies, who begged to know the ending. Tess would not reveal it, naturally—Ada wondered if the ending were even written yet—but she did hum "The Sea Sprite's Song," which the orphans were busy learning.

Lady Esther, in particular, adored amateur theatrics, and pleaded to have the drama enacted for Lady Ashmead's company. The ballroom at the Meadows would be perfect, she insisted, and Lady Ashmead was sure to give her permission. Ada could not disappoint the eager young lady by telling her that pigs would fly sooner, unless Tess wrote Sebastian out of *Sebastian and the Sea Goddess*, or found a different actor for her hero. Neither was likely. Tess, though, was intrigued by the possibility.

"I could invite that acting troupe director, yes, and the manager of Drury Lane and Mr. Murray from the print shop, and anyone else who might come. Someone would be bound to make an offer for the piece, and I would not have to depend on Leo to pay for the production and publication. I would not have to go to Leo empty-handed."

"Leo doesn't care, Tess. You told me so yourself."

"No, but I do."

Ada could understand her sister's feelings. "Perhaps Chas

could convince his mother to stage *Sebastian* for the entertainment of her company," she said, sounding unconvincing even to herself.

"I'd rather put my money on the heiress," Tess answered, nodding her head to where Lady Esther was creating the perfect mask for the perfect shepherdess. "Especially if I give her a part in the play."

Tess was adding gold braid to the silk scarf Leo would wear as the pirate for the play, and for the masquerade ball.

"Are you so sure he will be back in time?" Ada asked, not wanting to express her fears for her brother's health.

"He'll be back." Tess added another loop around the eye slits.

"You sound so sure. Are your souls in some kind of communion, then?" Ada wondered. Then she wondered if she really did love Chas, for she had no idea when he'd be back from hunting, even. Not only did his soul not communicate with hers, but he'd hardly said a word to her in private in ages. Granted he always had one or another of his guests along when he called, but Ada thought he might have made a point of visiting on his own, if he truly wished. She envied her sister, who was so much more sensitive to such things. "Do you have such rapport with Leo that you can share his thoughts?"

"Don't be a ninnyhammer, Ada. A messenger came from Leo this morning while you were busy welcoming the company. He'd reached Portsmouth, packed up Emery and another officer, and was on his way back. If the weather holds, they will arrive on Friday, the day before the ball."

"And Emery? He does well?"

"As well as can be expected, Leo wrote, in the rat-infested, foul-aired ship that carried him. He'll do better now. Leo promised."

Ada blotted at her eyes with a scrap of fabric she was supposed to be using to trim her own costume. The mask was no bother; the crown was giving her difficulties. So far she had a mass of gold-painted wires with beads strung on them, bands of sequins woven through them, and lace and silk flowers trailing off them. The blessed thing weighed so much she'd be Pitiful Princess Pinch-Neck before the first dance.

Chas had his own worries. According to the men who had unloaded the boat last night, the word was that Prelieu had fled from Paris, taking with him a great deal more than valuable information. The avaricious old fool had embezzled a fortune from Napoleon's coffers, and half that country was looking for him. Half the English smugglers were, too, to collect the reward the Frogs were offering, or to confiscate the cash in Prelieu's cold blood.

Damn, but the man could have slipped away quietly if he hadn't turned greedy at the end. The British government had agreed to finance his relocation—at Viscount Ashmead's expense, naturally. It was not as if they expected him to take up clerking at a bank. Who would hire him anyway, after he'd embezzled a fortune from the French army?

Well, at least Prelieu wouldn't be needing Ada's windfall, if he ever made it to England. Wellington was needing the Viscount's promised report, though, so where the deuce was the fellow? He wouldn't be nodcock enough to think he could hide out in the French countryside, not when the people were filled with hunger and distrust. He might have decided that, with a price on his capture, the usual smugglers' route was equally as dangerous. Prelieu would have made other, less obvious plans, although Chas still believed the exchequer administrator's aide was headed for England, where he had friends among the emigre community. With enough money, monsieur could have bought himself a bloody boat to make the crossing.

Thunderation, Chas swore to himself. He'd wanted to bring the French finance man to London, then shut down the smuggling operation. It was time Leo's activities became strictly legitimate if he was to take on a wife and family—or wife and fine arts. Chas was too old to be clambering up cliffs half the night, too, especially when he had to be the gracious host at breakfast, and a hunting guide all afternoon.

So here he was, beating the bushes with a bunch of Bond Street beaux. They were looking for birds, Chas was looking for bankers. He'd rather be at Ada's. Gads, he'd rather be giving pony rides at the orphanage than listen to these empty-headed idlers make odds on who bagged the first bird, who shot the most birds, and when Chas would declare for Lady Esther.

He could not tell them that he would announce a betrothal to Lady Esther Wrentham when the cowth came home, not without insulting the lady. So he smiled, as he'd been smiling for days, it seemed, smiling at the Ravenshaw heiress, smiling at all the other pretty hopefuls so no one could accuse him of singling Lady Esther out for attention. Now he was smiling at gentlemen he'd be happy to see at his clubs in London, at the races at Epsom, or at a mill, at any other time. Today he'd rather see them at the devil.

Chas was too busy being a host to woo Ada. They never had a moment apart from the others, never a moment of privacy. Whenever he managed to slip away from his mother's guests to call at Westlake, the orphanage as an excuse, a deuced orphan was always underfoot. Having experienced a few stolen kisses of her own, Tess Westlake suddenly developed a taste for propriety, it seemed, and made sure Sarah was on hand to play dogsberry for her sister. Just what Chas needed, more interference in his campaign to win Ada's heart.

At least she was aware of him as a man, now. She'd kissed him back, aye, and pressed herself against him for more. Any more and his blood would have boiled, and he'd have borrowed one of Leo's boats to sail her away to Scotland. If he were any more aware of Ada, of her scent, her softness, the golden flecks in her eyes, he'd need two cold baths a day, perhaps three, to avoid mortifying his mother.

They were not friends; not even Ada could make that addlepated claim now, not once they'd had those too few kisses. Chas could not answer for Ada, but he'd never wanted to rip the clothes off any of *his* friends. Chas wanted to spend his nights with her, yes, but he also wanted to spend his days in the warmth of Ada's smile, caring for her, sharing a life with her, making new life with her.

Instead he was bear leading a flock of fribbles through the forest. With firearms. Looking for a fleeing Frenchman. Faugh.

He got to take his dog along for decent company in the woods, at least. He'd made sure that Algernon Johnstone jackanapes wasn't there to shoot her.

Chapter Twenty-one

Leo and Emery did not arrive by Friday. A storm had whipped the coastline with winds and heavy rains. There was still no word by Saturday, not even when it was time to get ready for Lady Ashmead's masquerade ball.

Tess did not want to go; they'd ought to wait at home to welcome their injured brother. Ada did not want to go; Chas might announce his betrothal to Lady Esther. Jane threatened to beat both of them with a stick—with the sea goddess's gold trident, in fact—if they did not go. Viscount Ashmead was sending his own carriage to Westlake Hall to fetch them, and Jane knew it wasn't her own blond beauty he expected to see step out of the coach.

"We have accepted Lady Ashmead's invitation, and we are going. We are not going to disappoint the highest ranking woman in the neighborhood, and that is final."

"Lady Ashmead has invited half the county," Ada reminded her sister-in-law. "She would not even notice if the party from Westlake Hall did not attend. In fact, she'd likely be happier if we did not."

"Well, you are not going to disappoint me," Jane ranted, "now that I am out of mourning. You might have tossed aside your chances with the viscount, Miss I'd-Rather-Stay-a-Spinster, but there are other fish in the sea, and a whole school of them will be swimming at the Meadows tonight."

The way her chest was puffed out, Jane obviously intended to do the breaststroke.

"As for you," she went on, pointing her painted finger at Tess, "there is no saying your smuggler will arrive home tonight, if he ever returns. Lud knows a moment's reflection would frighten off the most caper-witted suitor. And Emery's been gone from home this age and more. He cannot expect a welcoming committee at this late hour. Furthermore, you said yourself that you needed to advertise your misbegotten opera, especially after whetting the young ladies' appetites. If you have the slightest hope that Lady Ashmead will agree to stage its premiere, you'll be there tonight, showing off your so-called talent."

When they were all dressed and assembled in the hall, Ada wasn't quite sure what talent her sister was intending to demonstrate. The talent for trouble, most likely. "Good heavens, Tess, your nipples are showing . . . and they are green?"

"No, those are the fish scales I painted on. They are all over, see?" She twirled around in a cloud of blue and green gauze that had more to do with the ocean depths than with decency. Ada could not immediately discern just what Tess had painted the scales *on to,* praying for a pink undergarment of some kind.

Ada also prayed Lady Ashmead had not invited the bishop this time.

"That's revolting," Jane declared when she caught a glimpse of the stately Tess, whose flowing auburn locks covered more of her than her gown did. "Immodest, immoral, and imbecilic, if you hoped for Lady Ashmead's notice."

The viscountess would notice, Ada had no doubt. Her sister-in-law's ensemble left almost as little to the imagination. Her blue domino was everything pleasing, if Jane hadn't tossed the fabric over her shoulders to reveal that her own considerable cleavage was barely covered. If her peach-colored gown had been cut any lower, Ada thought, Jane's navel would have been showing, not to mention her nipples.

Ada was pleased enough with her own gown, despite its high neckline. After all, no depth of décolletage could display what nature had not endowed. She liked how the gold velvet sleeves ended in points at her wrists, and how the train could be caught up in a loop, so she would not be tripping her dancing partners—if she had any. She thought the embroidered frontispiece was lovely, if Lady Ashmead did not recognize the work, and the gold chain at her hips added the proper historic touch, if no one touched it and the gilding came off on their gloves. Her crown was another matter, redone so it weighed slightly less than a small ship's anchor.

"It adds inches, dear," Tess reassured her. "Height, dignity, regality."

It gave Ada the headache.

Jane's uncle Filbert had donned a new waistcoat for the occasion, eschewing a costume. The waistcoat looked like a cow had chewed it. The thing had green and orange wiggles on an ecru background, with violets embroidered on top. Johnstone should have saved his gambling winnings, Ada thought, to pay for his London digs. Then again, he most likely had not paid his tailor, either.

Algernon had already gone out to the carriage, his father announced, to take his seat up by the driver. He wanted to avoid crowding the ladies in the coach and crushing their skirts, according to Uncle Filbert. He most likely wanted to badger the driver into letting him take the reins, fretted Ada. Ashmead's servants knew better, she hoped.

Enamored of the goddess Diana's bow, especially when he could not find the guns Ada had hidden, Algernon had decided to dress as Robin of Sherwood, with a green tunic and a feather in his cap. Ada made him remove the points from the arrows.

Before they could leave Tess had to make sure their butler understood his instructions, should Leo and Emery arrive. If Mr. Tobin was not too tired, he was to put on the costume Tess had laid out for him in the spare guest bedroom, figuring that Leo would come to Westlake Hall first, to deliver Emery. Then Leo was to come fetch Tess and Ada at the

Meadows. After a brief appearance, which could be none too brief for Lady Ashmead, they could hurry home to Emery, leaving the others to enjoy the rest of the ball. Old Cobble rubbed his bald head. He thought he could remember, all right. Hadn't Miss Tess repeated the orders five times over?

They were off. Ada tried not to chew on her lip while they drove to Chas's house, for what kind of princess had so little confidence? She prayed for enough backbone—or Tess's trident—not to collapse if he did announce his betrothal, as the neighborhood expected.

When they reached the door, which was opened ceremoniously by two liveried footmen, they were greeted by a host of other maids and footmen.

"Who's the cove in the hallway dressed like an MP?" Algernon whispered while they handed over their wraps.

"That's Epps, his lordship's butler," Ada told him, smiling at her old acquaintance and accepting his compliments on her gown. Epps kept his eyes averted from the rest of the party.

Since this was a masked ball, Lady Ashmead had dispensed with a receiving line but, since she was still Lady Ashmead, each guest was to be announced at the entrance to the ballroom. They were not, naturally, expected to give their own names.

"The Lady in Blue," Epps announced, thumping his staff on the floor for attention. "Or out of it," he muttered to himself. "And Mr. Waistcoat."

He rapped his staff on the floor again after Tess whispered in his ear. "The most revealed—er, revered—Sirenia, the Sea Goddess."

When the room was hushed once more, Epps intoned: "Her royal highness, Princess Pretty of Pitsaponia."

He looked back and dropped his staff altogether. Algernon had decided that Robin Hood was too tame by half. Not willing to give up his bow and arrow, though, he'd taken the classical route. A sheet, some high-laced sandals, and a woven band of greenery was all it took.

"Cu—Cu—" the butler choked, while Algernon prodded him with his bow. Epps gave up. "Eros, by Zeus."

"I always thought Eros was the Roman chap. Ought to be by Jupiter, eh?"

Algernon ought to be drawn and quartered. If this was Love, Ada thought, mortified, no wonder there were so many arranged marriages. Eros with skinny shanks and spots? Cupid with no wings, no chin, and no aim? Love with such low intellect? Heaven help them all, and Algernon Johnstone when she got her hands on him.

Ada was never so happy to wear a mask. She wanted to slink away into a corner so no one noticed she was with the gangly, gawky godling. She wanted to curl up behind one of the giant ferns Lady Ashmead had placed around the ballroom floor so no one recognized her as the hairy-kneed halfwit's relation. She need not have bothered, for no one noticed her or the dunderheaded deity. Every eye in the room was on Jane or Tess. The dancers started bumping into each other and the orchestra musicians started playing the wrong notes. A servant with a tray of wineglasses walked right into one of the ferns.

Lady Ashmead clapped her hands together like an Oriental potentate, beckoning their party to the raised dais where she was holding court. The viscountess was not in costume, but she was definitely in her element, finding fault with everyone. For once she did not have a piece of needlework in her lap, having exchanged her embroidery for a long-handled lorgnette. She surveyed the Westlake party through it as they traversed the miles-long—it seemed to Ada—distance across the ballroom.

As they walked, slowly, to accommodate Tess's fluttering, frondlike trails of gauze, and Jane's mincing steps, Ada got a chance to look around. She noticed Chas instantly, partnering a diminutive shepherdess in tiered layers of lace petticoats no farm girl could ever have afforded. Lady Esther looked like a wedding cake, while Viscount Ashmead looked like . . .

like . . . Ada could not think of a comparison. He simply took her breath away. His face was nearly healed, except for a reddish spot on one cheek. He looked magnificent!

Somehow his mother had coerced him into orange doublet and dark hose, under the richly embroidered surcoat. Nothing could show his broad shoulders or fine, muscular legs to greater advantage. Ada had to keep herself from staring at those limbs a lady was never supposed to notice, limbs that made Algernon's spindly stalks look like insect appendages. Chas's dark hair was combed down, over his ears instead of back, giving him a courtly appearance, like a true *parfait gentil* knight of poetry, of romance, of girlhood dreams.

Tess had to tug on Ada's arm before she came to a total halt on the dance floor. They continued on toward their hostess. Ada made an effort to study the room so she could compliment Lady Ashmead: the floral swags, the swathes of silk, the viscount's legs. Heavens, the heavy crown was muddling her mind! That must be it.

Ada nodded toward the vicar, whose only disguise was a scarlet face, but Ada could not tell if he wore such a blush for the sake of his rejected proposal, or for her sister's immodest appearance. Squire Hocking made her party a self-conscious bow, before turning back to his wife. Masks were their only effort at costumes, but since he wore an orchid in his boutonniere, and she wore one at her breast, no one was baffled as to their identities. Others of the company waved or bowed or curtsied, and a few of the gentlemen dared to ask Tess or Jane for dances. Only Lieutenant Nye approached Ada, to remind her of their promised set. The riding officer was garbed as a jester, an unfortunate choice, in Ada's estimation.

Then they were at the dais, bowing as if before royalty. The silence was awesome as Lady Ashmead inspected her neighbors through the looking glass.

"You, sir, are excused to the card room," she told Uncle Filbert. "Try not to lose your shirt, only that abominable waistcoat."

She pointed the lorgnette at Algernon. "As for you, I should send you to the nursery where you belong, but you'd likely move in and I'd have you on my hands for the next ten years. Go have some punch in the refreshments room. With any luck, you'll pass out under a table and we won't have to look at your knock knees." Algernon bowed, blew her a cheeky kiss, and left.

Jane stepped forward, simpering about the graciousness of the invitation, the grandeur of the setting, the glorious time they were all sure to have.

"You mean the gentlemen. Go." As Jane flounced off on the arm of a masked cavalier, Lady Ashmead muttered, "Bachelor fare, more bosom than brains."

Then it was Tess's turn. "Speaking of lightskirts, what are you supposed to be, missy, some kind of mermaid?"

"Sirenia, madam, of *Sebastian and the Sea Goddess*, my epic poem, soon to be a book and an opera." Not cowed at all, having survived many a lecture from Lady Ashmead, Tess spoke loudly enough for those nearby to hear, and hopefully remember.

"Humph. Sebastian, sea bastard, it's one and the same. At least your smuggler had sense enough to stay away."

Before Jane could say something unfortunate, Ada put in, "He is kindly fetching my brother back from Portsmouth for us."

Lady Ashmead snorted again and tapped Tess's nearly bare shoulder with her looking glass. "Well, if that outfit's art, I'll eat my hat." Her hat was a purple turban, with a diamond pinned to the side.

"Start munching, Mother, for I find the goddess exquisite."

Chas had returned from the dance floor, Lady Esther on his arm. The little shepherdess happily reclaimed her lamb, a stuffed creature on wheels, with ribbons and flowers around its fleecy neck, to match those that trailed from Lady Esther's straw bonnet. Lady Ashmead had adamantly refused to permit a live farm animal in her ballroom, no matter how much the heiress was worth.

Followed by a flock of young gentlemen baa-ing for her next dance, Lady Esther gaily wheeled her lamb off to the row of gilded chairs where her chaperone was napping. Chas did not even watch her go. He winked at Ada instead, begging her to laugh with him at the absurdity.

How lovely of him to protect Tess from another social disaster, Ada thought. And how delightful of him to ignore the heiress. She smiled back, at which he bowed toward Tess.

"I fear your divinity is too awesome for this poor mortal, goddess, but may I make you known to Apollo here as a suitable dance partner?" He whispered in her ear as the toga-clad gentleman bowed: "Rich as Croesus, my girl, and a shareholder at Covent Garden."

Tess floated off on the arm of the sun god, describing her grand opus.

Chas swept Ada a low, hand-flourishing bow. "Might a poor knight pay his devoirs to a princess, or is that aiming too high still?"

Ada curtsied to the ground. "Prithee, Sir Knight, rise, that I might know thy name."

"My name? I hadn't thought of—" He looked down at the family insignia stitched on his tunic, the winged lion and roses. "Sir Sewsalot."

His mother rapped his knuckles with her looking glass, but Ada replied, "A worthy name for a worthy knight."

"Worthy enough for a dance, Highness?"

Ada handed him two fingers, which he raised to his mouth in the courtly manner, but he kissed her fingers, rather than the air above them, then led her toward the dance area.

"Would you mind if we strolled a bit instead of taking our places in the set? I, ah, have to make sure everything is ready in the supper room."

"As if your servants wouldn't have everything in train."

Chas smiled, showing his even white teeth, and squeezed

her hand where it rested on his arm. "But look, dear heart, they are forming lines for the dance. We'd never get to talk, what with changing partners for the next half hour. It's been so long since we've had a moment alone."

Forever, it seemed to Ada, who would have followed him to the ends of the earth for one of those heart-warming smiles, much less the supper room, which ought to be empty enough at this time of the evening for them to share a kiss.

It was and they did, before the footmen came in to start filling the tables with trays of lobster patties and oysters. Chas led her toward the windows, damning the cold air that kept them from the gardens, the dark, empty gardens.

Out of hearing of the servants, if not quite out of sight, the viscount stroked Ada's soft brown curls where they tumbled down her shoulders. Ada had argued with Tess that, if she had to wear the heavy crown, she would wear her hair loose. She was glad she'd won the argument when Chas said, "I've been longing to do this since you walked through the door."

She brushed a lock of dark hair off his forehead. "Me too."

"You should always wear your hair loose like this."

"Silly, you know that would not be at all the thing."

"Surely a princess can make her own rules, can't she? What is the point of being royalty if you cannot have your wish?"

"Alas, I am only a make-believe princess, Sir Sewsalot."

He bent his head to kiss her again, saying, "Not to me, you're not."

Just as their lips would have met—or Ada would have demanded an explanation of those breathtaking words—they heard a commotion behind them. As they separated and turned, a small, frothy figure hurtled through the room and into Chas's arms, weeping against his chest and wailing: "He thot my theep!"

Chapter Twenty-two

"This time I really am going to murder him."

Chas awkwardly patted the sobbing shepherdess on the back. "You will have to get on line." Lud, if Ada had not been here, the crowd of guests who rushed after Lady Esther into the supper room would have found her in his arms, alone. He'd be betrothed before the beauty's next bleat. He did not think Lady Esther had planned to entrap him; he did not think she had enough in her brain box to plan such a scheme. Still, the viscount set her aside none too gently and strode across the room to where half his mother's company was now clustered. Lord Ashmead plucked one sheepish-looking sprig in a sheet out of the herd and dangled him in the air.

"You, sir, are a disgrace. You will get on your knees and apologize to the lady."

Unfortunately, when Algernon bent down, the guests behind him could see that the clunch was wearing as much under his short sheet as a Scotsman wore under his kilts. The ladies started screaming again. This time Chas grabbed up Algie's bow and snapped it in his hands, then every arrow in the quivering Cupid's quiver. "Your neck is next, you blithering buffoon, if you are not out of my sight in five seconds."

Algernon was gone in four, in such a hurry that the sheet billowed out, offering another view of less than heroic proportions.

The men were swearing, holding their hands over their ladies' eyes, and the women were squealing, between peeks.

Lady Esther was still weeping. Lud, Chas thought, her sheep would drown if it weren't already dead, stuffed, and skewered. Then he looked at Ada, standing nearby with her hands over her mouth and her shoulders shaking. The wretch was giggling! Chas tried to look stern, telling her to behave like a lady, like the other tearful, tittery chits. Then he realized, no, he did not want his Ada to be like the other starched-up females who never saw the absurdities of polite society. He liked her very well, just the way she was. Besides, he could hardly hold back his own hilarity. They both started laughing out loud, to be joined by an uncertain chuckle here and there, then a general cheer of merriment.

"They are not laughing at me, are they?" Lady Esther looked up at him with sky-blue eyes awash in tears, lower lip atremble.

"Never, my dear. Who would laugh at such an angel?" Chas patted her arm again, very much as he would pat his dog, and directed the servants to serve the champagne. As the footmen handed glasses around, and Epps poured the sparkling wine, Chas called for a toast.

The glass fell out of Ada's suddenly numbed fingers. He was going to do it. Chas was going to announce his engagement to the heiress—to the angel, she corrected herself. She felt like one of Algernon's broken arrows.

Chas saw Ada's glass fall to the carpet, and saw her sway on her feet, her face pale beneath the glittering mask, but he could not go to her, not while everyone was watching him. He raised his glass, even though some of the latest arrivals from the ballroom did not have theirs filled yet. "A toast," he called. "To poor lost lamby. May no one else who is pierced by Cupid's darts suffer so grievously."

Everyone laughed and drank and returned to the dancing, except for a few who stayed to sample the lobster patties. Lady Esther tripped off with a brown-robed friar, restored to good humor by his less than fatherly flattery.

Chas stepped toward Ada and picked her glass up from the

carpet. He set it aside and signaled a waiter for a fresh one, while he pressed his own into her hand. "Drink, Ada. You look like you can use a restorative. Are you all right? Shall I fetch Tess? Find you a quiet seat?"

"I am fine, Chas, truly."

"You did not look fine for a moment there. What happened? Did a goose walk over your grave?" he teased.

"You . . . you aren't going to offer for her, are you?"

Chas nearly dropped his new glass of champagne. "Who? That is, for whom am I not going to offer?"

"Lady Esther, of course. Everyone is expecting an announcement tonight at your mother's ball."

"Everyone? Not Lady Esther, by God. I made deuced sure she understood enough not to entertain expectations, no matter what my mother said or did. Even Lady Esther could hold that thought in her mind. Besides, I swore never to make another proposal of marriage, remember?"

Ada remembered all too well. She'd give her last breath to have those words back; perhaps not her very last breath, because then she'd miss Chas's closeness. She could smell the lemony scent of his soap, and the spices of his cologne. Why did they have to be at a ball with hundreds of people watching? "Silly," she told him now, "you only promised not to offer for me again."

Chas struck his brow in mock astonishment. "Deuce take it! Now I have no excuse not to offer for Lady Esther, except that I'd throttle her in a fortnight."

"Truly?"

"Knight's honor. Viscount's too."

Ada would have kissed him, right then, in front of whomever wished to watch, and to the devil with her reputation. She was already known to be related to the erratic Eros and the mystical—to be polite—mermaid and the blue Bird of Paradise. Let Lady Ashmead's guests think the rest of the family was as mad. She leaned toward him.

"Ahem." Epps the butler had banged his baton twice before, to get their attention. He cleared his throat once more to bring order to the supper room and quiet to the company, before his momentous introduction. "Sebastian the Pirate," he pronounced. "And Lieutenant Sir Emery Westlake."

Once more mayhem reigned as word went out of the two newcomers' identities, their true identities, that was. Leo Tobin, here at the Meadows? The Westlake heir home at last? Lady Ashmead's ball was quickly growing to be the event of the Season, in the country, if not the City.

Chas found a secluded spot in his library for the baronet's family to be reunited in private. Tess and Ada were weeping, while Emery was looking tired and embarrassed but pleased by his welcome. He was thinner than Ada recalled, with harsh lines across his forehead, but he did not seem to be ailing. His arm was strapped across his body—but he had his arm.

"It might not be good for anything again," he told them once they were all three settled on a couch. "Though it is too soon to say. Leo's first mate thinks exercise might restore some of it, depending on how many muscles got cut. I cannot go back to the Army, that is for certain."

"Thank God," Ada said, then quickly added, "Not that I am glad to see your chosen career ended so unhappily, of course. I am just so relieved to have you home safe with us again."

Emery understood. "Tobin explained how things were left in such a mare's nest. I'll fix them, Ada, I swear. I'll meet with the solicitors tomorrow."

Ada mopped at her eyes, having discarded the mask to get an unobstructed view of her beloved sibling. "They have waited this long, they can wait a day or two, dearest, while you recover from your ordeal."

Tess asked, "Was it an ordeal? I mean the trip, of course, not getting shot or lying in a filthy Army hospital."

"The sail home was fine, except for the storm, naturally. I like your Leo, Tess. At first I was upset, a smuggler and all, helping put funds in the enemy's coffers. But then he explained what he was doing and why, so I came to admire the chap for his efforts. And his deuced fine brandy."

"And the other?" Tess pressed one of her trailing seaweed fronds between her fingers.

"What, that Tobin is bigger and better looking than I am, and richer, too? Don't be a peahen, Tess. I forgave him all that when he rescued me off the troop ship right in Portsmouth harbor."

"You know what I mean: Leo's birth."

Emery put his good arm around his older sister's shoulder. "I suppose we'll have to thank heaven for his birth, if he's the one to make you happy, love." He handed her his handkerchief—Lud knew there was nothing like a pocket to her gown—and turned to his other sister. "What about you, Addie? I heard how you whistled a fortune down the wind and then found another."

Tess was still weeping and Ada was still explaining when Jane and her uncle entered the library. Jane hated to leave the dancing, but unless some cavalier was going to sweep her off her feet this night—and he'd better hurry, for her ankles were swelling—she'd be going back to Westlake Hall, Sir Emery's house. As Uncle Filbert reminded her, they'd better show some sympathy for the returning hero.

"Oh, do not get up, brother!" she exclaimed, rushing to his side, as if she had not waited to finish the dance set before coming to welcome him home. Bending over to kiss Emery's cheek, she almost smothered him in pink flesh.

Wedged between his sisters, Emery could only blush and nod as Jane and her uncle went on about his fearlessness and fortitude.

Jane was still pouring the butter boat over poor Emery when Chas and Leo returned from the viscount's office, where they'd caught up on the news.

"Here now," Chas said, "you ladies cannot monopolize our returning warrior all evening, you know. The rest of the company is eager to view the celebrities, too. Leo and the lieutenant are quite the lions of the night, Epps tells me." He turned to the young officer. "Are you up to greeting my mother yet, Emery?"

Emery grinned, having known Lady Ashmead for most of his life. "Of course. Greeting your mother cannot be worse than facing the French cannonade, not by much, anyway. She is certain to blame me for getting injured, for signing up in the first place, for old Rodney sticking his spoon in the wall."

Showing unusual diplomacy, Tess took Leo off in the opposite direction from Lady Ashmead when they reached the ballroom. Showing unusual acumen about such matters, she held tightly to his bare, muscle-corded arm. The ladies might stare at Leo's nearly naked chest, covered only by a black leather vest. They might even grow short of breath at the sight of his narrow waist cinched with a scarlet sash, his skin-tight pants tucked into high boots, the sword at his side and the gold hoop in his ear. Let them look, Miss Westlake's possessive stance said; he was hers. The other ladies could look their fill when the book came out—if they paid for the privilege.

Ada and the viscount flanked Emery as they walked toward Lady Ashmead's throne, greeting old friends and neighbors on the way, accepting felicitations and welcome homes. Ada kept wanting to touch Emery, to cling to his scarlet regimental coat, to make sure he really was home, relatively healthy, ready to take over some of the family burdens. Champagne was not nearly as exhilarating as seeing her brother. In fact, walking with these two men, Ada could not recall being so happy, so at peace with the world. Emery was home, and Chas was not engaged.

Emery was correct about Lady Ashmead trotting out all his faults as a form of affection. He'd simply not considered that she could blame him for Tess's outfit, Ada's unmarried state, or Cupid's misplaced arrows.

"My sisters' waywardness you might be able to lay at my door, Lady Ashmead, but I refuse to take responsibility for

Love's vagaries. If Tess and Leo love each other, that's enough for me."

"I am not speaking of those two," the viscountess said with a toss of her turbaned head. "I might never speak *to* those two either. I was referring to Lady Esther's stuffed sheep that got skewered."

Emery declared he was still all asea, and he'd been on dry land for hours. Lady Esther, sitting beside her hostess between dances, giggled, so Lady Ashmead recalled her duty and introduced the handsome wounded soldier to the beautiful blond heiress. No one needed a poet or novelist to predict what would happen next; it was inevitable. Emery fell at Lady Esther's feet. Literally.

One of the servants had located a shepherd's crook to replace the missing mutton, lest anyone be confused about the lady's costume and mistake her for a spun-sugar statuette. Lambikin's ribbons had been transferred to the rounded staff, which rested alongside Lady Esther's chair.

Overtaken by the loveliest sight he'd seen since leaving for the Peninsula, deciding on the instant that this was what he'd been fighting for in the first place, Emery was not watching his feet. He fell over the decorated crook, skidded forward, and landed half in the little beauty's lap.

Never one to refuse a gift, Lady Esther murmured, "Oh, my," and he was. Hers, that is.

They got Emery back to his feet, uninjured, then onto a chair with a glass of wine in his hand to restore the color to his cheeks. Lady Esther waved away her next partner, declaring that she would sit by the hero instead. That was the least she could do, since she had almost broken his head.

"Oh, dear," Ada whispered to Chas as he led her out for a dance. "I fear she'll break his heart next."

Chapter Twenty-three

"Even widgeons fall in love, I suppose." Chas shook his head at Emery, who was leaning toward the golden ringlets as if pulled by a magnet, hanging on every word that lisped through perfectly bowed lips. "They must, there are so many around."

"But nothing can come of it," Ada fretted. "Her father is an earl."

Chas shrugged. "Not everyone puts pounds and pence ahead of happiness."

If that was a gentle rebuke it missed its mark. "Her father is a wealthy earl," Ada repeated. "He will never give his blessings to a half-pay officer."

"Devil take it, Ada, they just met. The lad set foot on English soil mere hours ago after years abroad. Why not let him catch his breath before landing him in parson's mousetrap?"

"You are right, of course. I am simply concerned about him and his future."

"I know you are, puss, but Emery is a man grown, so let him do some of the worrying from now on. The whole world need not rest on your shoulders. Your lovely shoulders, with your hair hanging down. Tonight is a masquerade, remember? It's meant for flirting and folly and forgetting who you are. Tonight you are Princess Pretty, and I your gallant knight. No banks or brothers or bothersome house guests should intrude on our pleasure, only music and magic and champagne. Come, my love, dance with me."

His love? Ada floated into his arms.

The dance was a waltz.

The dance was not intended to be a waltz, Lady Ashmead predictably frowning on the licentious touching. Still, the orchestra definitely began the strains of a waltz, setting the young misses into a dither. Did the Almack's rules apply here? Were they supposed to keep the same partners who'd been promised the scheduled quadrille? Were they proficient enough at the new dance to dare it in public?

Ada looked about her at the confusion. "How did you convince your mother to permit a waltz?"

"Easily. I pay the orchestra, remember?"

Then he swung her into the lilting tempo, and Ada stopped wondering about anything. They danced together like well-practiced partners, for hadn't Chas been the one to teach the Westlake girls, after a trip to London? They turned and twirled, glided and flowed, without the need for words. Whatever they needed to say, they said with their bodies, nearly touching in the movements, and their eyes, never leaving each other's. Flirting, aye. Folly, perhaps. Forgetting who they were with? Never.

Magic, indeed.

While Viscount Ashmead waltzed with the lady who had turned him down so often and so openly, tongues wagged. Goodness, those two were not marking time to the music, they were making love! Lady Esther took note, and took another look at the handsome officer at her side. Lady Ashmead watched in disgust as her son and Ada Westlake made a spectacle of themselves, without one official step toward making her a grandmother. There was no hope whatsoever of Charles ever offering for Lady Esther, the viscountess was forced to admit, and there was nothing Lady Ashmead liked less than being forced to admit her errors. Besides, now she was stuck with the little ninny for another fortnight at least. To her additional aggravation, the other topic of conversation at her ball was her husband's bastard. Look at him, flaunting himself and his chest hair at her party. It was enough to make a body bilious.

The sight of Sebastian's strong torso had quite another effect on the ladies at the masquerade, who suddenly found themselves wishing to be marooned on a desert island with the pirate. Their gentlemen were equally as entranced with Tess, in her flowing, not quite transparent, costume. Talk swirled around the pair as they, too, danced.

Leo did not know the steps of the waltz, but that made no difference to Tess. She drifted around him like waves to the shore, eddying, ebbing, her lithe form weaving trailing fronds of green and blue gauze about his swaying figure, choreographing a ballet—or a seduction.

"It's part of the play," the chaperones whispered among themselves, to stave off being scandalized.

"It's only the lunatic Westlake chit following her Muse," others said knowingly. "Means nothing by it."

"No, I tell you, they are going to put on a production called *Sebastian and the Sea Goddess.* This is by way of being an introduction to the drama."

"Where can I purchase tickets?"

"Oh, it wouldn't be in public. The gel's a lady, after all. I heard they are doing it here."

"You don't say!"

"I say no," Lady Ashmead swore, when sweetly approached by her now *de trop* heiress, not even if the prattlebox had a starring role in the amateur theatrics.

She said no when the vicar, of all people, mentioned that the neighbors were anxious to view the play, an allegory of good and evil, he believed. She said no yet again when Ada offered to see to the arrangements.

"You could announce it tonight, for ten days' hence, say, and not even have to send invitations."

Lady Ashmead even denied her son's request, knowing full

well that he needed no permission, no payments, and no patronage of his mother's to hold a bacchanal orgy in his house, if he so wished. He might forget what was owed his lady mother for a waltz or two, she hoped, but not for flinging open the doors to the Meadows to the raff and scaff. Not twice.

Ada went off for her promised dance with the riding officer, and Chas left to lead another of the house party beauties in the boulanger. Claiming the headache, Lady Esther declined her next partner, to sit by Sir Emery, who was sympathetic to her great disappointment. Why, on top of her lost lamb, such a blow might be too, too much for her tender sensibilities.

Emery turned beseeching eyes to Lady Ashmead, who only turned her back.

Having been pirated away by Jane, who insisted on having at least one dance with the most dashing man in the ballroom, Leo reluctantly took his place in the set.

Tess approached her hostess and bluntly said, "I suppose they all asked and you turned them down."

"Hmph." Lady Ashmead pretended to be watching the dancers.

To Lady Ashmead's regrets, Tess spread her trailing skirt panels over the adjacent chair and made herself comfortable. "You might as well give in, you know."

"Why? Why should I permit my home to be used for such a shocking spectacle? Tell me that, missy."

Tess waved her arm around, catching Lady Ashmead's lorgnette in one of her fronds. "The place is big enough, for one."

"Rot. The cow barn is big enough, too. Hold it there."

"And everyone wants to come," Tess went on as though the older woman had not spoken. "They are all talking about it, you know."

Lady Ashmead did know, and it stuck in her craw. "Ladies,"—she repeated the word for emphasis—"ladies do not make a byword of themselves."

"Now who is talking fustian? Every hostess in London would leap at the chance to hold such an entertainment."

Lady Ashmead knew that, too, and was doubly irate.

"You could even make it a charitable act, asking for donations for the orphanage from those who attend."

Triply troubled, reminded of the children her neglect had made suffer.

"We don't intend to produce the whole thing, you know, just the bits and pieces an audience will most appreciate. I doubt we could successfully enact the fire-dragon scene here anyway."

"Fire? I should hope not!"

"Mostly, though, you should give your permission for your son's sake, so poor Chas does not have to choose between you and Ada."

"That minx already made her own choice. And your sister has nothing to do with my decision whatsoever."

"She should, ma'am. You see, if we stage *Sebastian* here, it will be talked about among the London producers. We might even be able to get one or two to attend, or perhaps a journalist reviewer. I do intend my play to get to London, make no doubt, to earn us a fortune. Well, mayhaps not a fortune," Tess amended, "but enough to give my sister back her dowry. With her portion restored, her pride will be too. She would be good enough for any man, even a viscount."

"Botheration, she could have had a viscount anytime these past three years."

"Five, I believe. She does love him, you know."

"Of course I know. Any fool can see that. Why do you think I filled my house with ninnyhammers, if not to make the simpleton see that for herself? Your sister is stupid, stubborn, soft in the head."

"And Chas loves her."

Lady Ashmead sighed.

"There is another benefit to putting on the play here, you know." Tess pressed her advantage. "If the play is produced in London, Mr. Tobin and I are likely to move there. You won't have to worry about acknowledging my husband."

"Bosh. You get my son hitched to that addlepated Ada and I will be back in Bath before that scapegrace Sebastian puts on a shirt like a decent smuggler. Then I won't care what the two of you gudgeons get up to."

Tess was not finished yet. She nodded to where Emery and Lady Esther had their heads together like bosom bows. "Your little house guest will likely throw a tantrum if she can't be in the play, you know. I've lived with Jane Johnstone for years, and I can tell you a tantrum is not a pretty sight. Then too, the earl's darling just might set her sights on something even more ineligible if she is denied, such as a hero in scarlet regimentals. She's already lost a chance at Chas; losing her part just might be the last straw."

"The chit has the sense of a camel, too. She might very well throw her cap over the windmill for a handsome face, if it's not too late. Lud, how would I explain that to Ravenshaw? I near broke his heart once, when I accepted Ashmead instead. This could be worse."

Tess laughed, loudly enough that heads turned in their direction. "Are we agreed, then?"

Lady Ashmead hesitated.

"I suppose I could go cry on Ashmead's shoulder. He's been like a brother to me all these years. It is his house, isn't it?"

"Blackmail don't become you, missy."

"Oh, that's not blackmail. Blackmail is if I threaten to perform the dance of the severed sea serpent's head in your supper room. On the supper table. You were serving eels in aspic, weren't you?"

The announcement was made during the supper break. It was not the announcement Lady Ashmead had been hoping to make, not by half. It was not the announcement the guests had expected before seeing Lord Ashmead dance with Miss

Ada Westlake, nor even the one they expected after that memorable waltz. The viscount's invitation to another gathering in a fortnight, however, was greeted with loud cheers, due as much to the flowing champagne punch, perhaps, as the opportunity to view a new play at his lordship's expense. The ladies wouldn't mind a closer view of the pirate, either, nor the men another glance at that sea goddess.

"The musical drama will be written, produced, directed, and choreographed by our own resident bard, Miss Tess Westlake, and will be held to benefit the Lillington-Folkestone Foundling Home. Your generous donations will make the lives of those unfortunates brighter, as I am certain our efforts will enliven your evening. A toast. To Miss Westlake."

Someone, likely Uncle Filbert who never missed an opportunity to lift his glass, then proposed a toast to their most generous host and gracious hostess. A toast to welcome the return of Lieutenant Westlake. A toast to the health of everyone present. A toast to good friends who were absent. The King. Wellington. Lady Arbuthnot's birthday.

The toasts went on for so long the orchestra members were tuning their instruments for the next interval well before the last cream tart was consumed. Finally the guests returned to the ballroom or the card room or the parlor. Some of those who had to travel long distances called for their wraps and made their farewells, promising to return for the play.

Ada was yawning, not used to such late hours or lavish suppers. Besides, she had already had her second dance of the evening with Chas, and was not going to get another, not without setting the whole neighborhood on its collective ear. She would have gone home, citing Emery's injury as reason enough, but Jane would not hear of it, not until the last unmarried gentleman with hair, teeth, and money had left. The hair and the teeth were mere options.

"What, leave before the unmasking?" She might have missed a potential *parti* under an ass's head.

"But you are not wearing a mask," Ada pointed out. "What can it matter?"

"A great deal. And what would you do?" Jane hissed, knowing Ada's weak spots. "Drag your brother away from the best opportunity he is likely to have to meet young women of means? Look at him, top over tails for Lady Esther. Nothing can come of it, of course, but the peagoose helped cut his meat at supper. She's also dismissed her other beaux, the fool, to sit out with him again."

Emery did not look tired to Ada. In fact, he looked eager, excited, entranced. Egads, he'd stay as long as Jane. Meanwhile, Tess and Leo were strolling about the perimeters of the dance floor, answering questions about the drama. That is, Tess was answering the technical inquiries; Leo was looking piratical. If any of the gentlemen looked too closely at Tess's fish scales, Leo's hand reached for his sword. They were obviously not ready to leave, not while there was a potential backer in the ballroom.

Ada yawned behind her hand and looked around for Chas. He was standing beside his mother's chair, saying good-bye to the departing guests, still the handsomest, most chivalrous of knights in her eyes. She thought she might go see if Lady Ashmead needed anything: a shawl, a glass of lemonade, a grandson. Ada thought she might have had one too many champagne toasts, too. She'd do better in a chair. Next to Chas.

Chapter Twenty-four

On her way toward the viscountess's raised dais, Ada heard a commotion at the door. A latecomer had just arrived, but the butler was not at his post. Epps was in the wine cellar fetching more bottles of champagne, the toasts having depleted his prepared stock.

The under butler was stationed at the front door, making certain carriages were called and wraps were found for the early departures. The junior footman left at the entrance to the ballroom did not know what to make of this gentleman who rushed by him without giving his card, his name, or his current persona. Neither did the other guests.

"What's he supposed to be?" one of the dowagers shouted to her nearly deaf companion.

"I can't tell, what with all those cloths wrapped around him."

"Is he part of the play?" the first one yelled.

"Lud, I hope so. Deuced attractive, this 'un, and more our age than that half-naked pirate."

"Hah! You haven't seen this buck's age in half a century either."

Other guests were also wondering, as the man lurched past them. "Could the fellow be dressed as one of those mummy chaps?" A fop in a faun's costume, complete with pan pipes, pulled out his quizzing glass.

His friend, a portly King Henry, answered, "If so, it's in poor taste, I say. Frighten the ladies, what?"

The new arrival more than frightened the females, he created pandemonium when he took his hand away from the wrappings on his side and the cloth fell away, bloodstained. Ladies screamed and swooned, gentlemen felt their stomachs turn; half ran toward the man to see better, half ran away to safety.

Tess and Leo happened to be nearby when the man staggered. He would have fallen but for Leo's strong arms under his shoulders. "Ashmead?" the man gasped.

"Close, but no." Leo half carried the man toward the viscount, Tess supporting his other side. She handed Jane the gold trident, to get a better grip on the wounded stranger. Jane could not decide whether to be faint or to follow, but the man was good looking despite his pallor. She followed, the better to find out what was happening.

Ada quickly got up from her chair to make room, thinking, Lud, Algie had finally shot someone, but Chas and Leo laid the man on the floor, as gently as possible. Chas shouted for servants, the doctor, towels. Lady Esther was already unconscious, so Ada ripped off one of her many petticoats. Chas stuffed it under the man's head.

"*Je suis . . .*" the stranger tried to say. "*Je suis . . .*"

"Bloody hell. Prelieu."

Leo had looked beneath the wrappings. "Too much blood to say, but it looks like an old wound, reopened, though. Bullet went straight through his side, so he should live if we can stop the bleeding."

"He better," Chas said, followed by words not meant for a lady's ears.

Ada tore another petticoat from the shepherdess's skirts and handed it to Leo. "Monsieur Prelieu? Isn't he the one who was supposed to retrieve the money from the orchard?"

"Our money?" Jane asked, dropping the trident.

Prelieu groaned as Leo pressed the petticoat against his side. "I know nothing of this orchard, *n'est ce-pas*? I was to come to the Mermaid Tavern for the money, but I do not need your little douceur, Monsieur Vicomte. I brought my own, *non*?" He laughed, clutching his injured side. "*Oui,* I did. Napoleon tips well, *certainement.*"

Jane stepped closer.

"Why the deuce didn't you show up at the Mermaid, then?" Chas demanded. "Or send a message?"

"But I did, *mon ami.* Only I made a *petit* error. After being so careful in leaving Paris, and so secretive about boarding a boat, I trusted one of your men to carry the message, Sim Fuller."

"Not one of my men," Leo said with a growl, helping the Frenchman sit up so he could drink the wine Chas held to his lips. "But I will take care of him."

Prelieu shrugged, wincing. "That was my error. The fisherman was working for your traitor, one of those on my lists of Englishmen receiving moneys from Bonaparte for information on the ships around Dover."

Chas and Leo both cursed.

"This *cochon* Fuller, he sent for his master. They shot me, and left me for dead in an old shack with the mice."

"I suppose they took the list?" Chas finally recalled the ladies present and did not express himself as fully as he intended. He pounded his fist on the floor instead.

"But of course, *monsieur.*" Prelieu smiled and tapped his forehead. "But the list, it is all in here." He reached down and tapped his high boots. "And the money, it is all in here."

Chas breathed a sigh of relief. So did Jane. Then, "This traitor," Chas said, "do you know him, other than by name? Would you recognize him again?"

"Would you not recognize the man who tried to end your life, *monsieur*?"

Everyone nearby was trying to get closer, to hear the Frenchman's tale of betrayal. Everyone but one man, who was trying to push his way through the knots of people near the door. Servants were rushing in, though, with a plank to be used as a stretcher, so he found no exit there. The man edged closer to the orchestra's alcove, knowing there must be a door behind the musicians, but the music had stopped and the players were standing close together to watch the events below. Finally the man made a dash for the balcony doors, which were a quick leap down to the gardens and freedom.

Prelieu raised his hand and shouted: "There is the *bâtard*! Filbert Johnstone!"

Now Jane fainted for real.

Tess yelled, "He's getting away"'

Chas set off after him. "Like hell he is."

Leo dropped Jane to the floor next to Prelieu and pulled his sword. He cursed when he realized it was the mock curved scimitar, then grabbed up Tess's trident. Emery's lap was filled with Lady Esther, and he could not have run far or fast at any rate. So he yelled for men to go below, to the gardens, to head the turncoat off before he reached the woods. Lady Ashmead just yelled.

Uncle Filbert, a traitor? Ada had always wondered where he got the money for his wardrobe. Now she knew. She also knew she was not letting Chas go out there empty-handed and alone—discounting Leo and a score of servants—not after a dangerous would-be murderer. Not even if it was fat and foppish Filbert Johnstone. She looked around for a weapon and saw the shepherd's crook that had tripped Emery. She picked it up and raced for the balcony.

Chas and Leo were there before her, wrenching open the door Filbert had slammed behind him, shattering glass onto the balcony. The noise joined with the screams in the ballroom.

"This way!" Chas shouted, racing down the balustrade to the corner of the house, where a set of stairs led to the terraced gardens. Leo was right behind him, but the trident caught on one of the ornamental urns and he went down, landing awkwardly. Servants were pouring out of the lower levels, but they could not see the fleeing man in the darkness.

"Fetch lanterns," the viscount ordered.

Up on the balcony, Ada could pick out Filbert's white shir
still in the gardens. "The fountain," she called as she tore pas
Leo. "He is headed for the fountain."

The fountain, one-time scene of Tess's solo ballet, was en
closed at the rear by a tall yew hedge. Footmen with fireplac
pokers and kitchen knives were coming at it from the eas
Chas skidded to a halt from the west, with Ada careening int
his back moments later. Trapped in the middle was Filbe
Johnstone, with a gun.

"Put down your weapons or I shoot Ashmead," he threat
ened. The servants dropped their utensils. "You, my lord, sta
where you are. Ada, my dear, how nice to see you. You ca
put down that . . . shepherd's crook—doesn't quite go wit
your outfit, does it?—and step over here. You are about t
become my passport."

"No!" Chas shouted, but Ada was already handing hir
Lady Esther's staff, the gaily trailing colored ribbons in star
contrast to the perils of the shadowy night. She took anothe
step away from Chas's side before he could grab her arm t
hold her back.

"I am coming, Uncle. Lower your weapon."

He didn't, but Johnstone trained the pistol on Ada instead
knowing that would keep Ashmead from moving. Then Ad
pretended to stumble on the paving stones. As she started t
fall, she yelled, "Throw it!" and flattened herself on th
ground.

The crook went flying through the air, ribbons and all. A
shot was fired. Leo's trident went spiraling past Ada, who kep
her hands over her head.

When she looked up, Johnstone was bleeding from th
cheek and the chin, but he was still holding off both men wit
the pronged gold trident, the spent pistol at his feet. The
would overpower him eventually, Ada knew, but she was tire
of seeing Chas scraped and bruised. The dirty dish was he
connection, besides. So she picked up that blasted heav
princess crown where it had fallen beside her, and threw it a

Filbert. She hit him right in the middle of that ugly waistcoat, too.

"That went well, I thought."

Ada thought her sister must have windmills in her upper stories after all. "Well? We might as well have tied our garters in public." Ada very much doubted that her sister was wearing garters this evening, or stockings. She thought she had seen bare toes poking out of soft sandals, with the toenails painted gold.

They were quite a different party going home from the ball. Uncle Filbert was too guilty to take home; Jane was too ill; Algernon was too foxed. Those three would be kept at the Meadows this night, under various watch guards. Emery was with his sisters in Lord Ashmead's borrowed carriage, but he was half asleep, with a dreamy expression on his face that made Ada distinctly queasy, if the rest of the night had not.

"How could you think the evening a success, after our familial connections ruined Lady Ashmead's ball?"

"Ruined it? Pish-tosh. The ball will be the highlight of the year, and people will be speaking of it for ages. Lady Ashmead should thank us for enlivening a rather dull evening, in fact."

"If she recovers from the heart palpitations."

"She will be fine. When we left she was already berating Chas and Epps and poor Rodney for marrying into the Johnstone family. I don't doubt she will tell the surgeon how to treat Monsieur Prelieu."

Ada had to agree with her sister's assessment. "Still, it was frightening to a lot of her guests."

"Of course it was, frightening and exciting, heart-pounding and heart-stopping. They loved it, even the ones cowering behind the potted plants. Oh, how I wish I could capture such heightened awareness, such intense storms of emotions. But that last scene, Ada dear, oh, my. I shall have to write it into the play somewhere, don't you think?"

Ada thought that if Tess had had a pistol aimed at her, or at the man she loved, perchance she would not find the drama quite so entertaining. The man she loved? Oh, yes, without the last, least shred of doubt. Seeing Chas in Filbert Johnstone's sights cleared whatever cobwebs might have been clinging to Ada's conscience. She loved Charles Ashford and wished to marry him, no matter what. She might be unworthy of him, she and her odd family might even be a burden to him, but Ada did not think she could live without him. Hadn't she been ready to give her own life to save his? Surely that was a valuable dowry to bring to the wedding.

The problem was, there was no wedding. Chas had sworn he would never offer for her again, and Ada knew he always kept his word, except for a few instances about which she was beginning to have doubts.

She had no doubts whatsoever, now, that Chas loved her, although he had not said it in so many words since that once when she'd ridiculed his avowal. He wouldn't have shaken her and shouted at her for putting herself in the way of Filbert's shot, Ada believed, if he did not love her. He would not have called her a turnip head, and he would not have kissed her as he handed her into the coach.

He could not say much, not with Emery waiting to step up after her, but his kiss had spoken volumes. For one thing, the fact that Emery was in sight made the short kiss as good as a declaration, the one Chas would never make. For another, the kiss was hard and fierce and full of relief that the danger was past. Ada knew it because she felt those same emotions herself. The brief touch of Chas's lips was tender at the same time—how that could be was a mystery to Ada—a gentle promise of tomorrows to come, of never being parted again.

While Tess went on about the changes she was going to make to *Sebastian and the Sea Goddess* for its debut, and Emery snored softly in his corner, Ada fretted.

How could she and Chas be together if not in holy matrimony? Tess might be willing to sail off with her pirate, sans ervice, license, or blessing, but Ada did not think she could lo so. Her life she might give, but not her principles. Other-vise, she feared, she'd end up hating herself and Chas for compromising them so badly. Ada saw only one solution to ner difficulties: Chas loved her but would not propose? Ele-nentary. She'd just have to make the offer herself.

Chapter Twenty-five

"Chas, I—"

"I am sorry, Ada, you will have to excuse me. I nee to go work on those lists with Prelieu now that he has ha his breakfast. The physician dosed him with laudanum las night before he could finish giving me the names we neec and I want them on their way to London as soon as possible Otherwise word will get out and some of the other traitor will go into hiding."

"I understand, of course." Actually, she was relieved.

Before he left, Chas told her, "Prelieu will be fine, inci dentally, so Johnstone will not be charged with homicide a well as treason." Since treason itself was a hanging offense the charge of attempted murder was moot. Chas headed pas Ada toward the stairs with a stack of papers in his hand "Mother has not come down yet this morning. The physicia dosed her with laudanum, too. I'll have to double the man' fee. Oh, and Jane is waiting for you in the Crimson Room.

He went up the first three steps, then turned and cam down, lifting her hand to his lips. "And did I tell you hov lovely you looked last night?"

"Chas, would you—"

He kissed her fingers and took the steps to Prelieu's bed room two at a time.

Ada and Emery had come to fetch their sister-in-law hom late this morning, and to inquire as to the viscountess's health as good manners dictated. That's what Ada told herself sh had come for, at any rate, in addition to proposing marriage to Lord Ashmead, of course. Emery had come to see if Lady Esther was as angelic as he remembered, and if she would step down from her cloud long enough for him to ask after her welfare, after the upsetting events of last night. He would not mind if she fainted in his lap again but that was beside the point. She hadn't minded that he'd only the one working arm to hold her.

Lady Esther was not a whit worse for wear, wearing a blue muslin gown that matched her eyes, tied under her rounded bosom with a pink sash that matched her rosebud lips. Ada was green with envy. She'd wager Chas had paid the heiress pretty compliments over the kippers and eggs.

The earl's daughter was more excited about what part she could have in Tess's play than in last night's events. Not being at all loath to discuss whatever the little beauty wished to, be it dress patterns or the polarity of magnets, Emery led her off to the viscount's portrait gallery to consider the possibilities.

Ada shook her head. Emery hadn't even read the script. He had not so much as recalled that his older sister was writing a play, despite numerous letters mentioning it, and was only reminded when he asked Tess about the odd costume she was wearing—albeit not wearing much of it—last night.

And Chas hadn't invited Ada to take tea with him, not even when she'd worn her prettiest dress—which of course could not compare with Lady Esther's—and screwed her courage to the sticking point with an extra cup of chocolate this morning. Which was now sitting in the pit of her stomach like the anchor of Sebastian's ship.

Chas could only say no, couldn't he? She asked herself that question for the hundredth time. For the hundredth time she answered that no, he could laugh at her, too. Ada thought she'd perish of the last, if the first hadn't already killed her.

She wished Tess had come along to give her courage. She used to think Tess was afraid of nothing, until she decided her sister never noticed half the perils in her path. Either way, though, Tess was off with Leo Tobin, consulting his ship's carpenter and sail maker about constructing a makeshift stage, with curtains, on the raised dais in Chas's ballroom. Two weeks was not a lot of time to produce a setting worthy of a London theater, much less rehearse her amateur players, make costumes for them, and finish writing the last act. No, Tess could not be bothered.

Neither, it seemed, could Chas.

Ada made her way to the drawing room where Jane was gracefully arrayed in a pink frock her maid had brought over this morning, selected, knowing Jane, to match the Crimson Parlor.

Ada needn't have asked about her sister-in-law's health, for Jane was looking the picture of well-being, but she did ask anyway, out of politeness. In return, Jane made sure that Emery had suffered no reverses.

"No, he is very well, thank you, except for his arm. He, and Tess and I, of course, want to assure you that you will always be welcome at Westlake Hall, and we hold you entirely blameless for your uncle's activities."

"Of course I had nothing to do with that unsavory business. Ashmead sees no reason to mention the connection whatsoever when he reports to London. Why, if I had known of that man's activities, you can be certain I would have protested."

Ada was certain Jane would have claimed a fair share of the filthy money. She had already heard from Leo over breakfast that Chas was doing everything he could to see that none of Johnstone's dirt touched her family. The viscount was arranging for Uncle Filbert to be shipped out of the country for the Canadian wilderness, never to return, in exchange for his silence, to avoid a trial and hanging. The government would be agreeable, liking such matters handled expeditiously also, without the public's knowing how easy it was to exchange information with the enemy. Whitehall might have chosen to give Johnstone the gentleman's choice of a locked room and a loaded pistol, but Chas could not count on Filbert being a gentleman.

According to Leo, the viscount had given Algernon the option of exile with his father, or a post in the Army. Algernon had chosen shooting at people instead of shooting at bears, there being more Frenchmen than fur-bearing creatures. They were going to try to have him assigned to Lieutenant Westlake's unit, where some of Emery's comrades could look after the nodcock.

Ada told Jane, "Emery says that you are welcome to stay here with us, or he will help pay your passage if you wish to travel with your uncle. I'm sorry, but there is simply no way the estate can restore your settlements, not at this time, nor renovate the Dower House for you."

Jane dabbed at dry eyes. "No, I cannot stay here after last night. I would never be able to hold my head up, with everyone knowing of Uncle's perfidy."

What she meant, Ada supposed, was that after last night Jane was forced to concede that there were no eligible gentlemen in the neighborhood, unless she considered the widowed vicar. No, that was not a good match. "Then you will go with your uncle?" Ada could not imagine Jane braving the uncivilized wilds, with nary a mantua maker in sight, but Johnstone was her only kin.

"To Canada? Don't be a cake. No, Ashmead has been everything kind. I still say you were a fool to turn him down, but that is water under the bridge now. No, I have decided to go to London with the viscount."

"The viscount?" Ada echoed. Her viscount? Her Chas?

"And Pierre. They plan on departing tomorrow. Pierre will need help settling in to London, making the proper connections."

"Pierre?" Ada parroted.

"Monsieur Prelieu. He is a very fine gentleman, don't you think?"

"He seems rather . . . charming." The last Ada had seen of

him, he was lying on the floor, shouting French maledictions at his near-murderer, which Ada wished she did not understand quite so well.

"And handsome."

Bloody and bone-weary and pale. "Indeed."

"Refined, too."

Were they speaking of the same Monsieur Prelieu? "Jane, the man is a banker."

"A very highly placed finance administrator."

"He is a French traitor."

Jane raised her chin, high enough that the one under it would not quiver. "Pierre is a patriot who deplores what the Corsican monster has wrought on his beloved homeland. He told me so at breakfast."

"For heaven's sake, your Mr. Prelieu is a common thief who stole secrets from his employers, and then stole money, too."

Jane shrugged. "La, you would not believe how much. Those boots? False heels. He is actually quite short, *mon petit* Pierre."

"Ada, I need—"

"Chas, would you—"

"—To ask a favor. I'm sorry, you first."

"No, my request can wait."

"Good, for I am in rather a rush to get ready for the London trip, besides making sure Johnstone is out of the country."

Reminded of how much Chas was doing, how much effort and expense he was going to so that no scandal reflected on her family name, scandal which could affect the reception of Tess's play, Ada said, "Anything, Chas. Whatever you need."

"Thank you. I knew I could count on you, my dear." He even kissed the tip of her nose in relief. "I need you to look after Tally."

"Your dog?" Whatever Ada had been expecting, this was not it. Call on his mother, organize the evening of drama with Epps and the Meadows housekeeper, keep watch on the orphanage while he was gone—anything but looking after his dog.

"Yes, Tally. You see, Tally cannot stay in the house because of Lady Esther's blasted cat. I'd take her with me as usual, but I intend to ride alongside the carriage, or ahead, to make sure no one else tries to do away with Prelieu. I'd leave her with Coggs in the stable, but I want Coggs with me in case of trouble. The other grooms don't know her as well, and she's liable to get away from them and come after me. You know how she is."

The dog was a scruffy shadow, always waiting outside Westlake Hall when Chas came to call. Ada nodded that she knew the creature considered herself an appendage of the viscount's.

"If she didn't follow me, she'd howl."

Ada had heard that, too. All the hounds of hell couldn't sound louder. The last werewolf on earth couldn't be more mournful. The grooms in the stable were more likely to send her after Chas than try to console the dunderheaded dog. She nodded again.

"Good. Then you'll take her?"

When had Ada agreed? She'd been agreeing that his dog was an unmanageable, miserable mongrel. "Why can you not simply lock her in the kennels with the hunting dogs?"

Chas wiped a speck of dust off his leg—or a dog hair. "Tally has never been caged. She isn't used to being confined like a . . . a . . ."

"Dog?" Every dog Ada knew was either out working or waiting to work—in a kennel. "You do not wish her treated like a dog?"

"I knew you'd understand!"

"No, I do not understand at all. Why can't you leave the animal with Leo, or some other friend?"

"Leo is too busy tying to shut down the smuggling operation, and practicing with Tess. Frankly, I don't think he can concentrate on anything but your sister. I thought about it, but you're the only one else I would trust. Besides, she needs a woman's touch."

"Do not be ridiculous. The animal has never known a woman's touch in her life. I am positive your mother never lets her anywhere near."

"Of course not." Chas frowned, as if wondering why Ada thought Tally would welcome Lady Ashmead's attention. Lud knew, the servants avoided his mother whenever possible, and Tally had to be at least as smart. "I mean that she needs you, now that she is in a family way."

"Your dog is increasing and you think I can do something about it?" Ada did not know whether to laugh or cry. She wanted to be his wife, and he wanted a nursemaid for his dog.

"You don't have to do anything, just take her into your home and watch over her. It's not like I am asking you to welcome a mob of unwed mothers, my love, just one enceinte mutt."

His love was not listening to the endearment. "Chas, you cannot have considered. No one tells unmarried women the least thing about giving birth. For all I have lived my life in the country, I don't believe I have ever seen a cow or a ewe or a mare produce their offspring either, although I am certain I have watched the hens drop eggs. Once. I would be no help to your pet whatsoever. Neither would Tess, nor Emery, I am certain. Why, not even Mrs. Cobble, our housekeeper, has borne an infant."

"That's the glory of it, my dear, you don't have to know anything, and you don't have to do anything. Tally will handle it all on her own. If something should go wrong, you can send for the midwife. I'll leave a purse."

"Now who is being ridiculous? Any one of your tenants' wives would know far more, yes, and be far more willing to play *accoucheur* to a cur."

"But I would feel better knowing that she is with you. Besides, Tally is a fine watchdog."

"I do not need a watchdog, now that Emery is home."

"Everyone knows Emery is injured. They might not have heard that you handed me Prelieu's purse, though. Tally will warn you if someone tries to break in. Then I won't have to worry about leaving you, or her."

"About that purse, Chas. Monsieur Prelieu said it was never supposed to be in any tree."

The viscount consulted his pocket watch. "Blast, I have to meet with the magistrate in thirty minutes."

In ten minutes, dog, blankets, leather lead, and sacks of marrow bones were stowed in Ada's cart. "That's my girl," Viscount Ashmead said with a wide smile as he waved them off

His girl? How lovely. Ada looked back to see Chas hurrying into the house. It would be lovelier still if he meant her and not the dog.

Chapter Twenty-six

"Dear Lord," Ada prayed at the side of her bed, "thank you for all your blessings and for bringing Emery home to us. I especially thank you for keeping us all safe at Lady Ashmead's ball. Well, perhaps not Jane's uncle Filbert, but I am sure you will do your best. Please look after Jane and Algernon and Monsieur Prelieu, and all the orphans at the Foundling Hospital, and please help us make Tess's play a success, for it means so much to her. And Lord, if you could bring Chas home while I still have the courage to ask him to marry me, I will be even more grateful. Amen."

Ada got up from her knees and saw the face of one of her worst nightmares looking down at her from the bed, drooling. She sank to her knees again. "Lord? I know it is not right to bargain with Heaven, but if I promise to help Lady Ashmead with the church's new altar cloth, could you please make sure Chas's dog doesn't have her puppies until he gets back?"

Progress on the play proceeded apace. So did Tally's pregnancy. The dog grew rounder and slower by the day, more content to stay by the fire in Ada's room, on her bed of blankets atop towels atop newspapers. Or simply atop Ada's bed, to Ada's horror. At least the dog did not howl or try to run away, not after Ada had a long discussion with her about keeping Chas happy. The endless supply of bones and tidbits from the kitchen helped, too. As the hound gained weight, Ada lost it, running up and down the stairs a hundred times a day to check on her unwanted roommate. Finally she assigned Sarah's brother Robin from the orphanage to be official dog handler for Westlake Hall. With Jane and Filbert and Algernon gone, there was less fetching and carrying for the lad to do. He could watch and walk the dog between rehearsals and lessons and set-painting.

Ada had given up, with pleasure, her role as the princess to Lady Esther, who was amazingly proficient at it, for a pea-goose. She even forgot her lisp, on occasion, in Emery's presence. Emery took on, with equal pleasure, the part of the one-armed soldier who rescues the fair maiden, in a touching duet, while Sebastian takes on the sea kraken. The dragon was four newly recruited orphans under a tunnel of green sheeting, with a fearsome, removable head. Six other children were in charge of opening and closing the makeshift curtains, and wheeling Sebastian's cutout boat on stage and off at Ada's cues. She was now the musical director, teaching the sea sprites their chorus and accompanying the songs and Tess's dance, besides being prompter, prop master, and assistant wardrobe mistress, when she wasn't helping to paint the underwater castle or the serpent's head.

Tess and Leo, meanwhile, were spending so much time in private, supposedly learning their lines, that Ada supposed they could have memorized the *Iliad* by now. They did decide that Leo was going to declaim his now abbreviated speeches instead of singing them, thank goodness.

They made Chas the narrator, since he was not there to refuse, and it was his house after all.

Ada was so busy she barely had time to miss Chas or worry if he missed her, or if they had a future together, if she could be brazen enough. She did remember him in her prayers every night though, and every morning when she awoke to find a whiskery muzzle next to her on the pillow.

"Get down, you miserable mutt. I am certain Chas doesn't let you sleep on his bed. And if he does he shouldn't. You are spoiled and smelly, and you snore. Get down, Tally, I say."

One night Tally would not get down. She wagged her tail and whimpered instead. Ada lit her bedside candle and whimpered too. "It's not even three of the clock. I cannot get up to let you out. And get off my bed."

Tally circled and dug and whined and circled and panted.

"Oh, no. Oh, most definitely no. We had a bargain, Lord, and you are not doing your part! On my bed?" She lit another candle and put another log in the fireplace and cursed at the missing viscount. "I wouldn't ask that man to marry me if he were the last male on earth. He should be boiled in oil, that's what, along with that black and white sheep-herding dog."

She fetched her scissors and some thread, and put her water pitcher next to the fire to heat. That was the extent of her preparations because that was the extent of her knowledge of these matters. Tess would be no help. Little Sarah might be, since she'd seen her mother give birth to three other children, two of them stillborn, before dying with the fourth. But Ada could not wake the child in the middle of the night, not for another gruesome experience.

"No, it will not be gruesome," she told the dog, and herself. "You will be fine. Chas said you know what to do, so get on with it."

Tally only whined, looking up at Ada with sad brown eyes, beseeching eyes. Ada's tender heart could not look the other way. Sighing, she climbed up on the bed, resigned to throwing the cover, the blankets, and the mattress on the fire in the morning, and making Chas pay for new ones. She gingerly stroked Tally's head, and the dog licked her hand.

"Good dog." Nothing seemed to be happening, so Ada got down to fetch some towels, the dog watching her every move. "No, I am not going to leave you alone to deal with the consequences of your folly, but let this be a lesson to you, Tally. Men are not to be trusted. Where is that Tippy now, I ask you? And have you thought about your puppies? Where are they going to find good homes, half-breeds that they'll be, neither fish nor fowl, or herd or hunt in this case. You should have thought of that sooner. I hope my sister-in-law does."

The dog just whined at Ada's anxious chatter. "No, I did not mean to worry you. Chas will see that your babies are provided for. He would never think to drown an unwanted pup, the way someone tried to be rid of you." The dog yelped louder. "Oh, dear. I'll take in the puppies, if it comes to that! Just don't die, Tally. Please don't die! I cannot manage to tell your master that I love him and want to marry him; how in the world could I tell him I let his dog die? Please, Tally."

Then something gushed out of the dog in a sack of slime. It had to be the ugliest, sorriest specimen Ada had ever seen, but she dutifully went to fetch her scissors and thread. And gloves.

When she got back, Tally had nipped through the cord and was eating it. Then she started on the puppy!

"No!" Ada shrieked, tossing the gloves aside, visions of the fox hunt flashing through her mind. Tally looked at her—Ada could swear the dog was laughing—and went back to licking the pup. She kept at it, rolling the unhappy little thing over to get at its eyes and ears and belly, until she cried out with the next birth.

When Tally began to clean the second puppy, Ada gently moved the first one, lest it get sat on. The baby fit on the palm of one hand, although she nestled it carefully in both. It was softer than bunny fur, with a pushed-in nose and eyes squeezed shut, and soft legs that tried to swim. The bottom of its feet were as pink as the strawberry lotion Jane used to slather on her face to prevent wrinkles. The infant made a mewling sound, so Ada set it by Tally's side, where it immediately found its first meal.

Ada picked up the second pup when Tally was finished with it, examining the next miracle. This one was Tally's foxhound brown and white in color, whereas the first had been black and gold. "You would never hurt a fly, would you, much less a fox? No, I know you wouldn't, precious thing that you are. We'll make sure you are never hungry, never thinking you have to kill something to survive. I won't let those stupid men make savages out of your brothers and sisters and you, no, I won't."

In her heart, Ada knew that a dog was going to chase a moving object, ball or butterfly or bounding deer. The dog was going to act like a dog, no matter how much she fed it. In her hand, though, she held the sweetest thing she had ever seen. She rubbed the velvety baby against her cheek before setting it next to its brother. Or sister. She hadn't thought to look.

After the fourth pup, a black and white one, Tally lay back, exhausted. Ada brought her a bowl of water and some fresh towels. "Four darling babies, my girl. You have every right to be tired." So did she, but she'd never get back to bed now, Ada knew, even if the new family wasn't on it. She decided to go make herself a pot of tea, and find some food scraps for Tally. If there were no leftovers, Ada decided, she'd cut her a plate of ham from the pantry. "Good dog."

When she got back, there were five pups. The new one, though, was smaller, not moving around, although Ada could see that it was breathing, but shallowly. "Oh, no. If we were meant to have five puppies, then five puppies we are going to have. Do you hear that, baby?" Ada was holding the tiny thing, warming it in her hands. Then she moved one of the first puppies aside and set this one to the teat. When the first complained she said, "You've had enough. Your brother needs some now. You are the biggest and strongest, you know, so you have to look out for your family."

In a moment the newest arrival was sucking away and Ada could actually see its belly inflating with milk. She started breathing again. Tally wagged her tail, reminding Ada of the ham. "Yes, you did well, Tally. I did too, didn't I? I did not cry or cast up my accounts or get fuzzy-headed, did I? Chas better appreciate that!"

* * *

Chas would have appreciated Ada's efforts more if she let him see the puppies. He'd arrived home days later than he'd planned, Whitehall having him track down some of the so-called gentlemen on Prelieu's list. He'd also seen Prelieu and Jane temporarily established at the home of one of his many married cousins, a curate's wife, who was convinced by a large donation to her husband's church to lend what countenance she could to a disgraced widow and an emigre embezzler. Prelieu was being hailed as a hero, though, and Filbert Johnstone's complicity had been ignored, in light of so much juicier gossip. Some of the names on the list were high in the government; others were high in Polite Society.

Chas had no idea what was to come of Jane's sudden attachment, but Prelieu seemed pleased with the company of the buxom beauty, not in the first blush of youth, but well-born. Chas did not much care what became of either of them, as long as they did not batten on Ada or pour scandal broth on her doorstep.

His own doorstep was being repainted when he finally dragged himself through it, exhausted and aggravated. The rest of his house was in an uproar, too, with preparations for the dramatic entertainment. An army of servants was washing and polishing every inch of the old pile, as if it hadn't just been in prime twig for the masquerade. Workmen were sawing and hammering, the kitchens were too busy to fix full meals, the gardeners were denuding every plant in the conservatory and his mother—

Chas decided to call at Westlake Hall to retrieve his dog.

Ada's home made the Meadows look like a peaceful haven. Most of the hustlers and bustlers here were laughing, though, singing or dancing or reciting lines while carrying paints and fabrics and ladders. Half of the workers barely came to his waist.

He found Ada upstairs in Tess's attic, hand-coloring a huge stack of programs that had Leo Tobin's picture, in pirate guise, printed on the front. The viscount's mood was not improved by the sight of hundreds of his half-sibling, half-dressed, nor by how fatigued Ada seemed, and pale, as if she hadn't been sleeping enough or getting any fresh air.

Her welcoming smile almost made up for the past week's botheration, like the sun coming out from behind the clouds, until she told him he could not take his dog, his own pet, home with him.

"What do you mean, you won't give me back my dog? I didn't give her to you, for heaven's sake. I did not even lend her. I merely asked you to watch her, dash it!"

"I am not keeping her, exactly, Chas. It's just not the right time to move the puppies. It's too cold out for one, and they are enjoying being cuddled by all the children, for another. You wouldn't want them to grow up unused to people, would you? As you said yourself, Tally is not permitted in your home as long as Lady Esther's cat is there. You couldn't drag the poor thing and her babies away to your drafty stables, could you?"

"My stables are not drafty, by Jupiter. And I meant you to find her a bunk in your kitchens, not your blessed bedroom. Why, I cannot even go see the babies while they are up there!"

"You could if we were ma—"

"And what the devil do you mean, making me the narrator of the pestilential play? I won't do it, and that is final."

Chapter Twenty-seven

"Once upon a time . . ." Chas began, looking out at the Lillington-sized audience in his ballroom. The viscount's voice faltered, so Ada played a few encouraging notes on the pianoforte. The violinist behind her, her butler Cobble with his fiddle, played a trill. Chas frowned at her, then at his mother, who hissed at him to stop acting like some niminy-piminy prig and get on with it.

Lady Ashmead was seated near his lectern at the side of the stage in her usual oversized chair, befitting the benefactress of the orphanage and patroness of the play, they had told her. No one, wisely, had told her she was to have a role in it.

". . . In a long forgotten kingdom"—her loving son continued reading from his script, one hand gesturing toward his mother's thronelike chair—"there lived an evil queen who was jealous of her own stepdaughter. The dead king's only child was to inherit the crown and rule Pitsaponia as soon as the young princess came of age to take a husband. The queen had Princess Pretty kidnapped the day before her fifteenth birthday . . ."

"Hah!" Lady Ashmead said, loudly enough that the first five rows of the audience could hear. "As if I wouldn't walk through hot coals to see my last child wed. Look what tomfoolery I am putting up with tonight."

". . . and carried off to the shore where the fierce, finned, fanged kraken hunted."

Ada played a fanfare and the stagehand boys, dressed in dark skeleton suits, skipped across the stage, opening the curtains.

The playgoers, villagers, Londoners, servants, and orphans, all went "Aah" when they saw the set.

"Aha! So that's where all my ferns got to," Lady Ashmead complained.

The greenery was banked along the rear of the stage, with vines and flowers and fanciful birds painted on the backdrop, which had last seen service as a sail. Blue wooden waves bordered the performance area.

Ada played the "Princess's Prelude," and Lady Esther ran onto the stage. Her satin gown dotted with colored rhinestones, she glistened as she turned, looking behind her. The jewels in her crown glittered like diamonds, as well they might, since the earl's daughter was wearing her own heirloom tiara. Esther looked more like a princess than Ada ever could have, although Miss Westlake could have done a better job of appearing abandoned on a deserted shore after a three-months' journey. The little beauty looked more like she'd just left her dresser's hands, which she had, but she shrieked quite artfully.

At the second shriek, Ada gave a nod, and the green serpent entered the stage. The audience went "Ooh." One of the children inside the fabric body went "Ouch," but Ada did not think anyone else heard. The first child rotated the huge painted head this way and that, searching for a tender morsel. The princess ran across the stage to the left; the dragon slithered after her. The princess ran to the right; the kraken followed. Left, right, while Ada played a scary, pounding tempo and the fiddle thrummed and Lady Esther shrieked.

The boys pulled the curtains across to thunderous applause.

Chas started reading again. "The dead king's ministers offered a great reward for Princess Pretty's return."

A shower of coins was hurled over the top of the curtain at the audience, one of whose members loudly called, "Bit of all right, I say. I usually have to pay to be so entertained." The wit had obviously missed the donation jars at the entrance, for the orphans' fund. Epps was watching; he'd find the fellow before he left.

"So the Scourge of the Sea, Sebastian the Pirate, set out to find the missing princess and claim the reward, which included the hand of her royal highness in marriage."

The curtain opened again, but this time the backdrop was plain, solid blue except for a single cloud where one of the helpers had spilled paint. Ada played the "Pirate's Theme." Then she played it again. Finally the prow of a boat appeared, with Leo balanced on the gunnel, shouting "Row, me hearties, an' there's an extra tot o' rum for the lad what spots land."

The boat rocked—unintentionally, Ada knew—and Leo sat down hurriedly, but not before the watchers had seen his corded chest and muscular thighs. Half the audience sighed. The other half elbowed their husbands, with their padded shoulders and spindly shanks.

"Sebastian and his band of pirates searched for days into weeks, weeks into months. They captured a warship and a whaler and a wealthy merchantman, but still they kept searching . . ."

"Sail ho," came from offstage.

"Hard abeam."

"Belay that, matey."

". . . until one day they came upon an island that was on no map. And there they found the princess."

"Oh, thave me, Thebathian. Thave me from the thea therpent!"

The audience roared and so did the children in the dragon costume. The princess rushed off the stage, shrieking, of course, and Sebastian climbed out of his boat, his sword flashing in the air. Swish! Slash! Slice! While Ada played and Cobble fiddled, Leo fenced and feinted across the stage, nimbly avoiding the monster's teeth in finest swashbuckler style. Finally he cut the dragon's head clean off, and strode away, offstage, to claim the princess, his bride.

Ada softened her playing. Cobble plucked a string here and there.

"Even the worst of us," Viscount Ashmead told the audience, "can be loved by someone. The kraken had once been the lover of Sirenia the Sea Goddess before he turned evil, and she came to mourn his loss."

Tess came on stage in her flowing robes, keening her lament. She picked up the severed head and danced with it, singing her troubled eulogy, showing her bare legs. She swayed, she spun, her voice filled the huge ballroom with young love turned bitter, with all the lost chances, all the wasted years. The audience was enraptured. Many wept. Ada herself could barely read the music in front of her through the tears in her eyes, tears of pride for her sister's success.

Chas cleared his throat to reclaim the audience's attention. "Done with her mourning, the sea goddess grew angry. Someone had dared enter her province, had dared take the life of her lover. That someone would pay."

Cymbals crashed, drums rolled, Ada pounded the keys of the pianoforte. The goddess stood at the side of the stage—the side as far away from Lady Ashmead as possible—with her hands raised in wrath, the trident pointing at the sky, calling down the storm. Sebastian's boat was rocked and bounced, then the bow was raised and the pirate was tipped out. The sea sprites draped the blue backdrop over him.

"Sebastian and his men were all taken to the bottom of the sea, drowned."

The curtains were quickly pulled, the noise drowning out Lady Ashmead's: "Good. Now can we have refreshments?"

"Some of Sebastian's men were still ashore, however. One of them was the officer from the captured warship, Captain Corazon . . ."

(Emery had refused to be Generalissimo Markissimo.)

Ada played a sprightly march.

"... who discovered the weeping princess on her island prison. Despite his injuries, the officer freed the damsel, but she captured his heart, and he won hers with his bravery and goodness."

The curtains parted to show the fern island, with the young couple ready for their duet. Emery was in some foreign uniform, with ribbons and medals and gold braid strung across his chest. His own injured arm was strapped against his body under the white coat, which did not do much for the jacket, or Emery's arm. Still he managed to put his good arm around Lady Esther at the end of the song, and drew her to him for a remarkably well-rehearsed and well-acted kiss that continued while the audience whistled and stamped their feet.

Before Chas could read further, there was a disturbance from the rear of the room. A well-tailored gentleman of mature years but less than impressive stature shoved his way through the standing servants at the back, down the narrow aisle between crowded rows of seats, forcing his way toward the stage.

"Thtop!" he shouted.

Thtop? Chas looked to Ada and whispered, "Did Tess rewrite the script?"

She shook her head.

The diminutive gentleman shook his fist at the stage and yelled to Emery, "Unhand my daughter, you cad!"

Lady Esther threw her arms around Emery and declared: "I am Princeth Pretty and thith ith the man I love."

"The devil it ith!" the Earl of Ravenshaw swore, waving his cane like a sword. The audience was confused, but they applauded anyway.

"Archie?" Lady Ashmead lifted her lorgnette. "Is that you? Stop making a fool of yourself. It is only a play."

"A play? My daughter ith no common performer!"

"But thith ith thtill the man I love."

"Oh, do sit down, Archie." Chas had signaled one of the servants to fetch another chair, which he hurried to position next to the viscountess's throne. "You can argue about it later, without that ridiculous lisp."

The play went on as the earl sat. He leaned toward Lady Ashmead. "Irmentrude? Who is that chap with his arms—one arm, by Jupiter—around my girl?"

She whispered back: "He is Sir Emery Westlake, recently of the Army, a nice, decent lad. A baronet."

"A baronet? Bah. Who's t'other fellow, the handsome one behind the curtain waving his sword like he knows how to use it?"

"That is none other than my husband's by-blow, who died in the last act. If I can stomach him, you can accept the heroic young baronet who loves your daughter."

Chas took up the narrative: "Seeing the young lovers melted Sirenia's frozen heart, like the first buds of spring awaken the earth after winter. She could not bring her wrath to bear against them."

While the young sea sprites sang their song, dancing around Tess, Lord Ravenshaw leaned toward the viscountess again. "How many butter stamps did old Geoffrey leave you with, anyway?"

She rapped his knuckles with her lorgnette. "They are orphans from the foundling home. Now stubble it, Archie. I want to see the end. Demme if the Westlake gel doesn't have something between her ears after all."

Chas frowned at both of them, speaking louder: "Repentant, the sea goddess decided to bring courageous Sebastian and his men back to the land of the living, with the help of her water fairies."

They dragged Leo's once more inert body across the stage, where Tess sang another stanza, affirming life. The pirate sat up and stretched, and espied a goddess. He went down on one knee to her, vowing his undying—unless he had a relapse—devotion.

"But what of your princess?" the goddess asked, pointing across the stage to the young lovers, standing so close together her father's cane could not have fit between. "The kingdom you could rule, the fortune she would bring?"

Instead of the baritone's aria that should have followed, Leo turned to the audience and slowly, carefully spoke his lines: "Leave them to tend the soil. I am a man of the sea, where my beloved resides. As for riches, what good is wealth if a man's heart is poor?"

They walked off the stage, hand in hand.

When the cheering died down, mostly from the members of Leo's crew and the ladies, and the curtains were drawn, Chas read the envoi. "The princess and her noble captain returned to Pitsaponia, where"—he improvised with a nod toward his mother and the earl—"the Queen and her ministers approved the match. The royal couple lived long and ruled wisely, and had many children to gladden their days."

"Hmph," Lady Ashmead snorted. "I hope they got more pleasure out of their brood than I get from my aggravating offspring."

The earl glowered at the closed curtain as if he could see through it, to where Emery and Esther were still embracing. "Amen to that."

"As for Sebastian and the sea goddess," Lord Ashmead continued, "they went on adventuring, ridding the high seas and far reaches of fire dragons, fiends, and tax collectors."

Lady Ashmead patted Ravenshaw's hand. "At least you can be happy you aren't *that* chit's father."

Ada struck a chord so Chas could finish.

"Everyone lived happily ever after, which is what we wish for you, dear listeners." He bowed, then added, "Oh, and the sea sprites all found good homes."

Chapter Twenty-eight

Bows. Curtsies. Applause. Hugs, kisses, more applause. More bows, more kisses, more bouquets. They were a success. The play was a masterpiece. Tess was a genius. Strangers from London were clamoring to talk to her, waving contracts and checks in front of her face.

Glowing with stage makeup and pride, Tess took up a post in the library, signing programs for all of those who did not want to know her in the past, but now wanted to prove that they did. Her future looked rosy indeed.

Tess put off the London businessmen, telling them she had to consult with her financial adviser in London, Monsieur Prelieu, before committing herself. Meanwhile, they were welcome to present their proposals to her business partner, Leo. The eventual checks, she made sure they all knew, were to be made out to Mrs. Leo Tobin.

After supper and celebrations, Mr. and Mrs. Holmdale gathered up the foundling home children, with two likely prospects of families for such bright, handsome, and hard-working boys.

The earl was seated in the Crimson Parlor with a glass of Lord Ashmead's finest cognac in his hands. He was scowling at his daughter, who was accepting her rightful homage from her court, from Sir Emery's right side. Emery had changed into his own scarlet regimental jacket, with his injured arm in a sling.

"At least the clunch has two arms," the earl conceded to Lady Ashmead, sitting beside him on the sofa.

"Does that mean he is two times as acceptable, you old dodderer, or that he will love her twice as much?"

The earl did not reply, looking for answers in the swirling cognac.

"Fustian, you old goat, and you know it. It's a good lad, Sir Emery is, solid as stone. Not like that here-and-thereian brother of his, Rodney, who married into a parcel of the dirtiest dishes he could find. Emery will do."

When Lord Ravenshaw still made no comment, the viscountess rapped him with her looking glass. "So the boy might not have vast lands, deep pockets, or high title. Isn't your girl's happiness more important? Did your own arranged marriage bring you any joy, besides the riches you did not need?"

"Brought me my gel," the earl pronounced.

"Aye, and I would trade my youth all over again for my own three children, no matter how much I complain about them. But do you not wonder, sometimes, what it might have felt like, wed to someone you truly loved?"

He put his hand atop hers. "Perhaps it's not too late, Trudy."

Perhaps not.

While Lady Ashmead was holding private conversation with the earl, her son had Ada stand beside him to accept the congratulations of their friends and neighbors. The viscount had not asked; he simply held her arm, holding her at his side as if she were the lady of the house. It was not quite the thing, of course, since there had been no formal announcement of a match between them. There had been no formal offer, either, to Ada's despair, and could not be, in all this crowd.

She could not outstay the company, especially since many were Lady Ashmead's house guests. The erstwhile sea sprites were yawning, besides, so Ada decided to take them home. Tess was to follow with Leo, but Ada knew better than to wait up. No matter how late they returned, she would not have to worry. Emery's future looked assured too, for the earl had shaken his good hand and invited him to come take tomorrow's breakfast at the Meadows. No, all she had to worry about was her meeting in the morning with Chas, in the orchard where they would not be disturbed.

Her prayers that night were particularly poignant.

The day dawned bright and warm for autumn, which meant Ada had no excuse for delaying. She harnessed Lulu to the cart and loaded into the back a basket full of puppies, wrapped in blankets with a hot brick underneath. Tally sat on the bench beside her, eager as always.

Chas was waiting at the edge of the orchard, even though Ada was early. Tally jumped down and raced to him, barking and leaping and running in circles.

"Yes, my girl, I am happy to see you. And you, too, of course, Ada," he belatedly added, too busy admiring the pups to hand her down from the cart. He picked up each one, looking to see if it was a male or female, congratulating Tally on what a fine job she had done, telling her how big and sturdy they were, and wasn't five just the right number? Ada might have been a delivery boy.

He kept ruffling the new baby coats, assessing the size of the heads and feet and mouths and heaven knew what else. Surely Ada did not. Finally Ada asked, "Did you bring the money?"

He reached into his coat and took out the leather purse, which was larger than the black and tan puppy he held in his other hand. "Of course I did. I had to ransom my dog back, didn't I?"

"You have been watching too many of Tess's productions. You know you can't take them back yet, anyway, not with Lady Esther and the earl staying on another week. And we need to talk about their futures, too. The Holmdales would like the gold one for the foundling hospital, and Garden George thinks the brown fellow might help keep rabbits out of the vegetables. Mrs. Cobble's niece just lost her pug, so she would like a new dog, and I, well, I rather fancy this one, that no one else is likely to want." She stroked the littlest one, the runt, of course.

Chas grinned at her, tucking the puppies back under their blanket. He looked at the leather pouch and said, "Hmm. They'll cost you, you know."

"What, a litter of mongrel puppies? That's outrageous."

He laughed. "Seems to me like Tally's offspring are in high demand, for all their low birth."

Ada knew he was teasing, but she could not match his smile. She anxiously ran the leather drawstrings through her gloved fingers. "It is mine, isn't it?"

He pretended to misunderstand. "The runt?"

"The money, you gudgeon."

"Oh, that. Of course. Finders keepers, you know, not like my dog. I told you that weeks ago."

"But then Monsieur Prelieu returned."

"He never claimed the deuced thing, did he? It is yours."

"You never put it in the tree for him, did you?"

Chas busied himself with the basket cover. "Not precisely."

"Let me rephrase my question then. You did put it in the tree, didn't you?"

"That was not, perhaps, my most clever idea. I was regrettably castaway at the time."

"You truly fell off your horse putting it there." That was a statement, not a question. So was, "You could have been killed, you clothhead."

He shrugged. "Another miscalculation."

"You left it for me."

"The worst idea of all, it turned out. You did your best to get rid of it, though. How come you have changed your mind?"

"Because pride is a cold companion."

"Unlike my dog, right, Tally?" The hound danced around his legs, so Chas bent down and rubbed her ears. "I knew you'd bring her 'round, my girl, if she just got to know you."

Ada narrowed her eyes. "I thought I was doing you a great favor by taking in your dog."

“That too, I swear.”

Ada decided she would consider this new bit of manipulation later. “Anyway, I changed my mind about the money because I realized that I did have a good use for it, after all.”

“Why now? Emery will come about, and you know that Leo and Tess will gladly provide you with anything you require.”

“I did not wish to wait for Emery, or intrude on Tess. I need the money for my dowry.”

He was silent, staring at the ground. Lud, she was going to accept the vicar after all. After all their kisses, all their unspoken vows.

“You kept telling me that's what I should use it for, didn't you?”

He looked at her, bleak sorrow turning his heart to bitter cinders. “I was full of stupid ideas, wasn't I?”

“Here.” Ada pushed the pouch into his hands.

“Here? You made me bring your wretched windfall, just to hand it back?”

Ada fussed with the blanket over the puppies, making sure they could get enough air. “I want you to have my dowry, Chas. As Tess wrote, what good are riches if the heart is poor?”

The viscount just stared at her, his head tilted to the side.

“Dash it, Chas, must I spell it out for you? I am giving you my dowry because I love you and I want to—”

He stopped her with a hand over her mouth, then replaced his hand with lips that were cool from the air, then warm, oh so warm. “I love you too, my darling. I always have. Come.”

“But I—”

“Don't quibble for once, my pet.” He called Tally up into the wagon and made room for her in the basket. “We won't be long.” Then he took Ada's hand and half dragged her through the rows of gnarled apple trees.

Ada had to run to keep up, laughing, asking questions Chas would not answer. “But where—”

Finally she saw a tree with a pink ribbon around it. It was not the one that had held the windfall, but it was close by. A streamer of green hung from one of the branches, not a vine, but suspiciously resembling part of Tess's sea goddess costume.

"This time I used a ladder," Chas confessed.

"I don't understand."

"Pull the ribbon, my love."

She did, and a box tumbled to the ground at her feet. A small, ring-shaped, velvet-covered box.

Ada untied the ribbon and opened the box to find the Ashmead family engagement ring, the one she had tossed at his head.

Through happy tears, she told him, "Oh, Chas, I do love you. I always have. I just never understood how much."

"I was as much a slowtop, sweetheart, taking you and our love for granted."

"The ring really is mine?"

"Finders keepers," he said, tugging off her glove and placing the ruby and diamond ring on her finger.

"And you still want to marry me?"

"More than ever, my love."

Ada kissed her fingers, then touched them to the tree. "Then I do. I mean I will. I mean—"

Chas lifted her right off her feet and twirled her around. "I know what you mean, my addled Ada." He kissed her then, because words no longer mattered, or could express enough. When he put her down and stepped away, out of breath but not out of arm's reach, Chas straightened her straw bonnet. "Thank heavens you said yes, because I did not have time to finish my next plan."

He led Ada to the other side of the tree, where a hammer and chisel lay on the ground, among a pile of wood shavings. *Will you ma*—was carved into the old bark.

"I swore I would never ask you again, but you didn't say anything about the tree."

"I will. A hundred times, I will! I don't think I have eve been so happy in my entire life."

"But you will be, every day. I swear it, for you have mad me the happiest of men, my dearest. When? That is, when d you think we can be wed?"

"Not soon enough to suit me, but I suppose your mothe will insist on a lavish wedding for the Ashmead dynasty."

"No, she'll be too busy planning for Esther's Season i Town for the earl. If all works out, there could be a weddin in the summer. Perhaps two."

"We'd have to wait so long?"

"Not our wedding, goose. We can get married tomorrow i you agree. I bought a special license while I was in London in case I needed yet a third plan."

"What was number three?"

"I was going to kidnap you onto one of Leo's ships, the hold you there, kissing you and loving you until you said yes."

"I think I like that plan best. Did you have a fourth schem too?"

"Fourth, fifth, and sixth. Whatever it took. I would neve give you up, sweetheart, not unless I saw you walk down th aisle with another man. Even then, I would have shot him That was plan seventeen, I believe."

"Totally unnecessary, my love, for I would never let yo get away either. Not even I could be foolish enough to giv up a magician who can make money and jewels fall fron trees."

Then Viscount Ashmead showed Ada another kind o magic. They'd be at it still, except the dog barked.

ONYX

MAY McGOLDRICK

The acclaimed author of* THE THISTLE AND THE ROSE *presents an exciting new trilogy. Three sisters each hold a clue to their family's treasure—and the key to the hearts of three Highland warriors....

THE DREAMER

❑ 0-451-19718-6/$5.99

THE ENCHANTRESS

❑ 0-451-19719-4/$5.99

THE FIREBRAND

❑ 0-451-40942-6/$5.99

"May McGoldrick brings history to life."
—Patricia Gaffney

"Richly romantic." —Nora Roberts

Prices slightly higher in Canada

Payable by Visa, MC or AMEX only ($10.00 min.), No cash, checks or COD. Shipping & handling: US/Can. $2.75 for one book, $1.00 for each add'l book; Int'l $5.00 for one book, $1.00 for each add'l. Call (800) 788-6262 or (201) 933-9292, fax (201) 896-8569 or mail your orders to:

Penguin Putnam Inc.
P.O. Box 12289, Dept. B
Newark, NJ 07101-5289
Please allow 4-6 weeks for delivery.
Foreign and Canadian delivery 6-8 weeks.

Bill my: ❑ Visa ❑ MasterCard ❑ Amex ________(expires)
Card# ________________
Signature ________________

Bill to:
Name ________________
Address ________________ City ________________
State/ZIP ________________ Daytime Phone # ________________

Ship to:
Name ________________ Book Total $ ________________
Address ________________ Applicable Sales Tax $ ________________
City ________________ Postage & Handling $ ________________
State/ZIP ________________ Total Amount Due $ ________________

This offer subject to change without notice. Ad # N154 (8/00)

For only $3.99 each, you'll get to surrender to your wildest desires....

LORDS OF DESIRE

A special romance promotion from Signet Books—featuring some of our most popular, award-winning authors...

Arizona Gold by Maggie James
❑ 0-451-40799-7

Bride of Hearts by Janet Lynnford
❑ 0-451-40831-4

Diamonds and Desire by Constance Laux
❑ 0-451-20092-6

Prices slightly higher in Canada

Payable by Visa, MC or AMEX only ($10.00 min.), No cash, checks or COD. Shipping & handling: US/Can. $2.75 for one book, $1.00 for each add'l book; Int'l $5.00 for one book, $1.00 for each add'l. Call (800) 788-6262 or (201) 933-9292, fax (201) 896-8569 or mail your orders to:

Penguin Putnam Inc.
P.O. Box 12289, Dept. B
Newark, NJ 07101-5289
Please allow 4-6 weeks for delivery.
Foreign and Canadian delivery 6-8 weeks.

Bill my: ❑ Visa ❑ MasterCard ❑ Amex ________(expires)
Card# ____________________
Signature ____________________

Bill to:
Name ____________________
Address ____________ City ____________
State/ZIP ____________ Daytime Phone # ____________

Ship to:
Name ____________ Book Total $ ____________
Address ____________ Applicable Sales Tax $ ____________
City ____________ Postage & Handling $ ____________
State/ZIP ____________ Total Amount Due $ ____________

This offer subject to change without notice.

Ad # N153 (8/00)